Praise for *Dry Lands*

'Liv's daily battle against starvation and predators, human and otherwise, is visceral, and – thanks to Martins' gift for characterization – her evolution feels earned as she gradually adapts her ethics to keep Milo alive at all costs. The tenacious, well-shaded heroine elevates this above many similar efforts.'
Publishers Weekly

'A testament to the power of hope and motherhood in the worst of situations.'
Kirkus Reviews

T0288830

ELIZABETH ANNE MARTINS

DRY LANDS

This is a **FLAME TREE PRESS** book

Text copyright © 2024 Elizabeth Anne Martins

FLAME TREE PRESS
6 Melbray Mews, London, SW6 3NS, UK
flametreepress.com

US sales, distribution and warehouse:
Simon & Schuster
simonandschuster.biz

UK distribution and warehouse:
Hachette UK Distribution
hukdcustomerservice@hachette.co.uk

Publisher's Note: This is a work of fiction. Names, characters, places, and incidents are a product of the author's imagination. Locales and public names are sometimes used for atmospheric purposes. Any resemblance to actual people, living or dead, or to businesses, companies, events, institutions, or locales is completely coincidental.

Thanks to the Flame Tree Press team.

Cover image © Mike Martins 2024.
The font families used are Avenir and Bembo.

Flame Tree Press is an imprint of Flame Tree Publishing Ltd
flametreepublishing.com

A copy of the CIP data for this book is available from the British Library and the Library of Congress.

3 5 7 9 8 6 4 2

PB ISBN: 978-1-78758-905-6
ebook ISBN: 978-1-78758-907-0

Printed and bound in Great Britain by Clays Ltd, Elcograf S.p.A.

ELIZABETH ANNE
MARTINS

DRY LANDS

FLAME TREE PRESS
London & New York

To F.J., my guiding star

CHAPTER ONE

When the helicopter made an emergency landing in the wide forest pit, Milo was still sleeping. The panicked pilot ordered us to exit immediately, but my husband, Felipe, refused to leave. I held Milo outside in the stale air, bouncing him against my breast, waiting for Felipe. I was anxious for my husband to tell me we were safe; I waited for him as long as I could. But the rotor blades weren't slowing down quick enough. It was too much for Milo. Chaotic. I stayed far away from the helicopter, stopping at the edge of the woods.

"Mama?" Milo groaned. He quickly placed his head on my shoulder, as though we were simply walking from the rocking chair back to the bed in the dead of night. As though we were home. But we weren't home. Home was gone. Nonexistent. Our journey had been long. He was exhausted and in need of sleep. His head grew heavy against my face. His legs dangled at my hips. Behind me, the copter's blades began to slow down. Felipe and the pilot were still in the helicopter, assessing the source of the gas leak alert that caused the pilot to suddenly land. I urged Felipe to exit the helicopter with me and Milo, but he refused. "It's probably just something electrical," he insisted. "I'll be right there." Felipe was a talented electrician by trade; no problem was too challenging for him to tackle. I trusted his intuition.

Soon, the blades came to a pause. The forest was still. I heard Felipe's voice echo from the helicopter far behind us, and it set my nerves at ease. At last, we could finally figure out our next steps together. To reassess our plan. Luckily, Milo was limp enough for me to set him down in a cool bed of grass, with my diaper bag as a pillow. I shook my arms out. They'd held a toddler tightly since the start of our journey, since we first stepped onto the helicopter. I tucked a loose hair behind Milo's ear as he slept among nature.

When the helicopter burst into flames, Milo's head jolted from the explosion. My first thought was not of Felipe still in the helicopter but of our food supply. Felipe was strong. Felipe could survive anything. Food could not. I was not thinking straight. But as I turned to the flames, I realized no one was exiting the copter. Not the pilot. Not Felipe. I placed my sweater over Milo before running wildly toward the blaze, where Felipe was either being swallowed by flames or stumbling deliriously off the burning craft. Why couldn't he just let the pilot figure things out? Why did he always have to be so damn helpful? My heart pounded through my chest as I ran to reach my husband.

I tried to see past the fire and black molten smoke, to identify where Felipe could be. Maybe he was in the tail of the copter, collecting our luggage. Or maybe he was in the cockpit, trying to rescue the buckled pilot. I came as close as I possibly could. My face became singed. Smoke poured into my throat. The flames grew bolder and louder. I tried to march right into the belly of fire, but what good would it do for Milo to lose both parents on the same night? I screamed for Felipe until my voice broke. This was a battle I could not win even if I were a god. There was nothing I could do.

Nothing.

The fire covered the helicopter and crept into the nearby brush. The fire would come for me too if I wasn't careful. No screams came from the helicopter. Only whooshing flames and crackling fire. I told myself that Felipe was taken from the world instantly. The explosion – the gas leak that was definitely not an electrical issue – claimed him without struggle. He was at peace. He wouldn't want me to stand around and ponder his death, to pontificate on his pain. He would want me to take Milo to a safe place and keep us both alive. I ran from the flames toward the woods.

The night beyond the flames was a darkness I'd only heard about in stories. Like being lost inside a dripping cave, miles beneath the earth. I found a fallen tree to lean against as I held Milo with quivering hands. I didn't stray far from the flames – our source of light. There was nothing I could do but sit idly by, holding my son, keeping him warm while he slept through this nightmare. I wept until I didn't know who I was anymore.

It did not escape me that the flames that killed Felipe were the same flames keeping Milo warm that night, as the temperature began to dip. Milo slept as I watched the helicopter burn from a safe distance. I didn't want to sleep, but I couldn't fight it much longer. The exhaustion overpowered me. Foolishly, I imagined telling Felipe all about this in the morning. Like this would be any other event in our lives. In my sleep, I dreamt that Milo woke me with a soft hand and led me to a lukewarm river to drink.

In the silence of early dawn, the environment began to make itself known. A lush forest with wet rocks beneath my boots, the smell of a nearby creek, which reminded me of the bay back home. The soft scent of rain. Mushy leaves beneath my feet. A moisture in the air that opened my airways and mingled with the ducts of my eyes, making me unsure whether I was crying tears or creek water. With Milo tucked safely inside my Sea Isle sweater, I rose and left the sleeping boy on the wild grass. I walked toward the craft, which still crackled. I stepped over burnt ground toward the charred helicopter. I couldn't make out much from the craft. I didn't feel safe entering either. And I didn't want to see Felipe burnt. Not yet.

A growl came from behind me. A bear raised its head from a boulder just beyond and stared at my sleeping boy with predatory eyes and a mouth full of teeth. The bear lifted its beastly head as if to bask in the scent of a fresh human boy. As it hovered there, furry and huge, I felt murder rising in my bones. Felipe's gun. There was no time to ransack the still-burning craft for it. I grabbed the nearest piece of helicopter debris and marched toward my boy. I stood over him, holding the wreckage over my head, hungry for the bear to try me. The bear cowered and growled an understanding sigh before disappearing into the woods.

When Milo woke up, he said, "What happened?" and pointed toward the wreck.

"An accident," I said.

"I wanna see."

"No. Danger."

I wondered about food for him. As for me, I could not eat. But I wondered if our food survived the explosion. It was packed in a fire-resistant box. Did it work? It had been Felipe's idea to get the box. I scolded him about it at the time. "We don't have time for that!" I had yelled.

I wondered about that bear.

I wondered about Felipe. His body, his wishes. I could not function without him. My heart could not function without him. My husband was dead.

Felipe, dead. God.

Our journey had come to a tragic stop.

Milo pulled my shirt up and began to nurse. This was one thing to cross off the list. In the empty woods, no one was around to tell me to stop nursing a three-year-old. And yet, the silent, shrill voice of judgment still found its way to me somehow. Milo placed his hand on my stomach, twisting his finger around in my belly button. For some reason, his vulnerability made me cry. When he pulled away, he asked about the helicopter again. He watched the lingering flames and he looked at the woods where the bear had disappeared just moments earlier. I could not speak. I didn't know how to explain anything. Milo pulled my shirt back down for me. Then he sat up.

"Mama," he said in his sweet morning voice. "We at BeezBo's house now?"

"No, this is not your Bisavó's house."

"Oh. *Mama*?"

"Yes."

"Mama, where's Dada?"

"I don't know, Milo."

My hands shook.

"Oh. *Mama?*"

"Yes."

"Mama sad?"

"Yes, Milo. I'm sad. Very sad."

"*Mama?*"

"Yes."

"I make you better."

The boy gave me a peck on the cheek and waited a long, long while for me to stand up.

CHAPTER TWO

I laid my sweater on the grass just after Milo fell asleep in my arms and positioned him comfortably on the ground. While Milo napped, I investigated the rubble. The helicopter was charred debris, haphazardly positioned in a field of smoke, a clump of tangled metal. I neared the craft, stepping over the fallen door. The doorway was open. I peered inside and pulled away quickly. Felipe was hunched over the guts of a burned dashboard, unrecognizable, burnt. The image would be etched in my mind forever. Always a fixer, he tried to be of service in his last moments of life. The pilot beside him was frozen for eternity beside my husband.

Denial consumed me – for my own good. I had no time to think about the horridness of what I just saw. I had to move quickly to protect Milo. I gathered salvageable items and tucked them into my hiker's backpack, which I used as a diaper bag. I had no plan in mind, nothing. I didn't even know how far we were from our destination, or if we were close. I didn't believe we were, remembering the pilot saying we'd reach the target by morning. But my gut told me to gather anything I could, anything that survived the explosion. Scrap metal, steel wool, spools of wire, a small axe, anything that looked sharp. It went into the bag along with Milo's pull-ups, socks, snacks, juice bottle, and other random toddler items. Despite choppy breathing, I hunted for items obsessively and with focus; it took my mind off Felipe. When I finally packed enough, I looked toward the craft again, nearly catching sight of my husband. It was impossible to believe Felipe was gone, even after seeing him dead. We had been expecting death – I just didn't know Felipe would be first. I thought he was indestructible. He was the prepared one.

Yes, death was expected. One way or another. Felipe and I had talked through all sorts of scenarios if the floods reached us before we headed toward the dry lands.

"If I die first, take Milo to my grandmother," Felipe had said.

"Okay. And if I die first, make sure Milo knows how much I loved him."

For the most part, death had conquered our worlds – it took our friends, our family. It just hadn't hit us three yet. Till now.

I went numb. I would grieve when we had a roof over our heads. Emotion would not keep me and Milo alive. Action would. I kept looking back at Milo. The boy slept hard in the sun. Then, shuffling through the ash, I found the fire-resistant black box that contained our food and other items. I pried it open with a newfound gratitude for Felipe's preparedness.

When Milo woke up, he asked about Dada again. As we stood in the debris field, I thought about telling him what had happened to his father, about making him look. Maybe it could be a lesson on moving quickly, on listening to Mama. No, I could not make Milo look. We crossed over the broken engine, where I found a radio, but it was scorched. It would be useless anyway. Nothing worked anymore, burnt or unburnt. Electrical power was reserved for the elite.

We walked toward the back of the craft. I plucked off as many breakable aluminum rods as I could. I had no gun, only a small axe. But I felt a primal need for more protection. These airframe materials, with their sharp edges, would do. Milo stood looking around at the mess. I would have fallen to my knees and wept for the rest of time if I wasn't in survival mode. Ash was everywhere. The boy coughed and shifted his legs. He began throwing pieces of debris into an empty field.

"Just a little bit more," I said, continuing to stuff my bag with potential resources. Then Milo started walking around the front of the craft, toward Felipe. I dropped the bag and yanked Milo back by his shirt.

"Let's take a walk, Milo."

"Where?"

"Somewhere."

I couldn't leave Felipe, and yet I couldn't stand to be there either.

We left the food box in a crevice of metal and took off. Beyond the debris site there was dense wood. Beyond the wood, there flowed a river. Milo kept running ahead of me, tripping every so often. I tried to keep up with him, to keep him safe from whatever was ahead, but my body was weak and my voice hoarse. I begged him to stay close. He kept asking *why*. I had no energy to explain every fear, so I only said, "Bears." It wasn't a lie. I was afraid of everything, and bears were on the list. Did they roam in the day, morning, night? All three? There were no bears back home.

When I saw the river through the trees, I momentarily imagined using the salvaged wires in my bag to tie boulders to my feet. The sinking might feel nice. Milo found a caterpillar on a tree. "Mama, look! Look Mama! Cadda-pillah!"

On the edge of the river Milo tossed pebbles into the grinding water. Tall, fern-colored trees lined the banks, inviting my eyes to watch their slow-moving leaves. Smoke lingered in the air from the helicopter explosion. As Milo played, I sat on the rocky riverbank and tried to make sense of our location. Everything looked the same. Trees and water, water and trees. North and south did not appear different. East and west were arbitrary.

I looked ahead as far as I could, sometimes forgetting to breathe. I didn't know how close civilization was. And if it was nearby, were the people there like the ones I'd heard about on the news? The ones who killed without remorse? The news called them marauders. And was it true about life beyond the floods – that free men and women were captured and sent to encampments. Resources were reserved for the wealthy, the ones who smirked as they retreated to their bunkers built by their tech-giant ancestors before them. I looked at Milo, who pointed toward the river.

"Mama, I wanna go in there!"

"Not today."

I stared at the water, remembering everything we lost to the floods back home. Our home in Sea Isle, New Jersey – gone. The East Coast

– under water. The floods transformed the look of the Earth in a matter of days, turning land into the sea and sea into land. It was like someone took the Earth and twisted it like a Rubik's Cube. No one could agree on what caused the floods. Some said the Earth's magnetic poles shifted, while others said it was from climate change. Whatever happened, it caused calamities like severe floods and earthquakes. It came without warning. We simply called this change the 'Shift.' Everyone thought the Shift would occur slower, that it would consider our safety. It didn't.

Right before the waters came, I was arguing with Felipe about something trivial. It started off with a little water rushing into our flood-resistant home, rising from the basement. The water didn't stop. I wanted to stay, but Felipe started packing immediately. I thought it was just overflow from the bay after a heavy rainstorm. At first, I begged him to stop packing. But the water grew severe. It was not just overflow from the bay; it was astronomical.

Felipe had been prepping for years for a disaster. He never wanted to live so close to the coast and he had begged us to move west. But I had no desire to leave. In his bones, he knew to be ready for something. He looked at everything as a threat. I loved and hated this about him all at once. Civilization was crumbling with disease, war, and economic disparity from decades past, so it wasn't that unusual to meet a prepper like Felipe. Still, his readiness reminded me of my own mortality – *Milo's mortality* – and so I shunned it.

Before the water became too much to bear, we packed as much as we could into the car and left. We reached the edge of town, sitting in our car like doomed cattle, waiting to be directed to the nearest safety zone. Felipe smacked the wheel and cursed.

When the land beneath our tires cracked, dropping away suddenly, water came without warning to submerge almost everyone on that highway, and the nearby safety zone too. Our tires became lodged between the fractured pavement and rushing floodwater. Waves gushed by with bodies in them. Felipe and I were screaming at each other, unsure what to do. Milo roared from his throat. A large chunk of road suddenly jutted upwards, as if it had a spasm. The movement propelled us towards a section that hadn't suffered damage yet. We were momentarily spared from the flood that swallowed others. My vision blurred. Peripheral sound faded into obscurity. All I could see were Milo's tears. All I heard was *"Mama!"* I yanked him with force until he was free from his car seat. We managed to get out and cling to the hood, watching the world drown around us. Those who survived were rescued by helicopters and taken to a hotel somewhere in rural Pennsylvania.

During our long stay in the hotel, the water slowed. There was hope that the floods only came for the shore towns, that Pennsylvania and everything west of it would be spared. But those less optimistic knew it was coming sooner or later. Even though disaster was imminent, we still talked of things like home insurance, time off from work, preschool registration, and medical bills. We still talked about holidays. My boss still rang me and asked for my digital marketing strategy reports. I still brushed my hair. Food and supplies were flown to the hotel a couple times a month, then once a month, and then every other month. Every time a shipment arrived it was a mad rush for supplies. Felipe turned the hotel bathroom into our personal storage unit. In the hotel, shells of men and women hobbled through the halls like they were fever drunk. Babies wailed into the night. Disease eventually came to the packed hotel. Masks were scarce. There was no medicine. The news was all bad. Whole cities were wiped out from the floods. People shouted "Hoax!" daily, even as people dropped dead in the halls from sickness or malnourishment. We thought about leaving, but we didn't want to lose our room and the floods were getting closer, blocking any viable routes. The floods were blamed on every political leader and every country that wasn't ours. There were impossible conspiracies that held no merit. We blamed everyone and anything except the god of randomness. We read obituaries every day. Then, the power went. There was no backup plan. We boarded ourselves up in our room until we went mad. A year passed. The triviality of life and its insistent schedules and immaterial goals were exposed. Felipe came to me, delirious in the middle of the night, bloodshot eyes, telling me he knew someone who could help us. A pilot. There was just a certain price to pay. A price I've questioned since then.

We left the river when Milo started to whine. He needed to eat. We moved back to the debris site and huddled near the food box. I took stock of the food – bagged beans, rice packets, granola, oats, protein bars, chocolate, water. There'd be enough here to sustain us for a month, maybe less. Maybe more if I ate every other day. The box also contained a fire-starter, water purifier, and compass. Oh, Felipe.

When night crept in, I put the food box under a burnt sheet of metal from the debris. I didn't know much about bears, but I knew not to sleep near our food source. I made a camp in the dirt under a loose piece of sofa-sized metal blown from the craft. I positioned the metal sheet against a fat tree, creating an angled roof. I pulled Milo on my chest and coaxed him to nurse. I knew he was exhausted because he didn't protest. Wrapped in my sweater, Milo's mouth went still after a while. I adjusted the bag beneath my head and looked up through a gap in the sheet metal. The ink-blue sky was littered with thousands of stars, like someone had wildly flicked white paint all over the dark canvas. I counted Milo's breaths until my body powered down.

In the morning, we journeyed back to the river and drank from a pool of water, which gave me an opportunity to explain the water purifier to Milo. Standing at the foot of the river, listening for something – anything – I had a strange feeling we weren't alone. The river lapped against my boots, pretending it was just a friendly little pond. But I knew the gross power of water. How it gives life. How it takes it away too. An enchantress I feared more than anything.

We shared a protein bar and sat on some rocks; then Milo placed his palms on my knees.

"Can we see BeezBo now?"

I smirked. Hearing his pronunciation of Bisavó – or *great-grandmother* in Portuguese – as *BeezBo* made my chest momentarily light.

"Is that what you want to do?"

Milo nodded. "Yes, I do."

"Where is Bisavó's house, hon?"

Milo smiled sheepishly and said, "Um, that way!"

He pointed across the river, and there was really no way for me to prove him wrong.

CHAPTER THREE

It took a long time for Milo to settle down and accept that the ground beneath the sheet metal was a place to sleep. The previous night, he was easier to get to bed. He was exhausted and easily moldable. He would've slept on a tree branch. But tonight, he was more aware, more adjusted to the environment. This allowed for more stubbornness. He wanted to run off and touch everything. After I gave up arguing, he came to me. Huddled beneath the moon, shivering, Milo lay next to me, nestled inside my sweater. We were lucky it was summer. Still, night brought its dew and windchill. It brought its ear-scorching bugsong and impenetrable darkness. What would we do come fall, winter? How long would we live in this debris field? Was it lunacy to think about other seasons so soon? Or, was it exactly the right thing to think about? No one was coming to rescue us. This was exactly the right thing to dwell on. Felipe would have thought well past the immediate seasons and into the next decade. He'd already be cutting down trees to build a home. I bit my nails down to the skin as Milo slept, making a mental list of every fear. And then, I didn't think about anything at all. All that mattered was keeping Milo alive another hour.

I could feel the darkness clawing at me, taunting me. I rummaged in my bag for my sun-powered flashlight. I clicked it on and positioned the flashlight beside us. Milo's face in the small light reminded me of home. I thought about our sink for some reason. How I labored there, consumed with resentment. How Milo brought his toys over to me, asking me without words to give them life. How I wished Felipe would wash just one dish. Just one fork and I'd shut up. I'd be able to play with Milo, cross-legged on the floor, giving him the connection he craved so much.

Milo awoke.

"Mama?"

"Shh. Be quiet."

"Why quiet?"

I whispered, "We have to be careful of bears."

"Why?"

"Because they could eat us."

Milo finally whispered too. "Why they eat us?"

"Close your eyes, shh."

"Mama?"

"Yes."

"What we doing?"

"Sleeping."

"What happened to hell-copta?"

"Fire. Accident."

"Mama, I coldddd."

"Can you climb inside my shirt?"

Later in the night, he woke up whining.

"Mama, I want big bed."

"So do I. Shh. Bears."

"They eat us?"

"They could. That's why we have to whisper."

"I want milk."

"Come on."

"Mama, milk's not coming!"

"Shh, Mama's boobies need to sleep."

I lay awake for hours listening to the wind in the woods. Keeping tabs on the world. How could I sleep? What mother would sleep? It was like the first few nights after bringing Milo home from the hospital – couch-laden, wide-eyed, watching movies as Milo slept soundly in the bassinet lodged into the sofa crook. All four pounds of him.

The ash of the craft carried a bleak scent as it escaped into the void of open air. Carried away to mountain trees and their cold secrets.

I imagined Felipe and our pilot, resting together – forever. Milo's breathing became snoring. Sustained by the hopeful sound of his breath, I told my heart to loosen up. My body forced me to sleep, and we lay together like a single lump of clay.

I woke before sunrise and watched a shrew hobble across the debris field, curious and thorough. While Milo slept inside my sweater, I carefully removed myself from our cocoon and stood in the great open dawn. I came closer to the wrecked helicopter. Felipe's tomb. I knelt and talked to him quietly.

"You did it. You got us to dry land." My shoulders heaved with inward sobbing. "You were brave," I said through tears. "I'm sorry. I love you."

I swallowed, hoping to keep the sound of my tears from reaching the ears of bears, men, and most importantly, Milo. I'd never talked to him about death before, even though it happened all around us. If he didn't ask about someone, I didn't bring them up. The loved ones of his toddler-hood life were slowly being pulled out of his mind like loose string, and I let it happen. And soon, Felipe's string would be pulled out too.

I raised my head and asked the brightest star in the serene sky for help. *Will you guide me? Will you show me the way? Will you stay with us? Oh God, help me. Help Milo.* I spoke quietly to myself or any specter that would listen, until the shrew disappeared, and Milo woke up.

We moved back and forth from the river to the debris field for several days. This became our routine. Milo promised never to get too close to the charred craft where his father lay. He asked about Felipe often.

"Dada had to go somewhere," I explained.

"He coming back?"

"I don't think so."

"But I want him to!"

He let out a cry I'd never heard before and looked toward the helicopter. Milo was a smart boy.

"Just remember that Dada loved you so much. Okay? That's all you need to know."

Felipe had a grandmother in Tennessee. He called her Avó, or grandmother, while Milo called her Bisavó. I simply called her Ana. She lived in a remote tranquil mountain town on a high cliff. The town had never made it onto any map and was secluded. Its plateau was inaccessible by car due to its narrow roads. In years past, we would take special motorbikes to access the cliff town; sometimes a helicopter if we had the funds to rent a pilot. The old woman kept chickens and goats and would have us vacation in summers. She met Milo when he was six months old. She smoked a pipe and worked in a glass studio at the base of the mountain. Her home was lined with black gum trees and stood beautifully haggard atop the deep, dark tones of a tenacious mountain range. Heaven. The periphery of her property was protected by sturdy land, land that had weathered tornadoes, heavy mud, and root-eating insects. But never floods. Never intruders. The town was called Sweet Gum. No one knew about Sweet Gum. Before the world lost its power and its dignity all at once, she spoke to us, bragging about the stability of the land. Her home became a symbol of hope to Felipe and me. A grand pedestal in a world that was quickly sinking. Tall and hidden.

The trees in the wood must have wondered what we were doing, going back and forth to the river. This was obviously not a place that humans frequented lately. Humans would have come by now. The smoke would have brought someone, a hiker would have stumbled upon us. Not that anyone hiked anymore or did anything for leisure. This was a desolate place, which was good for our safety, yet also aroused a feeling of doom.

Milo picked up a large stone in the river and turned it over, finding a trout beneath it. It was floating in a shallow pool on its side, half dead. Milo tried to kick it, but I held him back. "No boo boos for the fish," I said. Before leaving, I eyed the trout carefully. I'd never killed anything before. Would it have to come to that eventually? How strange to be thinking that way. I helped the trout back into the river.

We collected a few of Milo's favorite rocks from the shore and headed back to the debris field for dinner. We had been eating sparingly from our food storage. I could hardly get anything down though.

The evening felt heavy. There was a palpable change, a drop in the air pressure.

"Mama, I hung-ee."

"I know."

We didn't speak much as we crossed the open field toward the wreck. I held him at my hip. I looked forward to rummaging through the food box. I had collected some water in Milo's bottle and planned to heat oats over a fire, granted the fire-starter wasn't a problem. But someone, or something, had gotten to the food box first.

CHAPTER FOUR

Not all the food was taken. I wondered if it was a human or a bear that had gotten into our scraps. Both possibilities frightened me. Whatever creature came for our food, it spared us half. I looked for footprints as a clue, but it was a challenge with the high grass and wreckage everywhere.

We stayed at the debris site until the food was nearly gone. By then, we barely had enough for a mid-morning snack. We were going to die of starvation – of this, I was certain.

Although starving, at times I reveled in the pristine beauty and the quietness of our environment that asked nothing of me. One morning, I took Milo to a high point in the woods that seemed to lead to an open mountain range, and we stood and looked out over the expansive land. I had brought the compass with me. The treetops were losing leaves, and the remnants of ash blew from beyond. It was known that fires came from the west. When we were holed up at the Pennsylvania hotel, I caught wind from the news that the west wrestled with demons of their own. Alongside the floods, they battled fires in rare pockets untouched by water. It drove even more souls toward the dry lands. Seeing the ash reminded me of the trouble still thriving and waiting outside our wooden enclave, but we couldn't stay there forever. I spun myself around, pinpointing south with the compass. The home of Milo's Bisavó was south, marked by an unmistakable rock formation that stretched into the sky. I could picture it in my mind. The rocky cliff boasted a narrow waterfall that fell into a fresh, shallow pool. But the key to finding this rock formation was first locating Heaven's Dome, an observatory tower. The observatory could be seen miles away – the highest point in all of northeastern Tennessee. Whenever Felipe and I visited Sweet Gum, we cheered when we spotted the observatory, knowing his grandmother's house, her cottage above the cliffs, was just a few miles south. I was filled with a buoyant hope knowing I held the correct direction in my palm. It took several days to muster the courage to leave Felipe's body. Milo had become used to the trees surrounding us, and accustomed to sleeping inside my oversized shirt, both of us beneath an upright slab of sheet metal that acted as a lean-to. He knew where to lie when I changed his diaper. He learned what to touch and what not to touch. I, myself, had become comfortable conversing with the wreckage of the copter, thinking Felipe was listening. "My milk is running low, Felipe. The river is warmer than I imagined. I'm sure you'd have caught one hundred fish by now. Milo wants more to eat, but I want to save what we have. He got so upset he hit me." But diapers were running low. Wipes were half gone. What would we do once they were completely gone? I could not hold on to this fantasy that we had a permanent home in the woods much longer. Or that Felipe was of some imaginary assistance. Sooner or later, we'd have to leave. It would be tumultuous to travel by foot to Felipe's grandmother's house. I had no idea how to get there or how far we were from Tennessee. But if we didn't try, we would die. I was numb, but still – I could not let us die there.

On the day we moved south, I salvaged additional materials from the crash site. The faint morning light was glimmering and ghostly, with pink and amber streaks smudged across the sky. Milo pulled at my leg, surprising me by his sudden appearance. I usually knew when to expect his waking. The fact that he could stray from his schedule was unsettling. I realized I could not take anything for granted, not out here.

The trees by the river were beginning to sway, and the wind howled in my ears. Rain was brewing. How could we march into foreign land during a storm? I realized I hadn't consulted Milo on anything. He had become used to having a silent, sad mother. How long had it been since we landed? A week? Two weeks? I couldn't tell. Milo tottered between his imagined world and our reality, in which we purified water, ate ridiculously small amounts of food, left the diaper on longer than usual, and used our quiet voices. This was an almost impossible task. Milo sought play in everything despite our bleak state. He collected sticks, named them, and gave them conflicting scenes to play out. He asked about Felipe every day. Eyes closed, hands outstretched, rain droplets fell into my palm.

"Mama, rain!"

We moved back to the field of debris and huddled beneath our lean-to. Rain tinkled against the metal, slowly at first and then it poured mercilessly.

"Mama, I don't like this! Mama, I want Dada! I *want Dada!*"

My mind moved in and out of my head like a swinging pendulum as thunder crashed above us. Milo howled. When the rain quieted slightly, I picked Milo up and moved him out of the metal tent. I stood beneath a tall, thick spruce and paced back and forth. I cradled his head in the crook of my neck. I moved from tree to tree, hushing him until he went down for a mid-morning nap. I covered his head in a fresh diaper to absorb the rain from his hair.

We left the next morning. But not before Milo stopped at the tree where I normally changed his diaper. He held on to the fronds of a hemlock. He looked toward the helicopter.

"What is it, baby? Time to go."

"But I don't wanna leave Dada."

Milo was perceptive – perhaps more than I gave him credit for. He looked at the sky. The rain had left. His clothes were still wet. I didn't know what to do. My rain-drenched son, standing by his father's tomb. I joined him and knelt.

"I don't want to leave Dada either." I didn't know what else to say. "Bisavó has pictures of Dada at her house. I think you'd like to see them."

"Dada in there?"

"In where?"

"Pictures."

"Yes, he's in the pictures."

"I wanna see."

"You will."

"Okay."

Just an hour into our journey south, Milo sat at the foot of the hill and smushed his palms into the dirt. I took the opportunity to pause and inspect the area. The sky was filled with gray ash, blowing in with a westerly wind. Distant ridges were highlighted with green leaves tinged with yellow, apricot, and rust. I thought of government-run patrollers, coming to round up wanderers. Vivid and nightmarish scenarios came to me – being forced into an encampment, separated from Milo. Images of children being taken from their parents in the dry lands were the last images I had seen on the news – before the news stopped altogether. But we were alone. No patrollers, no marauders, no one. No souls. I wondered what state we were in, for the sake of direction. I knew that the mountain trail stretched from Pennsylvania to Tennessee, cutting through Maryland and West Virginia. But I wasn't sure where we were; I wasn't sure where the helicopter had landed. Either way, we'd follow the mountain ridge as far as we could, as long as food would allow. By my estimates, that was about a day or two. Two protein bars and some beans and oats. After that, I'd pray. Bisavó's home was our goal. Sweet Gum, Tennessee. But I wasn't insane either. I knew it was a lofty goal, something to keep myself alive, for Milo's sake. The real goal was staying alive another day. But we needed something to set our will on. *You just follow the trail through the mountains. Follow the trail to my grandmother's house.* Felipe's instructions.

"Let's go, Milo."

"No!"

After a while, I realized the only way to move my son was to empty some of the contents of my hiking bag and place him in it. I took out rods and other metal scraps I had thought I could use as weapons or tools. It opened up a lot of room. I left the junk on the side of the trail and put all the other important things, like food and diapers, into the front pocket of the bag to make room for Milo in the deepest compartment. I made sure to keep the axe though, tucking it into a deep side pocket of the backpack. Then I fashioned my Sea Isle sweater into a bag, closing the neck hole with wire and steel wool. Anything that wouldn't fit in the backpack, like our water purifier and fire-starter, went into the makeshift sweater bag.

"Get into the backpack."

"No!"

"You can pretend it's a plane."

"Okay. Brmmm!"

His weight was manageable on my back, but I knew it would catch up to me eventually. We wandered down a narrow dirt path with sprawling meadowlands on either side of us, the mountain range in full view. We would follow it to Bisavó or die along the way. *Take him to my grandmother.* It was Felipe's request. I was a woman of my word.

Milo was unusually quiet, but every so often, I caught him pretend-flying his stick in the air.

CHAPTER FIVE

The next day, Milo wanted to do nothing but collect sticks. More sticks than he could hold in his mud-coated hands. He ran ahead of me. I caught myself smiling as he ran freely through a grassy pasture. "*Mama!*" He stopped suddenly. I hustled toward him to see what had stopped his feet. Two men lay in the grass, their throats slit. "Mama, what's that?"

The bodies were pale, eyes staring skyward. I looked all around me. Quickly, I rummaged through their pockets. I removed their pants, socks, shoes. With the edge of my axe, I ripped off the fabric of their shirts.

"Mama, what you doing?"

One man had a small leather bag.

"Here," I said. "For your sticks."

Hurriedly, I helped Milo into the backpack, and we marched on. I worried about those men. Who had killed them and why? They had nothing of traditional value on them, so I assumed they were robbed and murdered by marauders. Not patrollers. Patrollers would have forced them into the nearest encampment. I told Milo that the men were dead.

"What's 'dead' mean?"

"Sleeping...forever."

"But why?"

"Someone killed them," I said bluntly. It was the first time I talked so directly to my son about something so macabre. It was a test, to see what he could handle. To see how I might eventually tell the story of his father, and not scar him.

"Like bugs?"

"Yes, just like bugs."

"Mama, why they do that?"

"I don't know. Because they're big bullies."

We stopped at a large boulder before the sun set. The top of the boulder arched forward, providing something of a roof. I made a fire using sticks and leaves. The fire-starter worked well – Felipe had done extensive research on the best brand. At the time, I thought he was mad. It was hard to imagine that I'd never have access to my stove. When I poured Milo's sticks into the cluster, he wailed more than I expected him to. He almost jumped into the fire after them, but I grabbed his arm in time. Once he settled, I heated a full can of beans over the blaze, convinced I heard whispering from somewhere in the dark beyond. After we ate, the world felt somewhat hushed. Milo nursed and fell asleep inside my shirt.

Felipe came to me in a dream. His hair was blacker than normal, and his charcoal glasses sparkled. He wore a blue suit. He opened his arms, inviting me into his embrace. His eyes were mild and sweet, and I felt I could have stayed tucked inside his chest for eternity.

In the morning it was raining again. We stayed beside the boulder drawing pictures in the dirt with sticks. Staring into the sheet of rain and mist, I grieved the world as it once was. For Milo, that world was already gone. I drew pictures of things like swings and apple pie and friends to remind him of life's pleasantries. Milo became engrossed by a new stick, as I drew an image of a man in a suit with glasses – Felipe from my dream.

When it was time to go, I asked Milo to put the stick in his new bag.

"No!"

"Why?"

"Because you put sticks in fire."

"I won't this time. Is that your special stick?"

"Yes, it's Dada."

I looked into his sorrowful brown eyes. "Did I throw your other Dada stick into the fire?"

"Yeah."

"I'm sorry. Do you forgive me?"

"Yeah, this not Dada anymore. This is *Doo-Doo*-Dada."

"I like that name a lot. I won't put him in the bag. You can hold him."

We plodded on down the dirt trail, keeping the ridge to our right and the compass positioned south. I feared Milo was being too loud. When I asked him to quiet down, he began singing a bedtime song at full blast. It was the first time all day that he sounded merry. I asked him to sing in a quieter tone and thankfully he did. I sung with him, harmonizing.

At the foot of the trail there came an abyss. An old town could be seen down below, about a mile away. Grim, flesh-eating birds circled the town with its scorched rooftops and burnt trees. But there was a lake. It was too far away from our trail, and the ghostly birds did not give me any hope.

"What's that?"

"It's a town."

"What for?"

"People used to live there."

"Where they go?"

"They went somewhere new. They left."

"Killed?"

"I don't know. Maybe."

"Bullies?"

I knelt to my son. "Milo, things weren't always this way. Before you were born, people lived in towns and went to school and work and parties, and no one thought about bullies at all."

"Mama, I did this?"

"No, of course not. Never mind. Come on this way."

Before the Shift, we would visit the Tennessee countryside with Felipe and his family, and watch the flight of geese and heron, with smoky mountaintops in the distance. Birds flew by the shoreline of a lake, and we admired the changing colors all around. I tried to think of that, to hold on to that.

We moved on, aligning ourselves with the ridge, staying on the trail. Milo wanted to be a butterfly. After lunch, he ran forward, waggling his hands like wings.

"I'm a *crazy* butterfly!"

"Take your time!"

"Mama, you be a crazy butterfly too!"

"I'm tired."

"*Mama!*"

I beat my wings, running after my little meadow insect, muttering nonsense. There was no one on the trail except for two crazy butterflies.

CHAPTER SIX

We came upon a wooded path with a North, South, East, and West sign at the foot of a rock wall. The sign was a comforting thing to find after an arduous hike with Milo sleeping on my back. The wooden post informed its readers that one was standing in Maryland. This was the most information I'd received in weeks. I refrained from kissing the post. A far-off sign boasted a nearby hotel: Mountain Lodge. We couldn't get within an arm's length of the hotel though. Patrollers and marauders occupied the dry lands, and there was rumor of cannibalism there. Facing humanity would be a final resort. We were safer alone.

Following the South Trail, I pressed on, while Milo slept. His snoring was soothing in my ear. My feet began to drag sluggishly past twisting green and lavender thistles and alarmed chipmunks. We were in complete isolation except for the occasional appearance of a rodent. My stomach rumbled. I could feel my intestines gurgling. I needed food. Water, too. In the distance, a cabin sat in a wooded brush like something out of a painting. I stopped abruptly. Milo began to stir in the bag as I peered cautiously at the cabin from behind a great oak.

"Mama, I wake now. I went poopie."

After quietly changing Milo by the oak, I dug a hole to dispose of his goopy diaper and wipes. I noticed again that we were running low on diapers. This would prove challenging not just for Milo – but for me as well; I planned to use his diapers as pads for my upcoming period. I needed a place to settle for a day or two, to take stock of our belongings and to figure out how to gather more resources. I also needed a goddamn break. I needed to think, to plan. We would need coats for fall, new underwear, socks. How, though? I caught myself hoping I'd stumble upon more dead bodies. I was rummaging through my hiking bag to restore a sense of order to it, when Milo ran ahead toward the cabin. He charged forward, laughing. As I ran after him, my heart thumped rapidly. I imagined him running right into the clutches of a hungry marauder. "*Milo, stop!*" Laughing ridiculously, he started for the cabin's steps, but he fell into a covered hole before he could reach them.

Milo wailed from inside the hole, "*Mama!*" It was a trap for small animals. "*Mama! Boo boo!*" His cry stung. It was raspy and from his gut – it meant he was really hurt. My heart was in my throat; I worried he broke something. Then, what? I leaned over the hole, which was much deeper than he was tall. If I stood in it, however, I'd be able to peer out. Milo lay bent and unmoving.

"Can you stand up?" I asked, panicked.

He cried.

"Baby, I just need you to stand up."

The sun shone through the trees and onto his sad head. The pit had sticks that were whittled to sharp points burrowed into the ground. Milo was lucky. He seemed to land in a safe spot, where a few sticks had already fallen over. Still, I worried one of the sticks stabbed him. I couldn't see if there was blood or not.

"*Milo!*" I yelled. "Please stand up!"

"Mama! *Out!*"

"Shh. Please, baby. There might be bullies here. Please."

Milo quieted, trying to contain his whimper.

I looked all around before entering the hole. I hoped I wasn't falling right into someone's trap. I slid into the hole until my boots touched the ground on either side of sharp sticks. I picked Milo up by the waist and thrust him up until he was able to squirm over the edge to safety. Getting myself out was the hard part. Milo looked down at me, tears in his eyes. I tried to climb out, but anxiety consumed me. The dirt was slippery. I looked to Milo. Something caught his gaze. I worried it was patrollers, coming to take us to an encampment. He wouldn't take his eyes off whatever he saw. I would not let anyone take my son. Filled with adrenaline, I thrust one of the sticks from the ground and drilled it into the side of the dirt as something to step on. Rolling onto the dirt, I grabbed Milo and pulled him to my chest. Then, I realized what had caught his attention. It wasn't patrollers. It was a sound. Flies.

I quickly inspected Milo, ensuring nothing had been broken. His right leg was covered in scrapes and his left one was bleeding, but his limbs seemed to bend as they were supposed to. I pressed my hand against his skin until the bleeding slowed. He was shaken up, so I used the opportunity to tell him to sit quietly on the cabin stairs while I inspected the source of the sound. Whenever Milo got hurt, it always took him a while to bounce back. I gave him his sticks and told him not to move. He sat still but cried out that he was hungry. I worried that he'd gone too long without eating a good meal.

I walked anxiously to the back of the cabin, following the sound of buzzing flies. A dead horse and man who had been shot lay at the back of the home. Holding in a shriek, I held on to a rail to throw up the previous night's beans. We could not stay at a place where a man had just been murdered. However, I noticed the dead man had an empty revolver holster. Perhaps a marauder killed the man, took what he needed, and left. I looked at the horse.

Milo cried from the other side of the cabin. I ran to him. He was okay, just flustered by his bloody scratches. He needed rest, a place to relax for the night – as did I. Surely, the marauder would not come back after this kill. Perhaps the scene of a crime was the safest place to be. I peered through a window glazed with dust and mud. One room, with a loft. I jiggled the door handle and was surprised that it was unlocked. We stepped inside. I opened every cabinet, every drawer. No food.

"Mama, what you doing?"

"Just looking around."

"Is this our new house?"

"No. It's a cabin. It's like a hotel. That means we just stay for a night or two. Okay?"

He didn't answer.

I laid my sweater on the wood floor and sat Milo on it. I found old books in the cabin and tried my best to dab his wounds with sheets of paper. Then, I sat with him on the floor for twenty minutes, play-acting with his sticks, until his mood lightened. He had collected more twigs than I'd realized and had given each one a new name – Poo-Poo, Booger, and Boobie were his favorites. Doo-Doo-Dada remained a staple. Once Milo was satisfied to play on his own, I went outside to see the man and the horse. "Stay here," I instructed him. "I'll be right back."

I lingered by the horse, which was buzzing with flies. For some reason, I didn't vomit when I saw the horse again. My mind had gone blank on the matter. I only thought of our pitiful scraps of food left in the hiking bag, barely anything left. I craved food intensely. A hearty meal. A steak. A heaping pile of lasagna. My stomach swirled with hunger pains. Milo screamed suddenly from inside the cabin. My heart raced. I ran back to him. His face was drenched with tears when I returned, and he was lying on his side.

"What is it, baby!"

"Mama, I hung-ee!"

He held his belly. I rubbed it, terrified of how thin he was becoming. I held him in my arms until he cried himself to sleep. While he slept, I sobbed into my hands, not knowing what I was going to do. I walked outside and stood on the porch of the cabin, hyperventilating. Tears streaming, I walked around the bend back to the dead man and horse. I imagined our dwindling food. Milo's hunger. My hunger. I stared at the horse. Meat. No sign of decomposition. But how could I slice into a horse? Impossible. I was not a person who sliced into animals. Sure, I ate meat before the Shift, but never like this. Eating meat was like eating candy. I never thought about where it came from or how it got there; it was just delicious and filled me up. I remembered Milo's Bisavó Ana made us jumbo shrimp once. The eyes were still attached, round and sable. Seeing its beady eyes made me realize the life behind the food. When Ana wasn't looking, I moved my shrimp onto Felipe's plate.

I just couldn't eat something with a face. If it were missing the eyes, I might've eaten it. Funny how the mind is willing to block out the truth for comfort. Now, I'd kill for shrimp – eyes or not. But there was no shrimp here. Just a horse. And our lives depended on it. Its behind was beginning to look appealing. My old way of thinking seemed to be put on hold for the moment. I'd heard of people lost at sea, suddenly filled with urgency to bite blindly into a raw fish head. I understood this feeling now.

I paced. I couldn't do it. I couldn't cut into a horse. I sat on the cabin steps, my head in my hands. The flies buzzed fiercely. I crept back inside the cabin to escape the thundering sound of flies. I stared at my sleeping boy. He whimpered in his sleep, and it broke my heart. Nothing mattered anymore except keeping Milo alive. I needed to bury my fears. I eyed the axe I'd left on the kitchen counter. I grabbed it with purpose and left the cabin.

I rounded the bend to where the man and horse lay still and dead. There was no use delaying my act. Crying, I brought my axe down into the horse's behind. I hated myself for doing it. But I told myself this was what living beings did. I didn't create this world, but I was a player in it. Carefully, I sliced off meat, trying not to heave. This was not who I was. I didn't even want Milo to kick a half-dead trout, and now I was cutting into the thickest part of the horse. Hunger had clouded my perspective. More importantly, I thought of Milo's hunger. I brought chunks of meat back into the cabin and set it aside carefully. Then I found a couple of tattered books and dry twigs and arranged them in the cabin's empty fireplace. I took out my fire-starter, sparking a flame to life. My hands were shaking, paralyzed with disbelief on what I had just done. I put the flesh onto sticks and roasted the meat until it was charred. Soon, Milo woke up.

"Mama, you cooking?"

"Yes, I'm making something special for you."

"What?"

"Nuggets."

The day was lost. Soon, it was night. In a strange and wonderful turn of events, Milo said he wanted to sleep. He leaned his nose into my shirt, requesting milk. I noticed light sniffles and a warm forehead. I couldn't leave this place. Not yet. We needed the warmth.

"There's a bed up here, Milo."

We climbed to the loft, which was littered with hay.

There was a window. I spent the night watching the dead man and horse in the leaves, making sure they stayed put. I was losing my hold on reality.

I awoke in the dawn to a yelp from outside. I exited the cabin and found the source of the sound. A fox had fallen into the pit and impaled itself. It was on the edge of death. I waited for it to take its last breath. Once it stopped moving, I scooped the fox out with a long stick I had found near the cabin. While Milo slept, I axed its head off and threw it in the woods. I wanted its body to seem like an object. Just a blob of dough and bones. Axing the horse had given me confidence. I spent the morning skinning the fur off its rusty back with my axe. Milo needed a coat or shawl or whatever we'd call this hunk of skin and fur. As for me, I wiggled the dead man's coat from his back. It was made of suede and lined with raccoon fur. We stayed at the cabin for three more days, feasting on horse. Milo's congested nose went from clogged to clear, with the help of breast milk that I dripped directly into his nose for its healing properties. The horse meat had helped to replenish my milk supply. We left when the lingering scent outside the cabin was too much to handle.

The following day, I managed to carry us about three miles south of the cabin until we came upon a large lake surrounded by wild brush. I stopped and fell to my knees.

"Mama, you okay?"

"No, Milo. This is hard."

The boy crawled out of the bag and stared at me. His lips were chapped and peeling. His hair stuck to his eyelashes. Snot was glued to the edge of his nose and scattered across his cheek like a slug's trail.

"I think it's time we take a bath."

"Where?"

I pointed to the lake. Milo frowned.

"Don't you want to go swimming?"

"No."

"Why? It'll be fun."

"I scared."

"What are you scared of?"

"Bullies."

"There's no bullies in there. It's just for Mama and Milo."

"It cold?"

"It might be. But you're brave. Aren't you?"

"Yeah, I brave."

I smiled.

"Mama?"

"Yes."

"You brave too?"

"Yes, I'm brave too. Can you help me up?"

He reached his hand out for me, looking unsure how to physically get me to my feet. But as soon as he touched my hand, I stood up as though his touch were magic. A smile blossomed on his face. He kept his little hand in mine as we walked toward the lake.

CHAPTER SEVEN

We slipped out of our clothes and took them into the lake with us. Milo splashed in shallow water as I drenched our clothes, turning them inside out, scrubbing the mud spots and skid marks. I inspected his wet diaper among our pile of dirty clothes and decided to remove the chemical-laced padding from it. Perhaps if I washed and dried it, I could reuse it. As for Milo's poop, I decided the best course of action was to catch him before he went. That way, he'd soil fewer diapers.

Afterwards, I laid our wet clothes on a rock and walked into the water with Milo. I held him at my chest and sunk further into the cold lake. Beneath the smoldering sun, Milo laughed after reciting words like pee-pee and wee-wee and poo-pee. I splashed water at his tiny nose, admiring the crinkle of his button face. He began slurping at the water, which made me nervous. Knowing he'd only do it more if I told him to stop, I eased him out of the water. As we left the lake, sunny wind fluttered against our naked bodies. I thought of water parks and boardwalks, summertime ice cream and backyard sprinklers. Milo would not remember these things. Maybe they weren't real anyway. My foot became trapped in a tangle of grass and roots. I fell into a jagged rock, slicing my lip. Milo came to me with a leaf and plastered it against my bloody mouth. Then he peed, watching his newfound stream with amazement. The sun was kind. Clouds were displaced by a neon-blue sky. I made a fire and bundled our clothes over a stick to dry them. Yet, when they were ready to wear, I left Milo's pants off. I let him walk around pantsless, exploring. When he needed to urinate, he opened his legs and watched the dark amber stream make a tiny divot in the dirt.

In the late afternoon, Milo found a shallow pool where minnows gathered in green shimmering lake water, bumping noses, lost. They were trapped by roots rising from the mudbanks. He dipped his finger in, laughing as they dispersed. I placed the bean can into the pool and collected some.

"Why you do that!"

"Milo, we're going to eat these fish."

"Why?"

"Because we need to eat to stay alive."

"Alive?"

"Yes."

"What's *alive*?"

"It means we get the chance to spend another day together. Okay?"

"Okay, Mama."

Milo gripped my hand, giving me his stick named Doo-Doo-Dada to hold. He reached into the pool.

"I get more fish," he said.

I made a fire and roasted our minnows.

"Crunchy!" Milo sang.

When dusk came, the fire crackled and snapped. Milo lay in my lap, staring at the blaze. The calm hoot of a dove sounded, and Milo asked what it was.

"A dove," I said.

"What's a dove?"

"A dove is a bird. When I think of doves, I think of peace."

"What's peace?"

"No sadness. No pain. It means happy and safe."

Milo was quiet as he thought about this. "Mama?"

"Yes."

"I miss Dada."

I stroked his hair. "Me too, love." It was quiet. I struggled with what to say next. Guilt ravaged me. "Dada has peace," I said, trying my best to get my words out.

"Like dove."

"Like a dove."

We stopped talking and listened to the bird's beautiful coo.

When we were both in a trance, the sound of horse hooves and chatter sounded from afar. It was growing nearer to us. My heart pounded. *This is how we die*, I thought. *By the lake with bellies full of minnows.* I tossed the suede raccoon-lined coat over the flames. I grabbed whatever I could stuff into the hiking bag – fire-starter, water purifier, axe, compass, some leftover minnows. I couldn't grab everything. I pulled Milo away from our camp and trudged through the lake in the dark, holding Milo's mouth shut, whispering, "Shh. Bullies are coming. No talking. No noise." I held him against my chest and plodded through the black water, toward a lakeshore of wild bushes. Milo tried to cry once we emerged, but I held his mouth shut. We crouched in the damp thicket and watched from a great distance down the shoreline as two foragers on horseback stopped at the abandoned camp. A raw coldness ate at my skin. I prayed Milo wouldn't speak.

"I scared," he whispered.

"Shh. If you talk, the bullies will hear us."

I held him tightly against my body, his heart trembling on my skin.

We didn't sleep that night, not even after the foragers took off, clopping off in the moonlight. Milo fell asleep at dawn, shivering. I held him and rubbed his head. I blew hot air against his cheeks for hours. Beneath his eyelids, I imagined the world that was blooming inside his small, growing brain. The boy deserved so much more than this. He whimpered in his sleep. The sound brought an ache to every part of me.

When Milo woke up, I made another fire to warm us. Everything trembled. Him. Me. Everything. Our world. Then the chill left as the fire dried our clothes and skin and bones.

Milo looked fearful of what I might say or do next.

"It's okay," I said. "We're safe now."

The foragers took almost everything. Holding back tears and exhaustion, I left the lake and got back onto the trail. With Milo back in the bag, sleeping, I began to feel his weight. It hit me all at once, just as the water did. I didn't know how much further I could go. I had to sit. In the tall grass, staring, I left my body until buzzing sounded. I was beginning to despise the noise. Buzzing meant death. Bones were tossed carelessly in a pile. I reached for my axe. If we came upon any sinister scavengers on our path, I would show them no mercy. I was hurting, starving, void. But I was done caring about pain. Done with feelings. The only one who mattered was Milo.

I tied the small axe around my wrist and passed out.

CHAPTER EIGHT

I woke up to a calloused ice-cold hand toying at my leg. I sat up and met a shocked, grizzly face. Without much thought, I hurdled my axe into the man's neck until he fell onto me, blood splattering. Milo didn't stir. I rolled the man off. His quivering corpse was wearing my burnt suede raccoon coat — one of the foragers from the previous night. I slipped my coat back on with a strange delight. The man wore several layers, and this, I realized, meant that he'd killed someone for them. He was alone. Had he murdered his partner? I slipped his revolver out of his holster right as he locked eyes with me and died. I looked out toward the vast field of fog, wondering where his horse had gone. Nothing could be seen through the heavy white mist. I wiped the man's blood off Milo's face and watched Milo continue to sleep soundly until he finally became conscious.

Later in the morning, I asked Milo to walk beside me. His thirty-four pounds were wearing on my body. When he refused to walk, I challenged him to chase me down the gully that moved in lockstep with the mountain ridge. His laughter brought a lightness to my chest, but I needed something to ward off my dizziness and general feelings of malaise. I needed food. Something substantial.

. I had no way to know what lay ahead — I wanted to stay far away from towns, from people. As much as I feared the wild men who roamed the dry lands, I feared the organized ones even more. I could handle wild men — especially now that I was carrying a gun, now that I understood the vulnerability of a jugular vein. I empathized with them in a twisted way. Hunger and desperation had led them to insanity. Men with badges, the patrollers, had full bellies and warm beds and still did what they did. My hope settled in the fact that Bisavó

Ana's mountain village remained impregnable by those escaping the coasts. Not many people made it this far. And those who had made it were already corralled into the camps. While people on the coasts were pulled into the water, those in the midlands were plagued by the onslaught of bodies pouring in to escape a watery death. This brought disease. It brought the encampments. Our timing was good. We were lucky to escape the floods and miss the encampments. Yes, lucky. I continued telling myself that, as we rested in a bank of dirt. Each spot we rested might be our last. *Keep heading south,* I told myself. The more we walked, the safer I felt. Perhaps it was a delusion. A sick game I made Milo play. Perhaps it was just a way to pass time until imminent death.

Milo began ripping at the earth as I surveyed the land through the mist. "Look, Mama," he said. "Flowers." He brought me a fistful of dandelions. My eyes widened. I'd heard of dandelion soup. Never tried it though.

"Baby, we can eat that."

Milo helped me with the fire-starter. I held his small hands in mine as we lit the flame together. We fried up the golden buds using breast milk in our bean can. I tossed in some worms that Milo and I found. Teaching him kept him engaged. It kept him from wandering off. Where once I'd put the television on while I microwaved his dinner, now we were both scouring the dirt together for our food. It tasted like pure hell though.

We went on. Milo insisted on getting inside the backpack. I had rested enough to withstand his weight. Leaning into my neck, Milo started talking indecipherably about *Dada*. I wasn't sure if he was referring to the stick or the man. I was about to ask him to clarify when a high-pitched whimper sounded from behind us. Milo screamed. My feet came to a pause. A gray mist hovered in the air. I turned to the noise. From deep within the fog, the nose of a palomino punctured the dense veil of air with a snort.

I kept moving, ignoring the horse. I was hungry, but not hungry enough to charge after a wild animal. We moved on, leaving the horse behind. But as I marched on, I knew something was amiss. Milo was silent in the backpack, struck by something behind us.

"What do you see?"

"Horse."

I turned around. The horse nicked the ground with its hoof and blew air through its soft, big lips. It was still following us. A saddle hung awkwardly to the side. Its neck swung upward, as though the horse were politely requesting an adjustment of the burden. I wondered if the horse was a trap. Perhaps another forager was out there, waiting to attack. Was this a distraction? I didn't want to get involved. I scanned the area, ensuring no one was watching us, but I couldn't be certain. I walked on. The horse followed until the mist cleared. We walked until we found a cool stream with scattered rocks. I looked around and wondered where the horse had trotted off to.

The air was growing crisp. I questioned whether it was still August, or had we moved into September by now? I had no way of knowing. Hadn't taken time to tick days off on some makeshift calendar. My days were counted by the amount of times Milo smiled or learned something new. My days were measured in his increasing ability to understand the means of survival without destroying his spirit. I caught Milo looking at the stream.

"Mama, look! Fishies," he said, pointing.

We caught tiny fish in shallow water. It took all day. I didn't eat anything. Not after vomiting out a stream of putrid gray slush – dandelion soup à la breast milk and worms would not be on the menu anymore. Milo ate well. That night, I dreamt about Felipe again. In my dream, we never left our house. The water came and we didn't blink.

In the morning, my body was covered in red blotches from sleeping streamside where a nest of mosquitoes had taken camp. The itching was so intense it made me throw up once more. Milo was covered too. Our ruby-red bumps reminded me of a disease that ravaged through the hotel during our final days in Pennsylvania. Felipe talked crazy at the height of it all. Killing me and Milo first, and then himself.

If he hadn't met that pilot....
If I hadn't done what I did....

The horse came around again after we were bathed and standing naked.
I threw rocks in her direction and yelled a few choice words. I still
didn't know if the palomino was a trap. Even it wasn't, I didn't want
it drawing attention from anyone who might be looking for her or the
forager I killed. The horse grunted pleasantly as I held Milo at my hip.

"Go!" I yelled. "Get out of here!"

"Mama, horse not listening."

At every turn, Milo looked like his father. Somehow, I could
even see the grooves where his future crow's-feet might land. He
also inherited Felipe's fierce sense of observation. I shouted once
more at the horse, but she just sniffed at the roots and coils of an
upturned hemlock.

"No, she's not listening, is she?"

"Mm-mm."

We walked naked toward the horse. With a saddle made of
sheepskin, the horse waited patiently for my fingers to glide down
her creamy nose. When I did, the horse kicked at the ground and
quietly neighed.

"Mama, I like him," Milo said.

"I think she's a girl."

"But...why she don't listen?"

I snapped my fingers at the horse's ears. They remained still and
triangular on top of her weathered alabaster head.

"Because she can't hear, Milo."

CHAPTER NINE

In the afternoon, the water purifier was missing. I remembered Milo holding it last, near the stream. We had already made some significant tracks down the trail when Milo mentioned he was thirsty. I patted my bag. *Fuck, no.* When I told Milo that we needed to turn around, he protested by slapping my leg and screaming. My body was burning with aches. I could not imagine trudging upward, back to the stream with him on my back. I pulled at his arm as he rooted his heels into the ground. I wanted to lie down and never get up. But I needed to quiet him first. My fear was that his guttural toddler howls would one day reach the ears of someone waiting for such a cry, someone hungry. I yanked his arm. He stopped crying and gave me a strange look. I was not usually a mother who yanked. I kneeled.

"I'm sorry," I said.

"Mama."

"Yes."

"Why you do that?"

I crouched to my knees and nausea came on suddenly. I leaned forward and heaved until I spewed out some minnows.

"Oh God," I said, wiping my mouth.

"Mama, you sick?"

"I don't know. Maybe. I'm sorry I pulled your arm. I'm just... We need to go back to get that water purifier, and—"

"Okay, Mama."

Milo slogged behind me, doing the best he could on his short little legs. The more we moved up the hill, retracing our steps, the slower Milo became. I walked ahead, hoping he'd catch up. But soon, he took a seat in a pile of orange leaves. I walked back to him and helped him into the backpack. I wondered if I'd die by the hands of man or by the weight of my son on my back. I closed my eyes and counted my breaths, trying to escape the misery of my body. When the nausea returned, I took a break to heave by a tree.

"Mama, you sick. You need medicine," Milo said. I was too delirious to answer him. I walked on and didn't speak for a long time. I wasn't sure if Milo was following my lead or asleep in the bag on my back. I wondered if I might die.

"Look, Mama! Horse!" Milo shouted excitedly into my ear.

The palomino had returned to the stream where we last saw her. She didn't hear us as she lapped at the water. Bobbing between a triangle of streamside rocks lay the water purifier. I exhaled a long, steady sigh of relief once I saw it. The boy slithered out of the backpack and ran to it. The horse raised her head and wiggled her ears at the sight of Milo. I looked all around. No one was coming for this horse. She was just as lonely as us. I walked up to her slowly and raised my hand to pet her. She moved into my hand. Then I put my forehead to her nose. She blew warm air on me. It filled me with hope. A pure soul among us. She wore a coiled rope beneath her bridle; I gently unfurled it and latched it around the base of a tree.

We camped in the woods on the far side of the stream with the horse. The wind had blown ash from the west as the night swallowed the day. Milo collected wood from a slope of grass where a tree had fallen, talking to me – or maybe himself – from the distance. I could not hear what he was saying, but at one point I heard him mumbling about medicine. Frogs and cicadas had begun to sing as I readied our last remaining oats over a fire. All other food was gone. Now, our only source would be what I caught along our journey. I looked at the horse, and then I filled Milo's bottle with hot water as he ran toward the sunset. When he was out of view, over a hilltop, I heard an agonizing wail. I dropped the bottle and ran to him.

"Milo. Milo. What happened?"

He was inconsolable, on the ground, holding his foot.

"Did you get hurt?"

"Yes!" he cried. His face was scrunched and strawberry pink.

"Can you tell Mama what happened?"

He continued to cry. I wanted to hold his mouth shut and send his cries deep into his body, down to his feet, until it made the ground tremble.

I reached into my coat pocket and found an acorn that I'd picked up earlier. I held it up to his eyes, hoping he'd concentrate on the nut's intricate grooves. The thing with Milo was that he was always looking for new information, new stories, new wonder.

"See this?"

Milo wiped his nose with his sleeve and nodded.

"It's a magic acorn. Do you know what that means?"

"Hmm?"

"It means that when you hold it, you're super. Do you want to be super?"

Milo nodded and took the acorn in his palm.

When we walked back to our campsite, Milo limped.

The boy didn't say more, so I didn't find out what happened to his foot. Maybe a trip, a twist.

When we reached camp, Milo said, "Mama, magic acorn is from Dada?"

And for some reason, I said, "Yes."

We stayed at the camp for four more days. I needed to be certain that Milo could walk safely. I walked the horse around, getting to know her. Milo and I ate frogs and dandelions. I continued to vomit. Milo kept his eyes out for medicine, bringing to me blades of grass that I pretended to eat. In the middle of the night, I heard a noise from somewhere in the dark beyond. A gunshot. I knew we had to keep moving.

In the morning, I packed up our belongings and triple checked the water purifier was stored. I urged Milo to try to walk. He hobbled, and

I tried not to cry for him. A cold wind blew, sending bangs into his eyes. I needed to cut them at some point. More importantly, I needed help. I looked back at the horse. A vision came to me – me and Milo atop her. I had taken riding lessons as a girl, but that was so long ago. Perhaps I could make it work though.

"Come on, Milo," I said, placing him on my hip.

"Where we going?"

"We're going to go give that horse a name."

CHAPTER TEN

The horse had been in our midst long enough to know we were kind. She let me on her back with ease. Milo was the problem. The idea of riding on top of a horse was ludicrous to him. I might as well have told him to walk upside down the rest of the way to Tennessee. It's a good thing the horse couldn't hear him, because she might've kicked him in the mouth, the way he yelled. I had to wait until he passed out in my arms for a nap. I rocked him to sleep, infant style, by a quiet stream. Once he was well into dreams, I used the fabric of the dead forager's shirt to create a sling and wrapped Milo around my body. I hoisted us both onto the horse and urged her onward.

I had a feeling we were somewhere near the border of West Virginia due to familiar town names on weathered hiking posts that we passed during Milo's nap. The horse walked for a good four hours or so, giving Milo a much-needed rest. At times, I patted the horse, swirling my hand over her neck, thanking her. We passed a small hidden mountain village that had burned. We didn't pause. I held my breath as we passed charred homes, hoping no one would spot us. But I knew no one in town had survived the fire. Whoever started the fire took the people away to the camps, or else the people died from the flames. I was sure I'd see many more scorched towns on our way.

At night, orange flames swirled from a great distance. We weren't alone along this mountain trail. It was growing dark, and I was relieved that the falling leaves were soundproofing our careful clopping. I hoped to move us onto a trail deeper inside the woods by morning. Milo began to rumble in my wrap. I knew he would wake with a newfound energy while I was wanting nothing more than sleep. Lumbering to the edge of a leafy path, the horse began to flip her tail. She needed

rest too. Milo peeked out of the wrap and saw his new view high atop
the horse. He crowed with spirited laughter that could only come after
a deep sleep.

I set up a camp near a cluster of logs. I asked Milo to collect sticks
for our fire and to keep thinking about a name for the horse. As he
worked on finding sticks, I connected bits of the clothing I'd stolen
from the corpses. I draped the makeshift fabric tarp over a waist-high
stump and a long, thick log. It wouldn't protect us from bugs, but it'd
be something of a roof. Carrying a bundle of sticks, Milo dropped
them at my feet and said, "Horse is Mama."

"The horse is a mama?"

Milo scrunched his nose. "No, horse's name is Mama."

"Hmm, that might get confusing, don't you think?"

Milo tucked his lips in.

I don't know why I said that to him. I should've let him call
her Mama.

I patted down the fire when Milo fell asleep in the night. I wished to keep
it burning until morning, but I didn't want to draw in any wanderers.

The morning chill came for our noses and toes. I rubbed Milo on
his fox-covered arms, wondering how we'd survive true cold. Milo
suckled at my breast in the morning, whimpering. My supply was
down again. I needed something significant to eat. At that thought,
I pulled the covering off my head and the horse came into my view.
She was nipping at grass. Seeing her filled me with hope. The rope
kept her in place through the night. But I had a feeling she would
have stayed either way. A silent tear fell as I imagined her a messenger
from God. The color of her creamy fur brought a flashback of paint
palettes into my mind for some reason. To think we once cared about
the color of our walls.

The horse graciously let us onto her back again. It was cold in the
morning when we left our camp. Chipmunks buzzed with activity
on the trail. A thick scent of gasoline hung in the air. More towns.
More burning. I tried to steer the horse up a hill to get deeper into

the woods. She protested for the first time. Clucking her mouth, she moved us forward with determination. I was beginning to feel like she was in charge, and not me. A part of me liked it. Maybe she was Mama, after all.

We came upon a small farm, burned, tucked at the foot of a yellow valley. A scorched barn, fields of dead hay, remnants of wire-framed coops in pathetic disarray. Nothing lived here. I tried to pull us back onto the trail, but the horse stomped her foot.

Milo asked, "What we doing?"

The horse stomped once more, nudging us toward the dead farm.

I kept the revolver tucked into the band of my pants as we moved slowly onto the pillaged land. I whistled into the void, waiting for a reply. This farm had been destroyed long ago. Nothing moved or breathed here.

"Mama, what is this?"

"It used to be a farm."

"What's farm?"

"Remember your book about the cows and chickens?"

"No."

"Okay, well farms are where animals live."

"Where animals?"

"They're not here. This farm is broken, Milo."

We slipped off the horse. I tied her up and surveyed the open land. I begged Milo to get into the backpack. He followed through without complaint. He was hungry, weak, too tired to test his power. His mouth was chapped. He needed food and water. My milk. I could feel his ribs when I helped him into the bag. We walked toward the barn.

"Mama, where Mama?"

"The horse?"

"Yeah." Milo laughed at the silliness of using both names at the same time.

I looked behind me. She wasn't where I left her; my knot wasn't strong enough. Perhaps she wasn't as loyal as I thought. Inside, I was a tangle of nerves. How could we go on without her? I whistled for her, only to realize instantly that she would never hear my call. I prayed she would return. I didn't want Milo to worry too, so I acted calm. "I don't know where she is right now. She is a free bird. She'll come back."

"What's that mean?"

"It just means she does whatever she wants."

"Oh. Mama?"

"Yes, baby."

"Why can't the horse hear anything?"

"Um. I don't know why. She hears in other ways."

"How?"

"She has special horse senses. She *feels* things."

"What she feel?"

"Oh, lots of things. She feels vibrations, wind. She can feel the hot sun or a cold chill. She can feel us too."

"How she feel us?"

"Through her heart. She knows we're just like her. Moseying along."

"What's that?"

"Mosey?"

"Yes."

"Mosey means to walk…slowly."

"Mama?"

"Yes."

"Horse's name is Mosey."

"Okay, that's a good name."

We turned and walked toward the dilapidated barn. We crunched over boards and skeletal wood that crumbled against my boots. There was nothing here. I may have looked longer if Milo hadn't told me he peed his pants.

Milo's soiled pants went into the backpack pocket. I hung

determinedly on to the fact that I was able to alternate Milo between three outfits. I also had extra underwear for myself, which I kept in the bag, but other than that I had no other options except the new clothes I'd taken from the dead. We needed water, a stream, a river, rain, anything. Somewhere we could wash our clothes. I decided to change while I was at it. Changing out of my underwear, wiping off the day's discharge, I realized I'd gone a long time without a period. Milo slipped away while I was putting my pants and boots back on.

"Milo, come back!"

Milo laughed while spilling into an open field with clumpy dirt. I ran faster than I wanted to. I didn't want to expend extra energy. I caught Milo by the shoulder.

"Milo, you can't run away from me." My voice was trembling. I needed to eat.

"Why?"

I yelled, "Because I don't want you to die!"

Milo looked at me strangely. I didn't know if he knew what I meant. He didn't ask.

Milo sat in the dirt. I sat beside him to rest. The light was gray. Milo began pawing at the dirt like a mole. The ground smelled like muddy stew. Something in the dirt caught Milo's attention. He dug tenaciously. I let him dig, distracted by my thoughts and concern over my missed period.

"Something in here," he said buoyantly. I turned to him with a lazy look. He picked up a small dirt-cluttered potato and held it up like a toy. Something in me woke up.

"What's this, Mama?"

"It's a potato!"

"What for?"

I kissed him on the forehead. "Baby, I'm so proud of you!"

"Why?"

"Because you found a potato."

"Why?"

"Because you are amazing. Let's look for more. Oh, I'm so proud of you."

The boy smiled at the potato. We spent the afternoon digging the dirt for more treasures.

CHAPTER ELEVEN

We ate roasted potatoes charred over a fire. Milo was impressed that the dug-up potatoes magically transformed into something edible. The field was plentiful with the tubers, which we stuffed to excess in the Sea Isle sweater bag. It was good to feel full again. It was good to see a smile come back to my son. Before the night came, I found a cardboard box in the ramshackle barn. It appeared to have once held an overstock supply of goat feed. It wasn't burnt. There were even some leftover pellets, which we ate.

At night I brought the box to the back of the blackened barn where part of the roof barely stood. I told Milo the box would be his bed for the night. The boy asked if the box was his new house. "No. It's just your bed." He looked at the box and then back at me. He wondered if I would sleep in there with him. When I told him that I couldn't fit in the box too, he began to weep. "But I want you to!" Sounding like the complete sadness of the world, he cried much too loud. I bounced him against my breast and hummed. "Okay. I'll sleep in there with you."

At night, I stuffed the box with clothing for extra warmth and comfort. I tucked Milo into the box once he was drowsy. Then, I shuffled my torso inside the box with my legs hanging out. I didn't like feeling so vulnerable, but I hoped he'd fall asleep quickly. Milo was doubly upset when my milk wouldn't come. "Sometimes milk doesn't come," I told him. "Sometimes milk stops." And then I told him a story about two crazy butterflies who were looking for flowers to eat in a great, big meadow. He interrupted me.

"Mama, we live here?"

"Just for tonight."

"Why?"

"Because we have to keep moving."

"Why?"

"Because we have to."

"Because of bullies?"

"Yes."

"Mama?"

"Yes, baby."

"Where's Dada?"

The boy fell asleep, leaving me alone with anxious thoughts. I cried into my sleeve.

I lay down on a floor of cindered hay, folding down the flaps of Milo's cardboard box. I wiped my nose and shouldered up closely to the box, and peeked inside every few minutes or so.

When Milo was born, he came eight weeks early. None of our friends were having kids at the time. It wasn't the thing to do. But I wanted Milo. I thought of him every night before sleep, manifesting him into being. I had heard of baby showers – my mother had one. So did my grandmother. They would make intricate cakes and play games and put their pictures online and in physically bound albums. But that didn't happen anymore. Not when Milo was inside me. The country was dying. The world, failing. No one knew the floods were coming, but it's almost as if people knew, secretly, to their cores, that something momentous was about to happen. A baby? Oh. Hmm. Good luck with that!

Life in the Neonatal Intensive Care Unit, otherwise known as the NICU, was lonely. No one understood. It took seven days before I was allowed to hold him. It never sounded dramatic when I told people this. Oh, wow, they would say. Hmm. But they didn't really know what that meant. But Felipe knew. And if he had been in the dilapidated barn lying next to me, he'd understand why I still thought about it three years later. I lifted the flap to check on Milo.

"Are you awake?"

"Mamá, I went pee-pee."

"Okay. Come on out."

I left Milo's pants off and covered him in my coat. I crawled inside the box and plastered the wet spot with hay. I fell asleep holding him, my legs dangling out of the box like a dead squid, ignoring the scent of urine.

In the morning, I slid my way out of the box and let Milo sleep in. His waking in the night disturbed his sleep cycle, causing him to sleep later than normal in the morning. I sat outside the box, thinking. He coughed in his sleep. I looked inside. He settled back to sleep with his little legs curled up in my raccoon fur coat. My lips were dry. Dirt dry. I needed to find water. I needed to find Mosey. I grabbed my bag and stepped outside the barn, holding my arms, breathing in the morning. I walked away from the barn, searching for the horse. The scent of mud and the creek became overwhelming.

A stream was just beyond the nearest trees. How had I not realized it was here? I was delirious with hunger, I told myself. Now, I could hear it. Smell it. I walked, keeping the barn in eyeshot. It had been forever since I was able to do our chores alone. I soaked Milo's pants in the stream. My underwear next. The bean cans. Kneeling, I swished our clothes and cans in the water, almost forgetting where I was for a moment. I crouched there in the cool water while Milo slept, and for moment it felt like home. My mind was clear. The stream was moving. A strange and eerie sense of peace and renewal came to me. I thought of our house before the floods. Me and Felipe on the sofa, after the baby went to sleep. Felipe would kiss my neck as I stared coldly at nothing. He tried to bring me back to homeostasis. But I wasn't the same after we brought Milo home. There were looping thoughts, dangerous thoughts. At times, we made love at night. But it wasn't the same. Felipe felt my distance. Soon, we stopped altogether. I couldn't remember the last time Felipe and I made love. I held my belly, feeling the nausea return.

I walked back to the barn with our damp clothes in a bundle. I would make a fire and warm our clothing. I saw a creamy figure in the distance. Mosey was bent down, snacking on grass. It didn't look like she had any plans of coming up for air. Seeing her brought relief to every nerve in my body. I stepped inside the barn. First, I'd check on Milo and then I'd tie up Mosey.

But once I stepped inside, a hellish scream came from the back of the barn. "*Mama!*"

A large creature was pawing at the cardboard box that contained Milo.

CHAPTER TWELVE

A large cat with the face of a demon turned its head to me with a hiss. Mountain lion? Cougar? Puma? I wasn't well versed in animals. But it appeared hungry and unshakably angry. The cat was studying the box with Milo in it just as I appeared. Had I taken a moment longer at the stream, how would I have been able to live with myself? I wouldn't have. I reached for the gun at my hip. I had never fired a gun before.

"*Mama!*"

"*Hey!*" I screamed. "*Get out of here! Shoo!*"

The cat turned to me as I approached, dragging a leg slightly behind itself, with gyrating shoulder blades as it moved out of the darkness. I aimed the gun, not knowing what in God's holy name I was doing. My body was on fire, my blood coursing. I left the world. All that existed were me and the cat. I tried to fire the gun, but it was stuck.

"*Get! Shoo!*"

"*Mama!*"

Milo peered out. The big cat swung its head back toward Milo and approached the box.

"*Get back in there, Milo!*"

"Mama?"

There was a large, jagged rock in the barn. I sprinted toward it and hurled it at the cat. Milo burrowed back into the box. The cat clawed at the box with rapid-swift paws. Milo screamed. I tried firing the gun again, but the hammer was too rigid. I couldn't figure it out. I should have taken the time to learn, but I never wanted Milo to know about the gun. I threw more rocks. The mountain lion, or whatever it was, sniffed the corner of the box, screeching at me. How dare I interrupt his morning catch? The cat turned to me with angry, disfigured eyes. I finally managed to push the gun's hammer rightly into place. The cat moved in my direction. With gunfire speed, he lunged forward, knocking me down with heavy paws. His claws dug into my arms. I whipped the gun against the cat's head and fired a single bullet. The cat slumped off and recoiled in the burnt ground, lifeless. My entire body trembled as I stared at the dead cat. It took a moment for me to realize that I wasn't breathing, and when I did, I gasped, filling my lungs with air. For some reason, I grabbed my belly and not my arms where the cat had ripped into me.

"Mama?"

"Milo!" I ran to him, breathless. I pulled him out of the box and held him, sobbing into his neck. He pried me off, trying to see the cat.

"Mama, what is that?"

"I'm sorry. I'm so sorry."

"Mama, stop."

"I won't leave again. I won't leave again."

"Mama, I don't like this."

I led Mosey and Milo to the stream. I tied up Mosey and then set to washing my bloody arms in the gurgling water. I plastered wet leaves over my wounds while Milo examined pebbles. After a time, the bleeding diminished.

We moved back to the barn and ate parts of the cat that I cooked over a meager fire. Mosey seemed content in our midst once more. Perhaps she felt safe near us. Perhaps she thought of us as family. When it came time to leave, the boy was crying. He kept looking back at the remaining carcass of the cat. How could I explain that the cat tried to kill him, that I killed it first, and that we ate it to stay alive? "I'm sorry," is all I said. "The cat was food. That's all. Sometimes we eat animals. We won't always. But now we do."

"Do we eat Mosey?"

Mosey clopped closer, dutifully. Bless her.

"No," I said. "Not her."

"Why?"

"Because."

At evening, we walked on with the directional help of the compass. Milo fell asleep in the bag. Mosey wanted to stay on the trail, but I kept pulling her off the path. I wanted to get deeper into the woods. The burnt farm was an attraction. And the new path we trekked across was the natural way out of the farm. We'd found it, which meant others would too. We crossed over a stone bridge that arched above a creek. I knew that coming across man-made things like farms and bridges helped us secure resources, but it brought potential danger too.

I moved Mosey into some pathless woods. It was harder for her to walk smoothly over coarse grass and birch roots. I clucked my tongue at her, forgetting her deaf ears. With a gentle pat, I encouraged her to keep going. We walked into the woods until it was black. There was no time to make a fire. I nestled us into a fallen cluster of leaves and emptied our backpack so Milo could sleep inside of it. For me, I spread out extra clothing as a sheet for my bed. As I lowered myself to the ground gently, my arms throbbed with a persistent sting from the cat's attack. Every shift of my body heightened the pain, yet there was no choice but to bear it. Milo fell asleep quickly.

In the morning, I lay looking up at a birch tree and a mischievous crow. The crow flew away, flapping with a disappointed caw.

"Mama?" Milo rustled from the bag.

"Good morning."

"What happened to that cat?" I knew this might be a topic we discussed for a while.

"He died. I shot him."

"How?"

"I have a gun."

"Can I see?"

"No."

"Please?"

"No."

I set up camp and cooked more mountain lion meat over a fire. I was certain that mountain lions were new to this area; mountain lions didn't want to drown either. There was much to explain to Milo, and no right way to do it. I might have used sticks or rocks to entertain Milo if I were thinking clearly. To make him feel that everything was normal. But I tucked my fingers into the cool dirt, to keep from biting my nails. I needed to hide my growing jitters from Milo. I needed to understand my body – the nausea and why I suddenly felt my breasts tingle with intense soreness. A soreness that out-matched the lion rips in my arms and mirrored how I felt when I was pregnant with Milo. I needed to wrangle my thoughts around my missing period. Something was happening. Life was growing inside me. A baby. But not Felipe's. This wasn't good. Not good at all.

CHAPTER THIRTEEN

The Shift happened on a Monday. Of course, Monday. That's what everyone said in the early days. In the Pennsylvania hotel, we watched the news, feverishly trying to understand what had happened. There were videos, posts, articles, groups, and forums expressing a thousand different views on the matter. I stayed up late reading theories, but every idea led back to the same thing – that the layout of our world was forever changed. It didn't matter *why* anymore; it only mattered *how* we would survive. Felipe blamed it on climate change and outdated infrastructure, but I simply thought the Earth was tired of us. She shrugged her shoulders, shaking off land like it was an oppressive shawl she never wanted to wear anyway. A tired mother. Others argued that Pangaea never stopped evolving – it had dipped into the sea and rose again millions of times since its inception. New York City would be submerged, but Atlantis would reappear again. The Yin and Yang of the Earth. A tipping balance, always changing.

Before the Shift happened, Felipe was preparing for catastrophe. He knew *something* was coming, but he could never say what. I blamed the doomsday sites he visited all too frequently. I didn't know how to help him or what new conspiracy of his to believe, so I decided to believe in nothing except what I could control. Milk in my coffee, a yellow shirt on Sunday, a new bedtime song for Milo. But Felipe scared me, the way he loaded our garage with rice and beans and cans of everything you can imagine. Jams, pears, apricots, batteries, bullets. I just wanted to feel sane, to stop the intrusive thoughts that had developed postpartum. To be a good mom for Milo.

"We need to be ready for anything," Felipe said.

"Okay."

"You don't look ready. You look like your head is in space."

"Sorry."

In those months leading up to the Shift, I would lay awake and listen to Milo breathing. Sometimes, I would hear flocks of migratory night birds, circling the charcoal sky, hooting chaotically. The birds were trying to tell us something, but I just shut the window.

Milo was born into a cold world. A divided world, dead upon his arrival. I always thought things would get better, not worse. My grandmother would tell stories about the height of disease and civil wars and economic warfare. She said we were lucky we didn't have to wear hazard suits anymore or walk around fearing the logo on someone's shirt. She made it seem that we were the lucky generation, the ones for whom the world was promised. She didn't realize that we were already long gone from the wreckage of generations past. She never talked about rising water, about shifting plates. We weren't prepared for this.

The speed of the Shift was unpredictable. The water rose quickly at first, wiping out the East Coast and some of the West Coast in a matter of days. The crust of the country was gone. Millions, dead. Other continents had their own trouble spots. No one was safe. And then the flooding slowed over the course of a year. That's when the coastal survivors poured into the dry lands, into the encampments. By then, Milo was three and his home had been underwater for a whole year without any signs of coming up for air. The hotel became home. Our one-room suite with a king bed. It's all he knew. We thought the Shift wouldn't come for Pennsylvania, but it did. It came like a thief, suddenly and without remorse.

I met the pilot the night the floods finally came to our hotel. The water was rising, already claiming five floors of the fifteen-story building. I didn't know where Felipe was at the time. Milo was asleep. I considered staying put if Felipe didn't return; letting the water claim us both. What was the use? But Felipe did come back. He returned in a sweat, shaking me, leaning over Milo.

"Shh, do not wake him. I beg you," I whispered. "Where have you been?"

I followed Felipe into the hotel hall where bodies were wrapped in Vellux blankets. Candles sparsely lined the corridor. Coughing rang through the hall and the scent of blood was in the air. Felipe looked deranged.

"Where have you been?" I asked him again.

He grabbed my arms. "I have a way out."

I looked out the hall window. The water was coming.

"I thought we said we would stay."

Felipe looked over his shoulder at the water. "Are you crazy, Liv?"

"I don't know, maybe. There's no escaping it. We'll all be together this way. A lot of people are staying."

"Stop. We're not dying here. I met a pilot. He's in the military. He has a helicopter on the roof. He came to bring supplies."

"I'm tired, Felipe."

"Of what?"

"Everything!"

"Liv…"

"Milo knows when I'm not next to him. I should go back."

"Me and the pilot traded cigarettes and bread. I got friendly with him. Told him I had a wife."

"I'm happy you're making friends."

"He wants to meet you."

Milo noticed me holding my belly. Then he saw the gun that I left in the leaves. I wrapped it in a bundle of ripped fabric and then tucked it into the Sea Isle bag. When I went to kindle a fire, I noticed Milo snooping near the bag. I wrapped the bag around my body, hoping not to make a big deal out of it. The more attention I gave to the gun, the more he'd want to investigate it. I gave him my compass to occupy him. I cooked leftover meat over the fire, and we ate breakfast with the music

of chickadee calls. Milo got busy collecting pine cones while I stared
through the wood. I felt safe among trees, far away from paths and trails.
Away from bridges and towns and signposts and any signs of comfort. I
wondered if this would be the spot to stop. To abandon everything. Part
of me knew it was the right thing to do. For all of us. I rubbed my belly.

"What do you mean he wants to meet me?" I asked Felipe.
   "I told him about my Avó's house in Sweet Gum."
   "Yes. And?"
   "He said he knows Tennessee. He can fly us there."
   "Let him take you there then."
   "Liv, stop."
   "I'm not leaving. You saw what was happening to people in dry
lands. I'd rather the water kill us, not men."
   "Stop it. You're being selfish."
   "You are. You're sending us to our deaths."
   "It's better than waiting for it."

Felipe and I watched the news religiously before the power grid went
dead. We saw the camps. The murders. The rapes. The dry lands were
clogged with people. Resources were thinning. There was no power.
Nothing. It was barbaric. We saw gangs shoot a family in crisp daylight
and steal their belongings. A hidden camera in the camps showed people
being whipped into submission, starved. Food production ceased. The
people who didn't starve in their own homes succumbed to the corrupt
encampments. Death was everywhere. I didn't believe Felipe about his
conspiracies, and now he didn't believe me about the terrors of the
dry lands.
   "The pilot will take us to my Avó."
   "And then what, he'll just live with us and your grandmother?
Happily ever after?"
   "I don't know yet. He's up for anything."
   "Why can't you just go? You and the pilot can fly off to your
deaths together."

"Goddammit, Liv. Because he's a bartering man. He'll only take us if we trade something."

"So, give him something. What does he want? Beans? Rice? Milk?"

"No, he doesn't want food."

"Okay. What does he want?"

"He wants you."

People who were floors below us shuddered with shrill screams. Glass was breaking. The water was rising. Instinctively, I ran back inside to Milo. I needed to take him higher. So, there it was. I didn't want us to die. My instincts begged me to survive. There was nothing else to do. Maybe I'd be good at it if I tried. It'd be nice to be good at *something*. We were already packed. We were always packed, thanks to Felipe. I imagined Felipe's grandmother. She was a fierce woman who cobbled together an impressive acreage deep in the unknown bones of Tennessee. "No patrollers here," she said. "No water here." She lived in a bubble, far away from civilization. It was her secret kingdom. Blockaded on top of a mountain that seemed to mark the end of any semblance of human life. That's how we drummed it up in our minds anyhow. My body began to shake. I lost focus.

"Felipe, I can't— I can't do it—"

He held my shoulders and pressed his lips to my forehead. "I know, Liv. I know. This is insane. But do it for Milo." He opened the door to the hotel room where our son slept in the middle of the bed. We called it 'big bed.' I imagined the water breaking through the glass. Waves pouring through the hall during his deep and innocent sleep. His vulnerable body being swept into the cold wet sea.

I tried to stop my shaking fingers by clasping them together. "Where's the pilot?"

"On the fifteenth floor. Room 1527."

"What if he kills me?"

"He won't. He's a good guy."

"What if you stop loving me afterwards?"

"Impossible."

"When do we leave?"

"As soon as he's ready."

"What if the water comes first?"

Felipe looked out the window. "We have some time if you go now."

"What about Milo?"

"He wants to see his Bisavó. He'll be happy in Sweet Gum."

"Okay."

"Liv, thank you."

"Stay with Milo."

I had finished with the pilot by the time the water reached the tenth floor. By then, Felipe had Milo slung over his shoulder, waiting for me in a puddle with our luggage. We ran through the soaked hall together and up the stairs to the fifteenth floor, where we awaited instructions from the pilot. Milo was still groggy. "Let him lie down for a little bit," I said. Felipe looked at the pilot's bed, where I had just made love, and then he put Milo down on the floor. The pilot was still buttoning his shirt when we came back to hear his earnest plan to depart at once from the rooftop. "In the morning, we'll be safe," he said. I couldn't stop staring at him or concentrating on his steady military voice. A voice that had grunted in my ear just moments earlier.

CHAPTER FOURTEEN

It was strange to be with a man who wasn't Felipe. A muscular creature with viewpoints and habits I knew nothing about. An angled jawline that looked familiar. I had met him before, but I never caught his name. I remembered entering his room shaking, unable to speak. I hated him and was thankful for him all at once. I wanted to be with my son, not giving my body up for some horny opportunist pilot. He gave me a drink to stop the shaking. The sudden appearance of his bare chest fired a peculiar spark in my brain. I expected to be his masturbatory plaything, but he leaned me against the bed and exercised his tongue. Guilt ravaged me. Then the drink kicked in. My son and Felipe were moments away from being with me again. But for the time being, I was raw and naked, pleasured for the sake of survival.

"Mama, what are we doing?"
    "Nothing."
    "I'm thirsty."
    "Me too."
    "I want milky."
    "Milky isn't working anymore."
    "But I want it!"
    "We need water."
    "Where?"
    "We have to find it. We have to leave."
    "Why?"
    "Because we need water to stay alive."
    "Why?"

"I don't know why."

"Mama, I want milky."

We moved back to a wooded path, stopping throughout the day to eat sparingly from a scant supply of wild nuts and leftover meat. The boy fell asleep in the bag, and I struggled to keep my head up. Mosey ambled along slowly. She made grunting noises. We all needed water. The day was packed with drifting warmth, and my skeptical mind knew it wouldn't last. The cold was coming.

Milo woke naturally when we reached a mountainside brook. He whimpered from the bag, and I pulled us both off the horse. He stretched his body slowly, eyeing the pistol at my hip. He looked up to see our new destination. He always needed to understand his surroundings, to know his bounds, to know what was new, what needed to be touched.

"BeezBo house," he whispered. I shook my head no, too exhausted to explain anything. He eyed the gurgling brook and its sparse rocks. He looked up at the footbridge that carried us down here. I didn't like being close to the bridge. But we needed to drink. We would fill up and then head back to the deep woods. Perhaps that would be our new routine, I thought. Winter was not far away. I knew we would need shelter. But how? It tormented my weary mind when I was able to take a moment to think clearly. Which didn't come often.

We stood in the shallow moving brook. Mosey stood nearby lapping at water. Something shuffled from beyond the footbridge that was just above the water we stood in, nearly fifteen feet up. A caravan on horseback. One man, three women, and a baby. Mosey looked up, flapping her nostrils. How had I not heard them coming? The exhaustion. The thirst. The man who led the caravan wore a helmet of steel, appearing brutish and serious. The women were cloaked in animal fur. Their faces appeared slim and starved. One of the women held her baby in a sling. They began to cross the bridge. I grabbed the pistol at my side and hid Milo's head behind my legs. The boy laced his fingers around my knees.

If they spotted us standing idly in the brook, I counted on the fact that I had exactly four rounds left. Earlier, I had found a moment to carefully open the barrel and inspect each bullet. The experience with the cat taught me I needed to understand my tool. Four bullets. I would spare the baby. But I really didn't want to give up my bullets. "Milo, don't say a word." Mosey grunted and the caravan turned to us, halting in syncopated steps. The woman with the baby met my eyes.

Milo crouched lower in the brook, holding on to my ankles. "It's okay," I said. But it wasn't. There was a terrible silence. I pulled my pistol out and held it at my leg. From what I could tell, no one had a visible gun. "It's okay," I said again. Lumbering like a creaking ship, the man at the front of the group shifted strangely against his saddle. I would have no way to quickly pack our items and remount Mosey without giving the caravan time to leave the footbridge and come for us. After a few minutes the man in the helmet cleared his throat. He raised his hand to give some sort of direction to his cavalcade. I froze.

CHAPTER FIFTEEN

The man pulled a pistol out from under his cloak and held the reins of his horse with authority.

"Please, we don't have anything," I said, my voice trembling.

"You've got a horse. A boy. Supplies."

"Keep your eyes off my son."

He slithered off his horse like a snake, holding his gun steady at his side. The man moved slow and direct, showing no concern for the firearm in my grasp. He moved across rocks and toward a small dirt hill that led to the brook where we stood. He looked at Milo. His eyes, beneath his helmet, were so sunken into his skull it looked like they might seep into his brain. His beard spilled down his chest like a bib and was the color of an old rat. He and the quiet women on horseback behind him appeared weathered and annoyed. The man hobbled down the path, still not caring about my revolver, now raised. He placed a boot upon a mossy rock.

"Been out here long?" he asked.

I cocked my gun. "Leave."

"I'm not looking for a fight."

"Then you would've kept on walking across that bridge."

"Listen, there's not many of us out here," the man said. "When we find each other, we need to pause and talk."

"I don't need to talk to anyone."

"You may think that, but it's not true. How long you been out here?"

"Leave."

I pointed my gun at the women. The man laughed.

"You know, we're close to an encampment."

"Go away."

"They'll find you sooner or later."

"I'll shoot you," I said.

"You could come with us and be safe if you want. Or stay and wait for the patrollers."

I raised my revolver higher. "Why would I believe anything you're saying with that gun in your hand?"

"Well, we both have guns, don't we? That's what people do these days. They hold guns and say crazy things."

"How long have *you* been out here?"

"Since the floods. We're from the coast."

I reached behind me to make sure Milo was still in place. "We are too."

"We have some things in common."

I narrowed my eyes. "I don't approach people standing in streams. I let them be."

"We're not as different as you think. We're all just humans trying to live."

"Yes, that's what I'm trying to do. Live in peace. Leave."

"Nice horse."

"She's deaf."

"But she can still feel a kick, can't she?"

"Only my kick. Leave."

The woman with the baby was jostling uncomfortably. The baby began to cry. The man shuddered but kept his eyes on me. I took my eyes off the man. I couldn't stop staring at the baby. I could feel my breasts filling up with milk. I heard a faint click from the man's gun. I turned to the man and shot at him before he had the chance to rest a hairy finger on his trigger. He dropped the gun into the stream. My bullet struck his hip, knocking him into a shallow bog of mud and rocks.

"Stay here," I told Milo. "Keep your hand on that rock."

I looked up at the women. Their expressions confused me. They weren't sad, shocked, or scared. They talked quietly to one another.

I walked over to the man and removed his helmet. Then I shot him in the head.

His death lingered in the air. The gunshot echoed like a cymbal clash. I looked toward the women.

"Do any of you have a gun?" I asked.

"No," the woman with the baby said. Her baby was still crying. "Please don't shoot us."

"He was going to kill me. I'm sorry I did that. You saw he was going to shoot me, right?"

The women didn't answer. They were still in quiet discussion.

The woman with the baby hopped off her horse. She tried to quiet the crying child while the other two women talked heatedly. The young red-haired mother took the baby out of the sling and bounced her into oblivion.

"She's hungry," I called.

The mother looked like she was going to cry, herself. She leaned her head against her horse's belly and sobbed.

"I'm sorry," I called. "I shouldn't have said anything."

The mother turned to the other women. "Let's go."

The baby's crying was uncontrollable.

"Feed her!" one of the women shouted.

"With what milk?" the mother cried.

"I'm sorry, I forgot. There's food at the cave."

Cave.

"Just go without me. I'll meet you there," the mother said.

"We're not leaving you."

I stepped forward. "I have milk, miss."

The desperate mother turned to me. "What?"

"I breastfeed my son." I pointed to Milo, who was dutifully holding on to a slippery rock. "My supply has been down. But hearing your baby cry, I feel that it's returned. I'm full of milk right now."

The women looked at one another. The mother walked toward the end of the bridge, bouncing the screaming baby in her arms. She trailed down the dirt hill and stepped over the dead man. She didn't look at him. She walked through the clear, glistening stream, bringing forth her crying tomato-colored baby.

"What do you think?" she asked.

"I think you've got one hungry baby."

I let my breast out of my shirt and held it up to the baby. I put my nipple into her crying mouth, remembering how difficult it was to breastfeed Milo at first. Not an easy thing to do. The baby's half-gummy mouth felt foreign on my breast as it continued to wail. This was an older baby – eight months? Nine months? I couldn't tell. Certainly not a newborn. She might fit well into one-year-old clothing even. The muscles relaxed in my body. My breasts tingled until they brought forth milk from within. When the milk landed into the baby's mouth, when she tasted its sweetness, she began to suckle. The mother gasped. Tears formed in her eyes, and she began to cry happily.

"Can you hold her?" she asked. I took the baby in my arms and fed her, standing up, as the midday sun beat against my head.

Milo waltzed through the water toward me. "Mama, what you doing? That's *my* milky." The woman laughed. I swayed in the stream, in the sun. All was quiet. The baby drank milk by the creek, near the dead man, near the women on horses. I was tired. Milo splashed at a minnow. "Mama, fishies!" The baby emptied my breast and I moved her onto the other side. Then the baby fell asleep as the mother looked on gratefully. I helped her get the baby back into the sling. Meanwhile, the other women hauled the man out of the stream and secured him to their now riderless horse. They laid him flat on the ground behind the horse and proceeded to bind his wrists around the horse's reins. Afterward, they prepared their own horses, ready to leave. They shifted their cloaks over their saddles. I caught the black shine of a pistol in the belt belonging to one of the women. A gun.

"Thank you," the mother sighed, still in the stream with me.

"Okay." I eyed the pistol on the woman on the bridge.

"Goodbye. Good luck." The mother walked through the stream, back to her horse.

"Wait," I called. "What would that man have done if I hadn't shot him?"

The mother looked down for a while. And then back at me. "He would have shot you and then eaten you."

"And why aren't you upset he's dead?"

"He's better off dead. He was a bad man," the young mother said. "It's complicated."

The mother left the stream with her quiet baby.

"Why didn't you shoot *me*?" I called. "I see your friend has a gun. Why don't you want to eat me?"

The women looked at each other and smiled.

"We only eat men," the mother replied.

"Why men?"

"Revenge."

"Well, I shot him. He should be mine."

I didn't have an appetite for the man. In fact, I couldn't even fathom how I'd explain the act to Milo. Yet, the words escaped my lips. Perhaps I yearned for their company a little longer, however strange it may be.

The women looked at each other.

"Come to our cave and eat with us," the young mother said. "Your boy will eat well."

As hungry as I was, I didn't want to go off toward a mysterious cave with a group of women who hunted men. How long until their hunger didn't care about the sex of their prey?

"Thank you," I said. "But I'm all right here. At least give me his clothes."

The women complied. The one who bore the pistol dismounted, then proceeded to untie the man, removing as many clothes as possible, including his bulky cloak. She left behind his helmet for us as well. After securing the man once more, she remounted her horse and took hold of the neck straps of the riderless horse, seemingly to guide it along with them.

The young mother sat straight on her horse. She looked at me from the distance above, searching my face. "Thank you," she said.

I thought I should be the one thanking them for the man's clothing, but I understood her thanks were directed towards the meal I provided for her child.

I nodded.

With that, all the women pushed their heels into their horses and trailed off to some foreign cave. A cave with one less burden on them. We spent the afternoon catching minnows and rinsing the man's clothes.

CHAPTER SIXTEEN

We came upon an abandoned zip-line course in the woods. It looked like it had been abandoned for years, even before the Shift. There were broken-down wooden structures and long, sturdy lines that hung from tree to tree. It reminded me of a zip-lining camp in the Smoky Mountains that Felipe and I had visited once – it was bizarre to remember a time of leisure and fun.

On Mosey, we trod carefully onto its grounds. The man with the steel helmet had warned about a nearby encampment. I was on high alert. I turned Mosey all around, trying to listen. I heard nothing except a woodpecker. We staggered throughout the site and finally dismounted the horse. I wiped sweat off Milo's brow and held him close. He was quiet. He only stared. This scared me. "It's okay," I said.

We stumbled more throughout the grounds until we came upon a tall wooden structure. Something of a treehouse, but not quite. A wooden platform wrapped around a tree like a wreath, held in place by secure beams. Timber boards were nailed into the tree to act as a ladder to reach the base of the treehouse. I imagined this was where brave souls might've zip-lined from. It was run down. I explained to Milo that we should climb upward, and he just looked out toward nothing. I kneeled into the leaves. I pulled him to me and kissed his neck. He didn't move. Hours earlier he saw his mother shoot a man, saw the man writhing in a bed of sludge. The trauma I was inadvertently inflicting did not escape me. I hated myself for it.

As the sun set, evening became bitterly cold. I held Milo close atop the zip-line platform. A cough sprang from his throat. He shivered. I quickly dressed Milo in the man's clothing. I wrapped his shirt in layers, creating a robe for him. I wore the man's cloak as well. We did not speak for a while. With the onset of dark, Milo began to shiver uncontrollably. I left him up on the platform and instructed him not to move. Then, I descended the ramshackle ladder and collected rocks and thick wood, bundling materials into my cloak. I put down a layer of rocks on the ground, zig-zagged wood on top, and set fire upon the formation. I moved Milo down to the fire to warm his bones. Once he was asleep in my lap, I moved him softly to the grass and then went back to the treehouse to prepare a bed for him, elevated and away from danger, where I could keep watch and shoot any potential threats. The platform was wet, so I laid my raccoon coat on the floor for Milo. I went back down and lifted Milo onto my chest and steadied him with one arm as I climbed back up the beams. I laid him down gently and then wrapped his head in the man's undershirt. Once I pulled away, I noticed that he was awake. I could see his eyes in the sparse light. He looked into the blackness and said nothing.

In the morning, I discovered that Mosey's knot had come undone, yet she lingered close by. Clearly, I needed to improve my knot-tying skills. I hurried to her. I felt the sodden length of her nose and sniffed her creek-scented nostrils. It was obvious she had gone off and enjoyed a mid-morning drink without us. I tied her rope to our tree. The boy woke from the platform and called out, "*Mama!*" I looked toward him, covering my eyes from the sun, and I went to him.

Later we moved throughout the site, inspecting the flora of the grounds. On a log I discovered a trail of sulfur shelf mushrooms. I cleared the lot of them and stuffed them into my cloak pocket. I paused frequently to listen to the land and check on Milo. Throughout the morning, I kept a close watch on Mosey, holding her out in the open, waiting for her thirst to kick in. I spoke to her repeatedly, scratched her side. Nothing. She was used to following my lead, not taking charge on her own. I wanted her to show us her secret drinking spot. After a while I started walking her, hoping she'd eventually pull me in the right direction. I looked back at the boy. "Come on, Milo," I said. He slogged forward and asked what we were doing. I told him that we were looking for water.

I realized it had been a while since I heard him laugh.

I secured Mosey and sat down in the leaves. I invited Milo into my lap. I cradled him. We looked up at the sun through the trees. There was a slight breeze, but it felt nice.

The boy's face was expressionless.

"Milo, talk to me."

"I want to go home."

I ran fingers through his honey-colored hair. "What home?" I had no idea what he considered home. Was it possible for him to have memories of his life before the hotel? Before all this?

"What home?" I asked again.

He pointed backwards toward the platform. "That home."

I laughed. "Oh, is that our home?"

He nodded.

"What do we call that home?"

"Our treehouse."

"Okay, how about we do a hunt and then go back to our treehouse?"

"Okay."

Hunt. It wasn't a word I had ever wanted to use around Milo. When he was born, I made vocal proclamations that he would eat only the best free-range food. After his bones grew with protein and milk, I told myself that one day I would introduce him to a vegetarian lifestyle. I hadn't mastered it myself, but it was something I always wanted to try. I scoffed at the way I used to think. Milo asked for milk, and I was happy that the baby from yesterday had brought back a bit of supply. I tucked Milo beneath my cloak and let him rest a while on my lap while I gazed at slow-moving clouds. I couldn't help but think it would be nice to freeze time, the minutes passing in between these empty woods with my son and a horse. Mosey kicked at the dirt. "Come on," I said, pulling Milo off my breast. I gave the horse's rope some slack, letting her take the lead.

"We're going to follow Mosey," I said.

"Why follow her?"

"Because she knows something we don't."

CHAPTER SEVENTEEN

I wondered often how this would all end. Would the dry lands remain untouched by the coastal waters forever? Would the water come for everything, even the highest mountaintop? Would there come a day when Milo would give me his final hug and kiss? His final request of me. His last need. Of course. And sometimes, I let this merciless thought eat me alive, tearing at my brain, pounding. "Mama is here. Mama is always here. Forever." A lie. There were times I held on to Milo with this deranged and cruel thought, silently sobbing into his hair. I struggled to pull myself together. I never made a noise when I cried in this way, but he always pulled away and looked at me with a deep understanding that toddlers aren't meant to have.

"What he doing?" the boy said. He looked at Mosey ahead of us.

"Mosey is a girl. Not a boy."

"Why?"

"Because she doesn't have a penis."

"Why?"

"I'm sorry Milo. I shouldn't have said that. She's a girl just because."

"Because why?"

"Because she's powerful. And really, really cool."

"Yeah."

Mosey led us through the woods to an open field. It looked like it had been plundered some time ago. Something terrible happened here. There were scattered yellow leaves and patches of burnt grass. There were scant objects in the field, like someone had dumped trash here and then a war broke out fighting over the random objects. Rags of clothing, toys, books, bones. My eyes lit up like a row of casino lights.

Mosey walked on. She still had more secrets to reveal. Dried blood was etched into light-colored pockets of field grass. Milo kicked through piles of plastic. He punted a skull off a toy car like it was a rock. He held the car up to the glow of light and flew it like an airplane. We passed a pool of mud and guts. I asked Milo to look at the clouds and tell me what he saw in them. "Clouds," he said. In the vast field there were three hawks standing. Their white and brown silken bodies stood upwards like stumps in the fields. Proud guards. Their legs were grand and ruffled as they lurched over prey of some sort. They turned their heads slowly to us, and then back the other way.

We moved through the field, passing mud and bones and more hawks. Mosey hurried into the unknown. Milo was beginning to stumble. He was exhausted even though we hadn't tackled much of the day yet. I hooked him into my hip and carried us onward. He put his head down on my shoulder as we followed Mosey down an embankment. I rubbed my bloated belly beneath my cloak. A growing child on my hip and a new life in my womb – I finally had to admit this to myself. I didn't know exactly how far along I was or that it mattered. I wished to perform a séance just to tell Felipe. *So, here's what happened from your grand idea! You died in a helicopter explosion. And now I'm pregnant with the pilot's baby. Good going.* Knowing Felipe, he would shake his head and laugh at me. At peace, in death, with nothing else to prepare, he would surely laugh. The reality was much darker.

"I scared."

"What are you scared of?"

"You."

Mosey stole my attention from Milo for a moment. She led us to a stream in the grass. The water was dewy and misting with steam. Milo must've seen it before I did. "Water!" I exclaimed.

Milo didn't answer. He was shielding his face from the water. He turned his eyes strangely toward the ground. I paused.

"What is it?"

"Mama."

"Mama what?"

"Mama shoot."

"Oh, baby. I don't shoot right now."

"You shoot in water."

The man in the helmet had stayed with him. That ghastly image of the bloody corpse in the water was etched in his brain.

I ran my finger over his head. "Mama only shoots bullies when I need to keep you safe. Okay? You don't have to worry. Right?"

He didn't answer.

Eventually, Milo scrambled toward the stream where Mosey drank. From my bag I procured our water purifier and pumped water through its filter. The warm stream water spurted into our bean cans at last. I was flabbergasted to taste its warmth. Milo shuffled along the edges after a hearty can of warm water and soon, I saw color return to his face. He began to talk, asking questions. Always questions. I tied Mosey up, and we moved into the water to bathe and wash our clothes. I held Milo against my bare chest and rocked him in the raw hot spring with lacteal steam. His feet knocked into my abdomen, and I wondered whether I cared. He began to trust the water and soon discovered its gentleness. We spent the entire day seeped in its warm glory until the hawks left and we were able to pick at their leftovers.

CHAPTER EIGHTEEN

We made it several more days and nights living by the abandoned zip-line park deep inside the woods. When we weren't sleeping, hunting, or eating, we spent our time dragging armloads of odds and ends from the war-torn field where the hawks feasted. We brought our treasures back to our treehouse. Milo loved calling it his treehouse. I loved that he was talking more.

As comfortable as we were becoming with this new place, I feared that the thick hemlock branches surrounding us gave us a false sense of security. Worrying made time move quickly; soon, a month or so had passed on by. We were like uninvited houseguests in this hidden place. By this time, the glow of the fire was the only thing Milo and I looked forward to every day. I always kept the fire-starter on my body as though it was my actual beating heart – remembering that without it, our lives would fade to nothing. We would die. Milo asked often when we would see BeezBo. I always told him, "Soon." I wasn't sure if leaving was best for us though. Surely, staying wasn't ideal either. Winter was imminent, and so was the life growing inside me. For the time being, I needed the reliability and comfort of routine. Milo did too. He needed to see his mother collect mushrooms and hunt for frogs, not shoot men in swamp water. We needed to move past the incident together, peacefully. I needed to see my son's eyes look onward with purpose, not fear.

On a day that brought unusual warmth, I organized the objects in our treehouse, while Milo napped. A helmet. Cans. An axe. Gun. Then, there were the new items foraged from the field of war and debris. Boots. Books. Toys. Blankets. Rope. Utensils. A larger hiking bag. It would be an upgrade for transporting Milo on my back.

While Milo slept soundly, I used clothing and blankets from the field to create a textile roof. Using a concoction of rope and rocks, I lightly hammered random fabric and clothing from railings to the pole in the center of our wooden nest. A rock was my hammer. Bolts from the war-torn ground were my nails. I kept parts open so that I could catch rainwater in the helmet and cans. I arranged the firepit below to be a bit larger, dragging a mid-sized log over as a bench. When I finished cleaning up for the day, I looked out from the wooden rail and surveyed the open wood. I was like a prison guard, always on the lookout. Should trouble come here, it would be over. Our tracks were all over this place. We were hidden from cats and bears. But humans, with their guns and knives, would see our fabric-lined treehouse at once. It would be the end.

Milo woke up with chattering teeth. I held him inside my cloak until he agreed to take a walk to the hot spring. He was out of character along our way. Even the shape of him looked different. He appeared hollow, or perhaps I'd been too busy becoming Jane of the Jungle that I hadn't taken time to notice my maturing son. There was a seriousness about him. He wasn't interested in my songs or funny voices. Everything was, "No, Mama. Don't do that." He didn't want to follow me down our usual path. He wanted to go in a new direction. A foreign path. I forbid it, and soon he was screaming. I covered his mouth with my palm and stroked his pale, tangled hair. When I removed my hand, Milo's face was stained with tears. *Please don't do this*, I begged with my eyes. When he looked at me, with a face contorted with pain, I could feel every bit of sadness and pain that ever existed in the universe.

Milo got his way. We ventured down the path he wanted. I kept my hand on the gun as we walked the brush-lined path. Milo began to hum. Golden leaves crinkled beneath our feet. The path led to an open field where rows of trees stood, waiting. Milo ran to the largest tree with sun-yellow leaves. The amber leaves were quickly falling from the branches. The autumnal glow of change. The top was nearly naked. The tree appeared to be wearing a bright yellow tutu. We heard the crisp crinkle of each falling leaf. Milo walked up to the tree as if it were trying to speak to him. I let him go. This was the first time he'd seen a tree shed its leaves up close. Soon, I sidled next to him.

"Mama, what's that tree doing?"

"The leaves are falling off. That means it's autumn now."

"What's autumn?"

"It means it's getting colder because we're moving away from the sun."

"Why?"

"I don't know. That's just how the world works."

"I miss it."

"What?"

"The sun."

"Me too."

We sat beneath the tree. The yellow leaves fell on us like fast snow. We were quiet, listening to the calming sound of wind and falling leaves. When we finally spoke again, Milo noticed me rubbing my belly. We hadn't talked about what was inside me yet. It felt too soon. I didn't want to accept it. There was a bulge, but it was mainly bloated belly. The beginning stages of growth. The boy laid a hand on my stomach and rubbed his small palm over me. Did he notice my growing belly? Did he know what pregnancy even meant? I smiled at him, thinking my son was the wisest, sweetest soul in the world. Here he was, in communion with an aging tree, foraging new paths, and appearing perceptive to my changing form. Then, he laughed.

"What is it, sweetie?"

"You ate a lot of frogs," he said, patting my belly.

CHAPTER NINETEEN

It was winter at the Pennsylvania hotel when I first saw the pilot. I had never told Felipe about this. I hadn't told him much about anything since the Shift. I kept things inside like a message in a bottle. One afternoon, before the waters reached us, I had hiked past the parking lot and into the woods where I could get a second to breathe. To simply exist and be in my skin for a second with no demands. I stood listening to utter silence. Then I heard strange noises from inside the white, foggy woods. The pilot was kneeling beside a dead deer. He wasn't *the pilot* to me then. He was just a man in the woods with a dead deer.

I watched him work in silence. He stuffed his hand into the cavity of the animal, pulling out its heart and liver. After he had taken everything he could from the animal, he placed the pieces in a cold box and cleaned his materials. He leaned over the remains and breathed deeply. "Thank you," he whispered. He turned to me, stunned.

"Sorry," I said shyly.

The man didn't answer.

I twiddled my hands. "I was just curious."

He looked at me. I felt like the deer. Gutted. I turned to leave, picking up my pace.

"You ever skin a deer?" he called.

I stopped, crunching on leaves. "What? No."

"You want to see?"

"No, that's okay."

"You ever eat deer?"

"I think so. Not like that though."

The man laughed, and for some reason his laughter was soothing.

"This is a good one. I shot it. No diseases or anything. Either way, you gotta roast the hell out of it. Dangerous, this stuff. Bacteria, parasites. It's a risk. But the alternative is bad too. We have no other choice, do we?"

I shrugged with a smile.

The man tucked his knife away and crossed his arms. "Sorry, I just – I don't talk to anyone these days. Just to dead deer, apparently."

"It's okay."

We looked at each other in silence for way too long. I saw Felipe in him. Another prepper. *They'd be friends if they ever had the chance,* I thought. This man was much rawer than Felipe though. More open. I wondered why I was comparing men in the woods when I should be with Milo. I turned away from him.

"Wait."

"Yes?"

"What's your name?"

"Liv."

"Do you want some? It's only me here. I don't want it to go to waste, Liv."

"I have to get back. I have a son. We have beans."

"Well, he can have some too. Might be a treat from beans."

"I've gotta go."

"Nice to meet you, Liv."

"You too. Enjoy the deer."

"I'll try to. Enjoy your beans. It was really nice to meet you."

In the parking lot, I looked up at the hotel and its dark rooms. No power. Long gone. I could hear wailing coming from an open window. The wailing never stopped. I turned back to the woods.

"Actually, I changed my mind. Can you show me how to skin it?"

The man laughed. "Sure. Come on."

With a sharp knife, he cut the skin over the rear of the hock and down the back of the leg toward the rectum. He used the knife sparingly. He ripped the hide with his hand using the knife as a base to keep his momentum going. I don't know why I wanted to stay and watch. Perhaps it was something animalistic inside me, begging me to learn.

In the morning I thought about the pilot, the man from the woods. If things hadn't ended up the way they had, if Felipe hadn't brought me to the pilot like some gift – would the pilot and I have found a way to each other anyway? There was that moment between us. There, in the woods in the gray-white fog. How he stood, holding me in his gaze. Just another one of his deer, but different this time. Not something to kill or eat. But something to take for himself, nonetheless. And now I was growing his baby. There would have been something between us; of this, I was certain. If we had lived in another time, another world, another dimension. Alas, it was the only way for me to make peace with my situation. It was the only way for me not to hate the life growing inside me.

Milo awoke in the morning with a newfound vigor and immediately wanted to leave the treehouse. He wanted to go to the war-torn field. We called it the treasure field. It was like visiting an expansive flea market. Always something new to find. I appraised the area from atop the treehouse. No movement of life, except Mosey and the birds. I lowered us down the planks until our boots crunched the ground.

We soon reached the treasure field with Mosey in tow.

"See anything you like?" I asked Milo.

"No."

I found a tin can on the ground. "What about this? You can put your car and sticks in here."

"I want a new toy."

"Hmm. What about this thing?" It was a piece of plastic. Its function, obsolete. Its purpose, unfamiliar. Did it hold something? Keep something in place? Was it the wrapper for a toy? Food? No idea.

"Yeah!" Milo cheered.

The boy took the plastic and flew it around the field in circles.

"What is it?"

"It's a horse! Like Mosey!"

"Oh yes, I see that now."

"Mama, where's your horse?"

"I have to keep looking."

"I'll find it for you!"

As Milo searched the perimeters for a horse for me I kept my eyes open for something to eat. By now, the hawks had left, knowing we always came for their scraps like some poor beggars. Food was scarce. I kept my eyes on the horizon looking and listening for signs of people. No smoke, no sounds. Nothing. How long could we go without the help of others, I wondered. Could we even go just a few more days? We couldn't. I blinked away tears, remembering the images on the news. The encampments. Babies dying without their mothers. Mothers pulled from their children and forced into labor camps.

A strange thought came to me – what if the encampments weren't real? What if it was a ploy – something to keep people away from the dry lands. To keep people in place, to wait upon their watery graves. I didn't know what to believe. I remembered the women on horses, the man with the helmet – they spoke of a nearby encampment. They spoke of it as a threat, not a sanctuary. This backed up my fear. Milo discovered a window screen and delivered it to me as a gift. I held it up and smiled.

In the afternoon, we collected as much food as we could – crickets, earthworms, silverweed, roots. I made a paste, but Milo refused to eat it. I managed to finally get some into his mouth through a fitful of tears had by both of us. Soon, heavy rain fell on us.

We left the stream and the treasure field, and we crossed through the woods on foot until we came across a crisp burning smell. Smoke hung in the air. I mounted Mosey with Milo and we galloped through the leaves, past trees, toward the treehouse. Fire had come to our camp while we were away. I must have forgotten to dampen our fire. I had always taken such good care of it. Ensuring it never got out of control.

The embers were so small, so insignificant when we left. Now a sizzle of smoke hung in the air; a fire had made its mark on our perfect treehouse. Flames had caught onto the fabric roof and left it scorched. The rain must have stamped it out before it could destroy everything. Suddenly, I was reminded of the helicopter explosion. Mentally, I was back where we were so many moons ago. Helplessly, I looked on at everything we worked so hard to build. I was most worried about the leftover smoke still rising into the sky, giving us away. Giving everything away.

CHAPTER TWENTY

I thought of my parents often. Not just how they were swallowed by the floods – but of our old life together. Growing up with a distant father and an overly critical mother left me with a sense of self-consciousness. Am I using the right utensil? Am I chewing enough? Have I said something wrong? Something that will cause a fight or the latest screaming match? Faint yelling still rang in my ears from those childhood years. Still, I loved them dearly. I even loved them during our NICU days when they hadn't bothered to check in on me – thinking I was selfish for having a baby in dark times. Maybe they were right. Sometimes, in my lowest moments of the day, I thanked them for showing me how *not* to parent Milo.

The rain came again and softened the smoke. During rainfall, we climbed the treehouse to take stock of the damage. The fabric roof was now useless, and many of our resources had burned in the flames. Half the treehouse planks were burned through. Black charred wood. The remaining half was useable for sleep, but we would have to be more careful than ever on them. I stomped on the planks, ensuring their security. Then I investigated our ruined material. I lurched over our melted water purifier and wept. Milo stood there looking at me. He came up to me with a bizarre look in his eye. He began beating me with his fists. He barreled his small hands into my chest and cried until he fell limp in my arms. I ran my fingers over his back. Too skinny. When the rain stopped, we moved back to the hot spring to heat our bones and hunt for water bugs. After a small meal, we sat by the spring and gazed upon the clouds.

Our trio spent the afternoon walking further through the treasure field. I told Milo we needed to find new supplies. I came prepared with my new backpack, but nothing came to us. We walked further until we came upon a canvas. Darkness was coming fast. Through the dim light, I saw the canvas was something that may have been used as a tent flap of sorts. We slid it across the field like we were dragging prey back to our cave. I held Mosey's reins in my free hand.

"I'm hung-ee, Mama."

"I know."

"I wanna eat."

"Yes. I do too."

"What we eat?"

"We'll figure it out in the morning. We need to sleep."

"Why?"

"Because we need energy."

"Why?"

"Because we do."

"Why?"

"I don't know, Milo. Sorry. I don't know why. I don't know everything."

I felt nervous walking through the woods back to our treehouse. What if the smoke had trailed from our treehouse toward the great beyond? We never walked the woods at night. I folded the canvas into my bag and picked Milo up to walk us along faster. The movement caused me to buckle. I suddenly felt nauseous, and a metallic taste swirled in my mouth. Milo looked at me through the darkness. Holding him against my chest, I could feel him shivering beneath his fox fur. He leaned in and kissed me on the ear. "It's okay," he said.

After I tied up Mosey, Milo and I slept in the half-burnt treehouse. The canvas from the treasure field spilled over us like a blanket, giving us acceptable warmth. In the darkness and the silence, I listened to Milo snore. His breathing gave me hope. I counted his breaths, remembering how I counted the number of times he suckled the small bottle in the NICU. Each suck, a count. "You have to count every suck," the nurse had told me. "You have to stop him when he reaches ten, or else he could suffocate." Sometimes, I still counted his sucks. I counted his sucks, his snores, his kisses – sometimes, it was the only thing that kept me tethered to reality.

Milo woke in the night whimpering. He climbed on top of me and placed his head on my heart. Below, footsteps clopped. Leaves crunched. I told myself it was Mosey.

"Mama?"

"Baby, we're okay. Go to sleep."

"Why we get new stuff?"

"Because the fire destroyed some of our things. We have to rebuild."

"What's rebuild?"

"It means we start over."

"Why we start over?"

I thought for a while on the best way to answer him. Sometimes, his questions led me to insanity. Other times, I found them to be extremely important, and a wonderful privilege.

"We gotta start over because some things are worth starting over for."

"Why?"

"Because it means we love each other and ourselves."

"Why?"

"Because I just love you so much."

"Why?"

"Because you are my angel."

"Why?"

"Because. Just because."

When we awoke the light was yellow, and the sun was present. The wild chirping of birds told me it was well past morning. We had slept decently beneath the canvas tarp. It packed heat well and kept us safe inside its sailcloth. I did not dare wake Milo, but I listened to his breathing to calm my heart. A buzzing noise trailed in the early afternoon air. I slithered out from the canvas and stood at the edge of our treehouse.

The buzzing was growing louder. I looked around for its source. This was a sound I could not place. This was a sound that did not belong in these foreign woods. I was certain I was losing control of reality. It sounded like a conveyor belt in a factory, a soft and idle sibilation. Milo shifted beneath the canvas. I stepped over a collection of our new finds – window screen, hammer, handmade mud bowls, onion roots, and a collection of belts. The buzzing grew loud and direct. I turned around, finally understanding the source of the noise. A black drone was hovering just over the canvas where Milo shifted. It was staring directly at me, recording my every move.

CHAPTER TWENTY-ONE

The drone scanned my face with a thin blue light. Paranoia consumed me. Furiously, I picked up my new hammer and launched it at the flying machine. Small and black, the drone cracked from the force of my throw but still flew. Through my tired, haggard eyes, I knew this machine belonged to the patrollers. The way it floated in the air, so cocky and close, I just knew it. The blue light flickered and faded. I picked up rocks that Milo used as toys and launched them at the machine until its blade ceased and the drone fell to the leaf-covered ground below. I leaned over the treehouse rail. The drone struggled to take flight and reeled with sounds of a dying machine. I climbed down the tree to get a look at it. I put a hand over its camera eye and ripped wires from its body until the blue light faded completely. I turned it over. A military-style typeface: EEMA. I brought it up to the treehouse like a chimpanzee who had found some new tool.

Milo stirred beneath the canvas and climbed out to see his mother hunched over this strange contraption. He rubbed his eyes and moved hair from his face. He spoke about his belly hurting, but I couldn't concentrate on his words. My head was swirling. This drone meant someone knew our location. We had to move. I turned my head left and right, trying to see if anyone or anything was coming for us. Milo put his hand on my shoulder. I turned around to see his ashen face. He looked unwell.

"Milo, what's wrong?"

"Belly."

"Your belly hurts?"

"Yeah." He rubbed his eye and pouted.

"What does it feel like?"

"Mama!"

"What is it, baby?"

Milo threw himself on the canvas and bent his body. I had never seen him do this before. He squealed and moaned uncontrollably.

"Maybe a bath will help. Let's go to the hot spring. Okay?"

"Mamaaa," he moaned.

"Okay, just lie down a little bit. I'll get everything ready."

"Mammmma. Hurttsssss."

"I know. I hear you. I hear you. I hear you."

"*Mamaaaaaaaaa.*"

Milo could not walk. I lifted him onto Mosey, and we trudged through the woods toward the spring. I talked to him to keep him engaged. I talked of bugs and sticks, birds and trees. Nothing warranted a reply from him. His moans were serious.

We made our way to the spring, where I immediately tied Mosey's rope around a tree and then laid Milo down in my coat over damp grass. Using a piece of canvas, which I ripped apart, I dipped it into the hot water. I massaged his belly with the hot cloth. I pushed on his stomach to see where the pain was. He rolled back and forth. I thought back to the pilot in the woods with the dead deer. *Parasites, bacteria*, he said. *A killed deer is better than a found deer.*

What had we eaten? An old squirrel, perhaps. We had come across it, already dead. Stupid Liv. Stupid Mama.

There used to be a time when I could look for answers using a device. Nothing like that anymore. It was just me, my son, and a rotten squirrel inside his body. I needed to get it out.

"Milo, you ate something bad. We need to make it come out."

Milo pushed me away with a weak hand. He could see panic in my face. I was making it worse. The sun was hot and sticky. I opened his shirt and let the sun heat him up.

"Mama."

"Yes."

"Mama, I sick."

I blinked away tears. There was nothing more terrible in the world than seeing him in pain. I prayed for the pain to leave his body and come to mine. The cruelness of the world, to cause pain in a child. I spat on the world. Who came up with such an idea?

"I'm here for you. Mama's gotta get that bad food out of you."

"No, Mama." He cried. I attempted to make him gag, but I couldn't bring myself to hurt him further. He started to cry so much he hyperventilated. I cried into his belly and pleaded for the pain to leave.

"Stop. Stop. Mama."

He was crying again. I could not gag my little boy. I needed to do something else. Wash it out. Cleanse him. I gathered my supplies and lit a campfire with a small bundle of sticks. I would boil water in my bean can and flush his system clean. For the next couple of hours, I could see nothing except Milo in front of me, writhing. Nothing else mattered.

We slept by the hot spring after Milo vomited well into the evening. He was exhausted. His body heaved up and down, holding on to life. Then the boy slept. I held him close, keeping my hand on his heart, counting every beat. Always counting. The fire kept us warm as we crouched there in the grass upon coats. I feared what was to come. The drone. Patrollers. The end was imminent. I held on to my boy, wishing I could hold on to him forever.

CHAPTER TWENTY-TWO

By early morning, sickness had come to me too. Milo was still pale, but the writhing had ceased. My prayers had been answered. By high noon, I estimated, we were both lying in the grass by the side of the spring. The boy looked at me often. I tried to conceal my pain.

"Mama, you ate bad food too?"

"Yes."

"Are you gonna sleep? Forever?"

"No."

"Why?"

"Because I need to keep being your mama. Okay?"

"Okay."

In the evening we moved back across the treasure field toward our treehouse. We needed to leave. We could not stay at the abandoned zip-line park in the woods much longer, no matter how familiar it felt to Milo. It had become home. And it would be devastation to leave. We knew each muddy trail, every morning birdsong, and where the mushrooms grew and berries blossomed. However, I could not risk the patrollers coming to take us. *Home is a state of mind*, I told myself. By the time we reached our treehouse it was the dark of night. The pain had entered my body like a wild beast. It spread throughout my abdomen and zapped my muscles with deep penetrative aches. After fastening Mosey securely to a nearby tree, I tried to help Milo climb our treehouse, but I didn't have the energy to lift him. I fell to the ground, right beside the dead drone, and I heaved whatever pathetic food was left in my body.

The world shrank down to the most basic particles. The dark leaves in front of me. Rotten vomit. The world was fading entirely. It was losing meaning. Where were we? How did we get here? What were we doing? Finally, I heaved something solid and thick. It was this heave that allowed my body to relax momentarily. I slunk into the dirt and rested my cheek against the cool leaves. My body convulsed with chills.

I didn't know where Milo was as I drifted off to sleep uncontrollably. I was convinced I was already dead, or about to leave the world. So cold. How could I have let it come to this? What could I have done to stop this? What could I have done differently? Why didn't I ask the three women where the encampment was? Perhaps, Milo would have had a chance. I hated myself with a fury as I lay there succumbing to death. I was a horrible mother. I would die one, too.

In the morning, I awoke to a cold hand on my face. Milo was trying to raise my eyelids. I could not lift my head, but I eventually could see him through squinted eyes. His rusted lips needed a drink of water.

In the hours that followed, I managed to drink a can of rainwater that I'd left on the ground. Milo drank too. Then he napped in my arms in a pile of leaves. Birds flew near to us, as we looked on like furniture. Good as dead. I managed to lift my head and surveyed the site. Mosey was gnawing at grass. My vision was off – everything came to me in twos and threes. I rubbed my eyes and wiped dried blood off the crevices of my mouth. A chilling paranoia washed over me. Were patrollers on the way to us? But I was too weak to worry. Milo's teeth chattered in his skull. He woke up from his nap with a confused face. Meanwhile, the muscles in my abdomen were pulling and stretching. I wasn't sure what I thought about that. I had forgotten the baby was there. Did it matter? I wasn't sure. Milo looked up at me every so often. When life came back to me, I said, "We're okay, we're okay." He looked at me with dry eyes and taut lips and asked, "Mama, are the people coming back?"

"What people?"

"The people that came here."

"No people came here."

"Yeah! They did!"

"No, it's just us here."

"No, Mama. You were asleep. People came."

CHAPTER TWENTY-THREE

I'd come to trust every word Milo uttered. He had no reason to lie. I am not even sure if he knew what lying meant. When Milo awoke and told me about the people who came, he did not provide any details. When I pressed him on it, he was more interested in haphazardly pulling his pants down to pee. Without diapers, he was forced to learn how to urinate freely. We'd been training along the way. He'd gone many days in wet pants until he was forced to learn. He held his stream far away from my head but drops still spattered against my cold, damp cheek. As for myself, I realized I was completely soaked. My own sweat and urine had consumed me during my sick night in the leaves.

"Milo, I need you to tell me – did people come here?"

"Yes."

"What people? What did they look like? Did they have helmets or guns or anything like that?"

"No, it was mamas that come here. Like you."

"More mamas? I don't understand."

"I hung-ee."

No food remained. I needed to muster the energy to hunt or forage. Pulling myself off the ground where I had slept, I grabbed on to a tree to steady myself. Milo walked past me, strutting toward a bundle of sticks with a confident swagger. His body was healing much faster than mine. I felt as though I might collapse. Silver stars twinkled in my vision. I was going to pass out if I stayed standing.

"Baby," I said, "I can't do this." Milo poked at the sticks, ignoring me. The weight of my demise was pressing down on me, the long claws of death were scraping at my insides. The boy sat down in the grass and began organizing his sticks by size, completely unfazed by my ruination. I put my hand on my belly to feel my stomach muscles twist and turn. Somewhere, the sound of a horse blared. Not Mosey. Something or someone was drawing near to us. I held on to the tree, on the brink of passing out. I slid myself back down to the leaves. Milo crept close to me. He brought the drone.

"Mama, what's this?"

"A drone."

"What it do?"

"I think it was spying on us."

"What's spying?"

"Someone was watching us through the drone."

"Who watching us? How?"

"I don't know. Milo, I need to talk to you about something. If anyone comes here to take you away, you tell them to be nice to you, okay? You tell them you're a good boy and you'll always be a good boy if they're nice to you. Do you promise to do that?"

Milo laid his cheek to mine and whimpered. "But I don't wanna go."

"Milo, I am not feeling good." I closed my eyes and listened to his breath.

"Mama, I make you better. I find food."

"Milo, I'm so, so sorry. I'm so sorry. I'm so…"

I shut my eyes for a long time.

I awoke to the sound of geese honking, flying in formation beneath the sun, bold against the autumn sky. It was still day. The blue air was crisp and breathable. I looked around and could not see Milo anywhere. I forced myself to stand, feeling the sensation of blacking out as I stood to my feet again. I stumbled onward, drunkenly, chaotically. I needed to find my son even if I was dying. I landed in a new coating of dirt, and there I slept until the following day.

I awoke to a hand rubbing my belly. Milo sat over me, staring. I blinked heavily, taking in his somber face, thankful I survived the night. The boy kept staring at me. I waited for him to talk. Something in him appeared broken. How could I make this up to him?

"Mama, I got you food," he said drearily. "But you were asleep."

"What did you get?"

"A mouse. See?" He pointed to a dead field mouse by his foot. "It's for you. Cook it."

"Where did you find it?"

"In the bushes."

"How long did it take you to find it?"

"All day. But then you were asleep."

"Where did you sleep?"

"Right here."

"You've been with me this whole time?"

"Yes."

"I love you so much. I'm so proud of you."

"Cook it."

There were moments I thought about the baby inside me. Could this last? Could I possibly do this? Milo was born premature under the care of professional doctors. What would become of this baby? Surely, it would be premature too. It was inconceivable that we could both survive, alone. The need to find the encampment was becoming more and more inevitable. As my son dangled a mouse in front of me, I prepared myself for the worst. Losing him.

"Milo, one day I might not be here."

"Mama, you being silly?"

"No."

"Where you going?"

"I don't know. I just might not always be here. You might have to be with other people."

"The mamas?"

"What mamas?"

"The mamas that came here. The mamas that got taken away."

"Baby, I don't know what you're talking about."

I looked up at our treehouse. Rainwater in the helmet was up there, but I lacked the energy to stand. "Hold on to my belly," I told Milo. "There's something I need to tell you." I held on to his small hand, preparing to tell him about the life inside of me. A brother or a sister. Yet, I didn't have the chance to speak these things to him. Beyond the modicum of mountain pine, there stood a woman with hair blazing red, boring into us with an impertinent glare.

CHAPTER TWENTY-FOUR

The woman with the red mane paced cautiously onto our grounds with a sleeping baby on her chest. She cleared a trail through the leaves with chunky boots, gently pulling a golden-brown horse that walked steadily behind her. When she struck a ray of light in the center of the grounds, I recognized her. I looked at her for a long while without speaking. Then I held my gaze on the sleeping baby. The small babe from the brook who I'd breastfed.

"I remember you," I said weakly.

"I remember you too."

"Where are your friends?"

"They were taken."

"Are you peaceful?"

The woman nodded.

The aches in my body were diminishing, but my throat was vexed, and I had trouble lifting my head. If this woman decided to hurt me, there would be nothing I could do to defend myself. The woman walked closer. She had a bounce in her step to keep the baby asleep.

The woman's horse clopped to a halt beside her. She pulled a bag from the horse's saddle and reached inside for something. Bottles of water and two plastic-covered packets. Food, perhaps. I hadn't seen factory-made food in an eternity. The young mother brought the items close to me and set them down nearly two feet from us. She was feeding us. But why? Was she connected to the patrollers? To the drone? Had she come to politely take us away to our deaths, to some eternal darkness?

I was on the precipice of passing out again. I was weak. Much too weak. I was half conscious as she stood before us begging me to take the food. Sound escaped my head. Words lost meaning. Milo sat up. He grabbed the packet and began gnawing at it. He drank from the water bottle. I slithered further into the leaves, too consumed with exhaustion to take part in this scene unfolding before me. I was crashing. Dried vomit and blood were stuck to me. I could taste it. I didn't want this young woman seeing me like this. I don't know why I cared. She knelt and opened the food packet. She nestled herself closer to me. "Open your mouth," she said.

The woman poured the food into my mouth. What was it? Some type of liquid goo. It was warm and welcome on my throat. I couldn't move my mouth. She helped close my mouth with my chin.

"Come on. Eat."

I managed to consume the entire paste.

"Why are you here?" I asked, my voice barely audible.

"Me and the others – the two other women you met on the bridge – we saw you at the hot spring the other day. We were just beyond the field when you were there with your son. You didn't see us. But we followed you back here. We were curious about you. We were impressed. Truly. Out here by yourself with your boy. We followed you back here, but you quickly fell asleep. We didn't want to bother you, so we turned to leave. But two patrollers were arriving at the same time. They captured us. I managed to escape when my baby girl started wailing and they told me to take her aside to stop the crying. I managed to escape back to my cave. I thought I should come back here to warn you. They could return. You're not doing well, are you?"

Milo sat up and looked wildly at the woman. "See, Mama? People came."

I stroked my boy's hair. "Yes. You were right." The liquid goo was giving my body a sense of comfort. I managed to sit up.

"Maybe I don't care if the patrollers come. We need help." I motioned toward my belly.

The woman softly eyed my stomach with understanding and then looked into my eyes with unease. "The encampments are more terrible than you can imagine. You would rather die naturally out here than in there. Trust me. I can take you back to my cave until you figure out something else."

I started to cry. I didn't want to. "What about this?" I rubbed my belly.

"Mama, why you crying?" Milo interjected.

The woman reached for my hand and squeezed it. "I understand. Really, I do."

Light rain began to fall. The young mother assured us her cave was within reach, a journey we could manage on horseback. An unassuming cave in the mountains. She told me she'd been in an encampment before. The 'death camp,' she called it. It's where her child came from. The baby was ten months old by now, and she only received the name *Virginia* in the last month or so. She called her *Ginny* though. An ode to her home – a state forgotten. Gone. Mostly under the sea. "It took me a while to accept what had happened," she explained. "I was in shock. I couldn't process that she existed." She met the other two women at the encampment. They too had been tortured, beaten, and set aside for labor or fertility purposes. "At least we weren't chosen to be eaten," she said. I flinched. "Yes, that happens," she asserted. Could this be true? Could the encampments have become more terrible than what I saw on the news? The young mother explained that the man I shot was the one who helped them escape. He was a guard who broke away.

"I'm sorry I shot him," I said, still feeling groggy. Yet, slowly coming back to life.

"It's okay. He was Ginny's father. Not by choice. He may have helped us escape. But he wasn't good. I'm glad he's gone. You did the best thing in my mind. Thank you."

"Okay. Good, I guess. Anyway, I couldn't impose on you."

"I would like it. I need someone to talk to," she said. "I have more of that food at the cave. We took it from the encampment when we escaped. It's like meal replacement food – something they give athletes and astronauts. It's like having a three-course meal in five minutes."

"But you also eat…" I gestured toward my body.

The woman suppressed a laugh. "You're too scrawny for me. I promise you and your little boy are off the menu."

I stared at her, unsure.

"Also, my daughter needs a friend. And perhaps your son may need one too, I think," she said.

I looked over at Milo, who was staring ahead at nothing in particular, not moving or blinking.

"It will be temporary," she said. "Okay?"

"Okay."

When my body finally pushed through the sickness, the young mother – I learned her name was Marisol – helped me collect our items. Marisol spoke more about the encampment – its terrors, its cannibalistic regime, its cold, bleak state. When I noticed the terrorized look on Milo's face, I asked if we could change the subject. Without hesitation, Marisol began talking about the lovely cedars leading up to the cave, the serene stream with a tranquil waterfall, the funny chipmunks that scurry back and forth in a frenzy outside the cavern.

"Ginny loves them," Marisol said. "I think you will too."

CHAPTER TWENTY-FIVE

The rain was pouring in thick by the time we left our grounds. I nuzzled my head into Mosey's nose. She was easier to lead away from the treehouse than Milo. Milo had no intention of leaving. He ran back to the half-burnt treehouse when I asked him to mount Mosey with me. He clutched on to the tree.

"But I can't go," he cried. "Dada is coming here."

The boy clenched his eyes, wishing me away. I could feel it.

"Come on."

"No, I don't want you. I want Dada."

"Come on."

"I don't like you!"

"I don't like me either, Milo! *Come on!*"

I ripped Milo off the tree and swung him over my shoulder. He beat his fists into my back.

We moved across the wet leaves and grass toward a path in the woods. Marisol led the way on horseback. Milo buried his face into my shoulder, weeping. He struggled to fit in the backpack. Soon, the boy fell asleep. I managed to save the canvas tarp and covered his head with it as we moved on. It provided some shelter for Mosey too. Milo picked up his head here and there in a foggy state of confusion. "I'm sorry," I told him. "I'm sorry."

We walked for a great length of the day through the rain. Marisol looked back every now and again to ensure we were still behind her. I caught her smiling at us. She appeared friendly, but the Shift had changed me. Trust in humans would have to be earned back, slowly. I ensured the gun at my waist was in proper reach.

Milo woke up when we arrived at the cave. Marisol led us to the opening. Tucked in a crevice of soaring mountainside, the cave appeared almost inconspicuous among the landscape. Marisol assured me that once inside, it opened expansively, letting campfire smoke drift away unnoticed. Marisol dismounted her horse and stood with her baby tucked beneath a long dark cloak. I shook out the tarp and folded it into a large square and furrowed it under my arm. Milo held on to my hand with a compact grip. The boy hid his face in my leg and whispered indecipherable complaints.

It was going to be hard convincing Milo to mingle with this woman and her baby. Or maybe it was going to be hardest for me. A new set of eyes, rules, needs. I wondered if we should hop back on Mosey and continue our journey to Tennessee, alone, starving, on the mend. Ginny started to cry. Milo pulled his face from my leg and stared at the crying baby whom Marisol pulled out from her cloak. I bent down to talk to Milo while Marisol consoled Ginny.

"We're going to stay at this cave for a little bit."

"Why?"

"Because we need some help."

"Because...we sick?"

"Well...no. We're not sick anymore. We just need some help."

"Why?"

"Because sometimes mamas need help."

Milo eyed the wailing child. "Who is that baby?"

"Her name is Ginny."

"Why?"

I hung my head down, and I looked back up at my curious child. "It just is."

"Mama, what's a cave?"

"A cave is a home inside of a mountain."

"What's in there?"

"Um, I don't know."

"Bullies in there?"

"No."

"Why?"

"Because I don't think bullies like caves."

Milo studied me, skeptically. Standing there, he seemed to have gained an inch of height; he drilled into my eyes.

"I won't ever lie to you."

"Okay."

"But we need to stay here for a little bit. And then we'll keep going. We'll go to Bisavó's house someday soon."

"And Dada's pictures are there?"

"Yes, Dada's pictures are at Bisavó's house."

"Mama?"

"Yes, baby."

"Does Ginny like sticks?"

I looked back at Marisol. Ginny was calming down.

"I'm not sure. Why don't we go ask her?"

CHAPTER TWENTY-SIX

Milo didn't want to enter the cave. "Too dark, Mama." He wasn't wrong. Marisol handed me her baby and disappeared into the cave's dark mouth. I stared at the round baby, surprised by Marisol's confidence in me. She returned later holding a wooden rod with a fire-blazed cloth wrapped at the tip. The fire spooked Milo. There was no way to smooth over his behavior. At first, he ran off. Then he shrieked fiercely into my ear once I caught him. He cried wretchedly once we returned. He stared at Marisol's torch. Its spiraling flames. Its dancing embers. He was more afraid of the fire than anything else. He must've remembered our half-burnt treehouse. He must've remembered the helicopter. I did too. Tight face and sunken eyes. My sad boy. Marisol walked close to us with her flickering fire.

"It's magic," she said. "It's only magic."

"We make fires all the time," I said. "I don't know why he—"

"You don't have to explain," Marisol said.

We walked into the cave and stood. There was a firepit right upon entering. Marisol set to work on it right away. There was a wagon filled with food and other resources and a clothesline tucked into grooves of the cavernous wall. A mix of dried animal carcasses and clothing hung from the line. There were crates holding bottles, cans, bowls, clothing, and a shovel. There were leaves and animal fur tufted inside cloth to create blankets and pillows. There was a section for sleeping, cooking, and playing. Then, there were rocks piled waist high in a straight line toward the far end of the cave. A way to keep Ginny from crawling deeper into the cave, I assumed.

"What's beyond the rocks?" I asked.

"Bats, probably," Marisol answered. She took Ginny into her arms and bounced her. The fire was blooming, creating light. Ginny glared wide-eyed into the flames. Milo held on to my hand, waiting for me to provide him with some answers.

"Have you ever explored beyond the rocks?"

"Zed did once."

"Zed?"

"The man you shot."

I didn't answer. I looked to Milo, who gave me a peculiar glance.

"He advised us not to go back there. There are some unexpected cliffs. Hard to tell how deep some of the holes go. This is a safe spot. But we can't let the kids go back there. Do you think that will be a problem?"

I looked to Milo. "No, it won't be a problem."

"I want to show you something," Marisol said, inviting me over toward a wall of crates. With her free hand, she dug into a wooden crate and pulled out a radio.

"Wow. What year is it from?"

"Who knows. But sometimes it works."

"Mama, what's that?" Milo said.

"A radio. An old radio. Do you remember how we would listen to music on our pods back home?"

Milo shook his head.

I nervously chuckled. I don't know why I felt embarrassed. Marisol had gone through her own version of hell, I'm sure. Why did I care that Milo couldn't remember what normal life once looked like?

"This radio," Marisol said, kneeling to Milo's level, "tells us what's going on in the world."

Milo stared. He wanted to grab the radio; I could tell.

"Who's on the other end?" I asked.

Marisol stood up and spoke seriously. "What remains of the government, I suppose. Patrollers. Sometimes I get a faint outlier. Someone spouting conspiracies. Sometimes there's an encampment insider. A guard. He calls himself Lincoln. People have found ways to communicate without a nationwide power grid. It's very hit or miss though. I get something every few days or so. It's solar-powered, so I put it outside as much as I can. But you never know if it's fully charged. It's not reliable. But it helps me feel connected…like, how things used to be. You know?"

I nodded. "What do they say?"

"They say that the coasts are getting worse. The water is coming for the midlands."

"What does that mean for us?"

"It means, things are going to get worse until they get better."

"What else do they say?"

"There's talk of islands appearing. Land split off from the mainland. Perhaps the patrollers will leave the encampments and invade the new islands. Get their sick hands on something else to conquer."

"You think?"

"I have to think optimistically. For her."

"But what if the water comes for us?"

Marisol kissed Ginny's cheek. "Let's hope it doesn't. Hungry?"

It took us a few days to get comfortable inside the cave. Marisol sectioned off a portion of the cave for me and Milo to call our own. We spent several more days finding the right materials to make our own bedding. It was getting colder, though. My pregnancy was making its presence known. Soon, I would have to tell Milo.

As we moved into a colder month, Marisol invited me to sleep longer than usual. In the mornings, she spread our tarp over us and rekindled our own fire. "You're surviving for three now," she said. I didn't know how to repay her for any of this. She had a good soul, but I still had my doubts about her. I still wondered if she would kill me and Milo in our sleep. And yet, every morning I awoke to her gracious smile from across the cave as she played a silly game with Ginny.

By the time December came, or what we assumed was December, there was no denying the baby inside me. I hadn't been sleeping well and Milo was getting bored with the cave. We ventured out into the mountainside one day to change our scenery. The snow had melted on the southern fields facing the woods. We stood upon a lookout. It had been ages since Milo mentioned Dada or Bisavó. This was our new life. The three of us, pillars of Earth, eating and drinking the riches from the land. Did I want to change this? Leave Marisol?

"Milo, I have to tell you something."

"What? Mama, look! Hawk!"

"I see it! Baby, listen." I bent down. It hurt to bend.

"Milo, there's a baby inside Mama's tummy."

Milo looked at me. "In there?"

"Yes."

"Why?"

I shrugged. "Because God wanted us to have a new baby, I guess."

Milo loosely ignored news of the baby. To him, 'new baby' was merely the word choice given to my bloated stomach. A strange name for Mama's growing belly. Until one day, I sat in the cave, rocking, singing a lullaby to my bump. As I was massaging my skin, Milo noticed my tenderness toward something else that was not him. Marisol was out foraging for fish with a net pillaged from the encampment. I was watching Ginny, who was sleeping sound and warm near the fire. Our eyes had adjusted to cave light by now; I peered over to see her chest rising and falling with the gentle movements of sleep. The boy ran to me and pushed me over with a grunt. I landed on a rock that dug into my side. I grabbed his wrist and wanted to smack him. I didn't. Ginny woke up, crying. I went to her and quieted her with soft hushes and patting. Milo was trying to go beyond the rocks. I ran to him.

"Milo, you know you can't go back there."

He was crying now.

I bent down and hugged him as his crying splintered my ear.

"I love you. I love you. I love you. Okay? I love you first. I love you last. You are everything."

"Mama, that's my song."

"The song I was singing to the new baby?"

Milo nodded.

"Oh, I see. Can I sing a different song to the new baby?"

"Yeah." He wiped at his nose.

"Okay. I will. Do you want to go outside and visit Mosey?"

I wondered how Mosey was doing anyway. Ever since we arrived at the cave, Mosey had been enjoying the expansive area just outside, where she was tied up alongside Marisol's horse. Milo smiled and said yes.

CHAPTER TWENTY-SEVEN

We learned it was January from the radio. Lincoln, the encampment insider, mentioned the date just before revealing news about a war. There would be a rush to conquer the islands that were going to rise from the sea. We were just happy to know the date. Marisol and I got to work using white rocks to chalk a calendar into the wall. Never again would we be lost, we joked. We had both come to love Lincoln, rushing to the radio when a signal appeared. We were like two teenagers fawning over a high school crush.

Later, we stood listening by a stream at the foot of the mountain. Milo clung to my leg, shivering. By now, he had grown out of his fox cloak. I knew I would have to come up with something new for him. "Shh," I whispered. We needed to make sure no one was around before we set to work on the net. Marisol and I held on to opposite ends of a large sheer net. We had become good at fishing together. But we were always on guard. Marisol nodded. It was safe.

"Stand back," I told Milo. He wanted to help. "Watch Ginny," I said to him. She was crawling in the snow. Milo ignored me and grabbed on to one side of the gargantuan mosquito net, and the three of us settled it into the half-frozen water. The mosquito net was one of the items stolen from the encampment. Marisol used to prefer a regular net. Once I noticed the mosquito net among her gear, I told her it would be more effective. I recalled Felipe using a similar method once while on a camping trip in Sweet Gum. Marisol kissed me on the cheek when she learned of this method. "I never even thought to use it for fishing," she said. "At the time, I was honestly thinking we'd use it to protect ourselves from mosquitoes. Ha, to think I cared about that. Remember caring about bug bites?"

Marisol talked a lot. Sometimes it got to the point where I had to block her out or pretend that Milo needed something. She talked as though silence was a disease. Sometimes at night after the children fell asleep, we sat by our firepit and reminisced about how things once were. We giggled to the point of bellyaches realizing we both knew the same societal jokes, the same trash entertainment, and so forth. She talked of her life back in Virginia. Her string of boyfriends. Parental issues. Career choices. All of it. She was a good caretaker to me, I told myself, listening to her talk into the night about her love of holidays, birthdays, and celebrations. She was lovely. But I wasn't sure how much more I could take. I was dozing off when she told me her birthday was the following day.

In the early morning before the sun rose, I created a birthday message for her on the wall of the cave. When she woke up, she stood looking at it for a long time. She walked to me before the children woke up.

"Liv," she said. "Thank you. I didn't even know you heard me."

"I always hear you."

She laughed. Her laughter echoed inside the cave, making the kids stir. "Sometimes I'm not sure."

"I'm sorry. Happy birthday."

"It means so much to me. Come here."

She pulled me into a hug and began stroking my neck.

"We should let the kids sleep in," I said, pulling away.

We spent the day inside the cave, tending to the fire. We had enough fish to char. There was a stash of wild onion and black walnuts that had been tucked inside the crates. In my section of the cave, I had a basket full of pine nuts that Milo and I had scoured. The woven basket was made by Marisol. One day she tried to teach me to weave baskets too. When she noticed my fingers were too swollen, she told me I could keep the basket and that she'd give me more weaving lessons after the baby arrived. It was then that I told her I had a history of prematurity. I would need to figure something out. She was great at weaving baskets, but she was not a doctor.

Back in the cave, we were smashing black walnuts and pine nuts while Marisol cooked brook trout. Milo kicked the walnuts, scattering them everywhere. When I told him to go to his bed, he pouted and stomped off. Marisol laughed it off and started rambling for some time. She reminisced about a Catskills cabin retreat she had once taken with her boyfriend, only to find him cheating with another woman in the common area spa.

I tuned her out once I noticed Milo was missing.

"*Shut up!*" I cried. Marisol quickly hushed, leaving only the crackling fish as backdrop noise. "Milo is gone." I searched the cave. "Oh my god. *Milo!*" Marisol set the fish aside and grabbed Ginny. We looked outside. A gunshot suddenly rang from inside the cave. We both ran back inside. I eyed the crate where I normally kept my pistol, and saw it was missing.

CHAPTER TWENTY-EIGHT

I stumbled over the rock pile as stones clacked against the cold cave floor. I ducked my head. The cavernous ceiling suddenly hung low. We used the area just beyond the rocks for extra food storage, but we never explored further into its dark pit of uncertainty. I could hear Milo yelling from an ungodly distance. I imagined the worst scenario – a sudden cliff, darkness eating him whole; me jumping in after him, the both of us lost in the mountain cave forever.

Milo called, "*Mama!*" My heart yammered through my throat. The boy was roaming through thick darkness with my gun. Marisol must have left the lock off the pistol. She had borrowed it to hunt a fox, leaving me with three bullets. Now only two. I crouched, holding on to the ceiling. I screamed for Milo as my voice cracked. I was afraid he was hiding in the dark, ready to shoot me. My boots clopped carefully over puddles. The cave began to smell hideous. My breathing was choppy.

"*Milo, do not move!*" I yelled. "*Do you hear me?*"

A light blared from behind me. Marisol was carrying a torch of light with Ginny at her hip.

"Jesus," I whispered to myself, as the cavern came alive with light and showcased a cavernous floor of human bones. My blood ran cold.

"Hurry," Marisol said. "Go to him. I'll follow you. Go, now! Zed said the cave has cliffs. He could fall, Liv." Her voice was trembling.

"Milo! Milo! Why aren't you answering!"

With Marisol's light behind me, I tore through the cave until I was able to stand up properly. The light revealed an empty, gargantuan space inside the cave.

Milo was standing there in the middle of the open space, holding the gun. Behind him, a cliff.

"Mama," he cried. "Mama."

My boy held the clunky gun in his little hand. He raised the gun and pointed it at me. I swore he was aiming for my belly. But the boy did not know what he was doing. It was what he saw me do with it. What else do you do with a gun but raise it, aim it, and pull its trigger? Marisol was breathing deeply, her steps tracing backwards.

"Put the gun on the floor, Milo. Do not move an inch."

"Mama, I scared."

"All you have to do is put the gun on the floor and Mama will take you out of here, okay?"

"Okay."

Milo rested the gun on the floor. I ran to him and scooped him up, my heart pounding. I held him and breathed, staring at the drop-off just a few steps behind him.

"Jesus, baby," I whispered through heavy breathing. "What the hell did you do that for?"

Milo cried into my neck. "I'm sorry, Mama."

Back at the campfire, Milo and I were alone. Marisol said she would take Ginny out for a walk. She had a disturbed quaver in her voice. She eyed Milo with unease, the boy who steals guns and runs into forbidden caves. But my boy was not violent. He was three. After a fish dinner, I gave every ounce of my attention to Milo. He carried on, showing me his sticks, moving on with life.

"Mama, you want to play too?" he asked. He had new sticks, new rocks. He looked toward me, telling me each object's name. "This one is a baby," he said. It was a smooth, tiny rock. He kissed it. "Shh, this one needs to go to bed." He tucked the rock under a leaf as though it were going into the crib for the night. I smiled, flabbergasted by his imagination and somber that I'd fallen so out of touch with his world.

"Milo," I said to him during a pause in our play. "Why did you take Mama's gun and go inside the deep cave?"

"I thought I heard bullies back there."

"What were you going to do?"

"Shoot them."

"You don't have to worry about bullies."

Milo was playacting with two sticks. He paused momentarily and looked up at me. "Yes, I do."

At night, Milo lay extra close to me. I thought he might be sleeping. My heart was pounding. I didn't know how I was going to keep this up. This life. This existence. The cave felt extra cold and small that night. The baby inside me wiggled so strongly, I thought it was trying to claw its way out. I held my stomach to keep from falling apart. I kept my tears inside. I couldn't stop thinking about the cliff inside the cave that Milo had come so close to. It worried me more than the fact that he could have shot me. The sound of Marisol snoring from across the cave provided a sense of normalcy. When she stopped snoring in the middle of the night, I longed for it to come back.

"I love you," I whispered into Milo's hair, not expecting a reply.

"I love you too," he whispered back.

We crawled slowly through the months of January and February. I lay most days, holding Milo through the cold. Some days, we hardly spoke. Marisol tended to the horses, relocating their posts closer to the cave where they could soak up warmth emanating from the fire within. She also took on the responsibility of hunting and made certain we all had enough to eat. She and I both realized we needed to raise our beds off the cold cavernous ground to keep warm in the night. We used tree limbs, fastened tightly with wild vines, and covered them with pine leaves and fabric, to raise planks for beds. By the size of my belly, Marisol estimated I had to be about six months pregnant. I bemoaned to her that I gave birth to Milo at seven months. She took my hand, as she did often, and told me we would figure something out. I was coming to realize that this *something* was not coming. There was nothing to figure out. I was terrified of having a premature baby without proper care. I feared not just for the baby inside me, but my own life. What would Milo do without me?

"Don't be afraid," Marisol said while the children were napping. We were sitting by the fire. Her fingers worked tirelessly, weaving a fishing basket from willow and boiled bark. "If the baby comes early, we'll wrap it in fox fur. Head to toe. We'll make a bed of fire rocks. You had no trouble breastfeeding Milo, right? You'll do the same for this baby."

"Me and Milo worked up to breastfeeding. He wasn't born a breastfeeding champ."

"This baby will do the same."

"Milo wouldn't have survived without machines."

"The machines were only doing what humans would do, just better."

I looked at her. Her bright green eyes remained so open. No crying. She never cried.

"How do you do it? How do you always remain so calm? So positive?"

She looked out toward the cave's opening. "Liv, because we're doing what we were meant to do. Do you understand?"

"No."

"We're surviving. We're living. Just as the deer. Just as the fox. The birds."

"What's your point?"

"Before the Shift, I worked sixty hours a week and went from abusive relationship to abusive relationship. I was so depressed I would just sleep to make the pain go away. I drank. Took pills. I was on suicide watch. That wasn't living, Liv. This is living. I'm not worried about this. This is real life. That other life was not."

She put her basket down and grabbed my hand. She picked it up and kissed it. Her lips stayed too long on my knuckles.

I pulled my hand away.

"Sorry," she said. "I'm here for you. I will protect you and your baby." She looked back at Milo, sleeping comfortably on his new raised bed.

"I don't know what to do, Marisol. I don't know what to do," I whispered.

"You're going to make it."

"I don't know what to do."

I started to rock. The cave was feeling all too small. The fire looked so warm, so inviting. I wanted to stick my whole head into it.

"Shh. I'm right here. I'm not going to leave you."

"I need to leave. I have to find Milo's grandmother. She probably knows a doctor. She has chickens and pigs and goats. We can eat well there."

"Shh. If you go, I'm going with you. I'm not leaving you. Why don't you sleep now?"

"I don't know what I'm going to do."

"Shh, come here."

"I'm so scared."

"Shh."

CHAPTER TWENTY-NINE

Milo came into the world at thirty-two weeks; a small pink child that could fit inside one hand. He almost didn't make it. He had trouble with his heart. Couldn't keep his temperature up. Had trouble swallowing. I stayed by his incubator, unmoving, as the NICU nurses gently guided me into motherhood. They told me to go home, sleep. *Don't you understand? He needs to grow. He needs the machines. You? You need rest. You'll be with him plenty. You'll hold him the rest of his life.* I stared cold and blankly and said, *I'm not leaving him. I'll wait until he's ready and then I'll carry him out of here.* So, I did. Stayed right by his bedside. Oh, he was so little. The grooves of his skull were still visible through his skin. When he was finally allowed out of his incubator and placed on my chest, he swiveled around, tangled in wires, naked, and lifted his head to lock eyes with me. *Oh, there you are*, he seemed to say.

In the night Ginny began shrieking hideously, waking everyone in the cave, including Milo. He lay listening. "Mama? Mama? Make Ginny stop." I pulled him into me, trying to press his ears to his head. I realized through Ginny's terrible screeches that Marisol had her own struggles. Pain was not just mine to claim. Ginny was still teething and had trouble with sleep lately. I worried about people hearing us. Marisol did too.

"Should I take her outside?" she asked, rattled. Her voice was strained. The past few nights had been rough.

"Come on," I said. "We'll sleep when she sleeps." The four of us sat around the fire, deliriously talking. Ginny stopped crying and stared into the fire. When she went back to sleep, so did we, just as the sun was rising.

No one knew why Milo came early. The doctors could not give me a reason. But I knew why: Felipe. The fighting, the arguing, the endless stress. It ate at my body, making me too weak and unstable to hold life inside me. Felipe was my world. But it wasn't always a healthy world to live in. His temper – I never saw it when we were dating.

"You did this," I told him weeks after Milo was born. I snarled. "You – with all the critiques and comments."

"Stop."

"You've got a temper. You did this to us. With your yelling. You did this."

I imagined him now, dead.

I had no idea what day it was. We'd neglected the wall calendar. My belly was my marker of time now, growing larger by the day. One day, Marisol and I tried to remember the date, but it was impossible. She had been too busy with Ginny. I had been busy waddling along, trying to keep the cave tidy, fishing, caring for the horses, ensuring Milo was content. Marisol and I went through our own respective hells at different times. Somehow our psyches knew to keep our hell days separate from one another's. At some point in the night, my mind betrayed me. I began to hear phantom noise from outside the cave. Buzzing. Drones. I wondered if I was dying. I looked at my hands, and I imagined them pale and wrinkled. I thought of the bullets in my pistol. Two left.

Marisol came to me and suddenly I realized I was shivering violently. I hadn't known until her warm hand grazed me. She brought me back to the fire and gave me broth to drink. I fell asleep by the common area fire, away from Milo. Marisol slept next to me.

When I woke in the morning it was almost light enough to see. Marisol was already awake and looking at me. I picked my head up to check on Milo, and then Ginny. Marisol mouthed to me that both children were sleeping. "Go back to sleep. You need rest." Her crimson hair folded around her face and neck like a warm knitted scarf. The cold alien world my mind had traveled to the night before was now gone. In the distance I saw the outside world beyond the cave's opening. A pink and yellow sky swept the horizon. I returned to the cocoon of my body and tucked my head into the heat of my chest. I felt the baby kicking, kicking, kicking. I could not sleep.

Marisol was close. When she got nearer to me, I could smell her hair. She smelled of pine needles and creek water. She looked exhausted but wore a smile. She leaned close to me and placed her hand on my belly, slowly rubbing until the baby moved into a comfortable spot. I went back to sleep.

In my morning dream, Felipe came to me. From beyond a great oak and dressed in rain-soaked clothes, he walked through dead grass and ash. His hands were calloused and broken. He met my face in the silence. Shrouded in fog, he slumped his shoulders forward. He walked away from me and found Milo crouched in a patch of fresh grass. Felipe sat down with Milo and put an arm over him. Milo melted into him and sobbed. He quickly pulled away from his father and bounced up to his feet. "Do you wanna play, Dada?" They held on to each other and played sweetly in the light grass field of my dream. I woke up sweating.

Milo didn't wake for some time. Ginny was having a restful morning too. Marisol was even closer now; the smell of her pine-scented hair was in my nostrils. We were lying together like two meadow fawns, holding each other much too close to keep the heat between us circulating. I told myself that it was good for the baby. It was keeping my stress levels mellow. I was at peace.

Marisol moved her mouth to my neck, pressing her lips against my skin. She moved a hand onto my waist and massaged my curled-up leg. Her lips moved onto my cheek and up my forehead. Faint gold light leaked into the cave. Our foreheads touched like magnets. Heat billowed between our bodies. I was unsure how we got into this position, but I reveled in this dreamy state. This sudden closeness. It was nice to be wanted, to be touched. In many ways, it was just what

I needed. Just what she needed, too. We held on to each other in a grave grip, entering the morning with newfound meaning. Without warning, Milo came from his bed and peered over at the two of us. He asked for broth in a loud voice that woke Ginny.

CHAPTER THIRTY

The grass outside the cave had turned into little spears of ice. I was glad to inspect the frigid icicles outside with Milo. The intimate morning with Marisol had left me feeling confused. We hadn't talked of our closeness since Milo came to greet us – or interrupt us, rather. And now the day had turned into late afternoon. Frost covered the land. Milo crossed the wild meadow and took a slippery trail toward the fishing stream. I waddled after him, asking him to slow down. The slower I became the quicker he was. Ice was everywhere. We were wrapped in animal fur and dead men's clothing. *Our clothing*, now. Our hands were covered in fabric from an old shirt, stuffed with fox fur. Fur mittens, we called them. I thought of Marisol the whole walk down to the stream. She stayed back at the cave, helping Ginny with her newfound love of walking. It was too soon to talk to her about what had happened in the cave. The strangeness of it all. Yet, I couldn't stop thinking about it. About her. Was it a fluke, or something more?

We went to the stream and marveled at its full glaze of ice. I kicked at the ice. Nothing. We needed an axe to break through. I thought there must be something sharp on me but there wasn't. I had left my gun back at the cave too. I was becoming too trusting of our immediate surroundings. My guard was failing. I pounded my heel into the ice. Not a dent. Milo tried too. I laughed at his sweet grunts as he pounded his foot on the frozen water. Then he tried again. This time he slipped and smacked his head against the ice. I went to help him and stepped onto the sheet. The ice broke into fractals, sending my foot into the frozen stream. The frigid water hit me. *"Mama!"* The water reached Milo too. Suddenly, my mind went back to the highway, back in the car with Felipe and Milo. Back to when water came rushing to sweep us all up. Maybe we should have let it. We backtracked out of the water with cold feet.

We walked back to the cave. Milo was complaining about his frozen feet, and I couldn't help but join in. On our journey up the trail, I told Milo that our feet took a bath in the stream. How it was for the best, since our feet were so stinky. Milo must've liked my comedy hour. He began cackling deliriously. Stinky feet. He laughed until hiccups consumed him.

Beyond the common area fire, Marisol was lying on her back, flying Ginny through the air like a plane. When we entered, I could feel the shift in the atmosphere. Milo broke the silence by telling Marisol the lengthy details of our afternoon. The stream covered in ice. How we kicked at it like fools. How we forgot an axe, forgot everything. How he slipped. The boo boo on his head. "Oh sweetie, let me see," she said. Milo went on. How Mama's boot eventually chipped ice and got us wet. How we had wet, stinky feet. Marisol listened intently to it all, looking at me after every sentence to wait for my nod of approval.

After snacking on grubs and the remains of a wild turkey and a scrawny bluebird, Milo agreed to play with Ginny. She was getting bigger, more aware. Not a baby anymore. The two of them were beginning to play nicely with each other. Milo didn't like to share his sticks and rocks with her, but they were satisfied to sit near each other and play independently. Sometimes Marisol and I caught a sweet gesture between the two of them, such as Milo passing one of his sticks to Ginny. Ginny leaning over Milo's shoulder to see what he was doing and copying his every move. We gave Milo the job of making sure Ginny never touched the fire or got terribly close. He did an outstanding job telling her to stay put, looking to us afterwards to bask in his job well done.

Marisol gave me her leftovers and begged me to finish. She asked me about my fall and then took my foot in her lap and kneaded the arch. We did not talk about our morning. Not a word.

In the night, a radio signal came through. Marisol and I dragged ourselves out of our beds and huddled by the fire listening to the radio. Then it stopped. Who was it? Static poured through. And then a voice. The deep tones of Lincoln cut through the long silence. His voice was choppy, as though he had just struggled through something. The urgency in his voice was palpable through the old black radio. "To whoever is listening," he said quietly and urgently, "there are more drones circumnavigating the dry lands, looking for more bodies to bring back to the camps to work. The drones are searching the mountain trails where there are reports of survivors from the coasts. Stay hidden. This is not a place you want to end up." He paused as screaming sounded in the background. Marisol and I looked at each other. God knows what was going on there. And then he confirmed what we had known for some time. "I can't speak for all camps, but this one is killing off the weak for food. There's no other options." He paused. Marisol and I looked at each other again, curious as to whether Lincoln was sobbing. He cleared his throat. "Our only hope comes from the new islands sprouting in the east," he said. "I can confirm at least three new islands are on the rise." There was sudden screaming, and then his signal ended abruptly.

Marisol and I sat by the fire staring at the bronzy red flames. How could so much devastation be taking place when the cave was so warm, so peaceful? How much longer until a drone came for us? We sat there a long time, not talking. Finally, I mentioned the ice-covered brook. Nothing swimming in there. "Do you know anything about ice fishing?"

Marisol nodded and told me she would go down to the stream in the morning and make a fishing hole. When I thanked her for being so resourceful, she leaned into my face without warning and placed two hands behind my ears. She stared at me, saying my name. "Liv – Liv, in this crazy world… In all this craziness, I met you. How did this happen? How did this happen? All of this led me to you." She laughed and kissed my lips, breathing fiercely. I turned my head to ensure that both children were sleeping. Then I grabbed her wild feathery hair and pulled her lips to mine. Each kiss was soft and perfect. She scooped her hand behind my back and held me close. Nothing had felt this good in a while.

CHAPTER THIRTY-ONE

In the morning, Marisol prepared to go down to the stream alone. She collected items in her wagon – axe, net, string, bait. Then she reached down and picked up Ginny for a tight hug and kiss. "You sure you want to go alone?" I asked her. She gave me a smile and nodded. She was about to speak but Ginny smacked her in the face for no reason. Marisol winced and plopped Ginny in my arms. "At least take a blanket with you. It's cold." Quietly, she got to wrapping her hands in fabric and fur. Her back was turned to me, but I could tell she was struggling with her hands. She never finished what she was going to say. She never complained either. Something was wrong with her fingers. I sensed it. She wrapped her hands completely, looking mummified, and then she set out toward the stream through crunchy snow with a makeshift blanket draped over her shoulder.

Marisol was gone for hours, but I wasn't sure what I was expecting from her outing either. I wasn't sure how long ice fishing took. We hadn't discussed her plan at length. We were quiet toward each other. Warm, but quiet. I began to miss her chattiness.

The children and I spent the afternoon sitting by the fire wrapped in fur and eating leftover turkey and nuts. We sipped boiled snow water from cans. With Marisol missing, I took the opportunity to focus on Ginny. She was very different from Milo when he was beginning to enter toddlerhood. Milo may have been quicker to speak, but Ginny seemed more focused on action. She was more rambunctious, more impatient to get to her feet. She watched everything that Milo did. He had become her entire world. Her noises were growing, mimicking sounds picked up from Milo. No words yet, but she was determined. She also picked up some of his more undesirable traits – hitting being one of them. But she was tough. Confident. She would soon be leader of the world; this I knew in my bones.

Milo kept his feet close to the fire as he played out a scene with rocks on the cave floor. In the distance I could hear thunder and after a while I realized too much time had passed. I walked to the edge of the cave and peered at the new sheet of rain. Why was Marisol gone so long? Were there no fish? Wouldn't she have come back and devised a new plan with me if that was the case? I wondered if I should gather the kids and look for her. It was getting dark. Ginny pulled at my leg. She had toddled her way over to me. She was shaking. I quickly picked her up.

"Oh, you're freezing, aren't you?"

Milo ran over.

"Mama, she cold?"

"Yes, she looks pretty cold." I felt her forehead. "But she feels hot."

Milo laughed. "That's silly."

"We need to help her."

"Okay, Mama. Like a doctor? Doctor Milo? Doctor Mama?"

"Yes."

It turned into a strangely long night. I dragged our bed made of tree limbs and pine toward the common area fire and had the children sleep next to me. Ginny lay between Milo and me. I wondered if she was coming down with something or just terribly cold. Soon, she fell asleep, and the shaking stopped. But a cough developed mid-sleep. This woke Milo, who was curious why the three of us were still lying in bed together next to the fire.

Milo drank some more snow water and turkey bone broth. He followed me to the cave's opening, as I looked out for Marisol. The ground was freezing, even in fur-lined boots. Marisol was out there, freezing too. I imagined the ice that Milo and I slipped on just yesterday. What if she slipped, alone?

By then, I was contemplating leaving the children in the cave and going out to find her. They would be sleeping. What harm could happen? I checked off the list in my head — bears, cats, patrollers, marauders, fire, guns, choking, or maybe just a toddler brawl of sorts.

"Milo, I might need to leave."

"*No!*" he yelled.

I looked toward Ginny. She was sleeping peacefully.

"Shh. I mean, I might need to go out and look for Marisol. She's gone too long."

"Why she gone too long?"

"I don't know. Maybe something happened to her."

"I come too?"

"No, I don't think you should. I need you to stay here and watch Ginny."

"Why?"

Milo sat down after following a crack along the floor. Then he said, "You said you never leave."

"Huh?"

"When the cat came, you said Mama won't leave anymore."

"You're right. I did say that. I'm sorry."

"Mama?"

"Yes."

"What happen to hell-copta?"

"I don't know."

"Accident?"

"Yes."

"And that's where Dada is?"

"Milo, I'm not leaving."

"Okay."

CHAPTER THIRTY-TWO

We entered the frosty morning after having only a little sleep. Rain had fallen in the night, creating an icy landscape outside our rocky grotto. I tried to pull Mosey into the cave, but she wouldn't comply due to its narrow opening. I covered her with everything I had and ensured she was as close to our heat source as possible. I went inside and sat Milo on my lap by the fire. We ate the last of the wild turkey. Ginny was stirring awake. I brought her a new cloth diaper made from old fabric, tossing the old one into a crate where we put our clothes to be washed at the stream.

"We need to find Marisol," I said.

"Why?" Milo asked, inspecting Ginny's bare behind.

"She hasn't come back. We have to find her. We probably waited too long."

The boy didn't answer. He locked eyes with Ginny. The two of them, bound to this situation that neither of them asked for.

I placed Ginny in the backpack and zipped her up to her chin. Milo held my hand, and we walked through the ice until we discovered horse prints. Marisol had taken her horse, Cherrypie, with her. Now her prints were preserved in the ice. I pointed them out to Milo to keep him engaged, looking for the next ones. The day was remarkably cold, and I'd forgotten to wrap my hands. I remembered walking through New York City in a miniskirt one winter vacation, amazed how blinding cold my body could feel. Memories from before the Shift came to me often. Imagine, a skirt. How silly.

We followed the horse prints through the snow until we were almost near the brook. Ginny coughed from the backpack. There were times when Milo would cough, whimper, or just stare blankly into space, and I become consumed by deep and sudden sadness, as though the world's goodness had failed him. This vulnerable, sweet soul. Ginny's cough had the same effect on me.

A trail of blood appeared without warning on the snowy ice trail. Cherrypie's prints turned into a tangled mess of blemishes. My heart quickened. It reminded me of a terrible dream I'd been having lately – Milo surrounded in a puddle of blood. I feared for what came next. Yet, we kept walking, quickening our pace. There was no turning back. We were already practically at the stream. Suddenly, Cherrypie's body appeared on the ground. Milo hadn't seen it yet.

"Milo, close your eyes."

"Why?"

"Just close them. Hold my hand."

The boy squeezed his eyes shut and held my hand.

"I want you to walk quick. Okay?"

"Why?"

"Milo, please. I beg you. Just listen to me."

"Okay."

We moved past Cherrypie. I could see a wound in her chest where I assumed she'd been shot.

"Mama! Can I open?"

"Milo. We have to be quiet."

"Why?"

"Bullies are here."

Milo stopped talking. I reached for my gun and pulled it out, holding it in my free hand. We moved past Cherrypie, and we neared the stream.

"Open your eyes now. Do you see Marisol anywhere?"

"Mama! Look!" He quickly placed a hand over his mouth.

"What?"

"Marry-sole over there!"

"I don't see."

"Over there!"

"Oh God, you're right."

"Why she is laying down?"

"Come here."

I picked him up and ran toward Marisol, who lay in the snow.

I scrambled to revive her. She looked like a pale corpse left carelessly in a wintry pile of snow. But she had a pulse. And she had a blanket. Without it, I knew she would have died overnight. I knew nothing of CPR but breathed into her mouth, nonetheless. She blinked and looked up at me with a terrible groan. Her teeth were chattering. I pulled her to a sitting position. She fell into me, apologizing. Looping thoughts plagued me. How could I have left her out here? What other option did I have? What happened to Cherrypie? Could I carry Marisol, Milo, and Ginny back to the cave? No, I could not. She was ice cold. I could feel my stomach tightening, blood rushing. I felt as though my temples might burst. I couldn't see straight. I needed her to tell me what happened. She was so groggy and couldn't move her legs. The people who did this were out there somewhere. I scanned my head side to side. This was borrowed time.

Marisol had a strange smile. A light and confusing smirk. I could punch her. Did she not know her horse was dead? Did she not know the graveness of this situation?

"Why are you smiling?"

"I did it. Caught us dinner." She pointed to her basket, filled with a striking mix of rock bass and hogsuckers.

"What happened to you?"

"Marauders came. Two of them. A man and a woman. I killed them, Liv. Killed them both. They came for me, but I shot the gun right out of the man's hand. They only had one gun. They put up a fight with me. It was terrible. I guess I passed out afterwards. I'm so sorry. But I won."

"Where are they?"

She pointed to the water.

"In there somewhere. I led them onto the ice and then pulled my gun out and shot them both. Shot at the ice until it cracked. They sunk. I think I'm out of bullets."

"You scared us. All of us."

I pulled Ginny out of my bag and laid her on her mother's chest.

Marisol had forgotten about Cherrypie when she first woke up. As we were walking back to the cave, it came back to her like a thrown brick. Cherrypie had been tied up while Marisol was fishing. The marauders killed Cherrypie first, and then they came for Marisol. She kept her mourning private. I told her that early in the morning, we would have a memorial for Cherrypie. Milo, holding on to my hand, kept looking up at us. He didn't say a word. We passed Cherrypie's body on the way up the snowy trail. We told the children to close their eyes. Cherrypie's body lay like a mound of fresh terracotta clay. Marisol didn't look. We both were thinking the same thing – that Cherrypie's meat would provide much-needed nourishment for all of us – but we didn't say it out loud.

"It would be a sacrifice of her love to you," I finally said.

Marisol didn't answer.

We reached the cave like a band of broken soldiers. Marisol set to removing her bloody clothes by the fire. I gave her space, tending to Ginny, who was still coughing. Each cough took me back to the Pennsylvania hotel, the disease-filled halls in the dim of night. "Mama? Mama? You okay?" Milo asked, half watching me, half playing with his sticks.

That night we collected mounds of snow and boiled it. We filled Marisol's solid-sided wagon and crates with sizzling water. Milo and Ginny received baths. Marisol and I used ripped shirts dipped in the warm water to wipe our bodies clean. Marisol was sore and unable to move as she once did. I took charge of caring for Ginny and Milo the rest of the night.

"Let's not go out for a couple days," I said.

"Agreed. We have enough to eat for a while," she said, hobbling toward her bed.

"I'll just need to go out and get the…meat…before it goes bad. I'm sorry. We can pretend it's not her. Pretend it's another horse."

"No, it's okay, Liv," Marisol said. "I'm a big girl. It's a sacrifice of love, like you said."

"Yes."

The next morning before everyone awoke, I left the cave and went to Cherrypie's body. I took as much meat as I could in one session. Milo was awake when I returned. He was not pleased. When I tried to explain that it was just a quick visit to the stream to collect food, he stared at me, shedding a silent tear. He gave me a sloppy hug that seemed to say *don't do that again*. I put down my basket of horse meat and hugged him ferociously. After we reunited, he helped me cut into the meat in our kitchen area. We laid the meat on slabs of slate rock. He was pleased to use an axe like a big boy. The smell didn't bother him. I wanted to puke. We looked back toward Marisol and Ginny, who were still sleeping. It was a relief to have a break from Ginny. To have this moment with my son alone.

A few days passed quietly. Marisol lay in bed recuperating. I hadn't stopped moving. Caring for Milo and Ginny was difficult. Everything required double the energy, which was more than I wanted to expend. My body was growing larger. My hands, swollen. The stress from Marisol's event had left me with a strange shortness of breath. I worried about my blood pressure – about the baby coming any moment. I kept my complaints private. Marisol was struggling. Her legs were sprained. Her head was concussed. Plus, her growing arthritis was flaring up. She'd kept it a secret from me until now. She was a mess. I needed to be the coolheaded one, the strong one. God, I was so tired. It was too much to handle. I coped by eating extra meat. I needed the strength to forge another day. For Milo. Always Milo.

CHAPTER THIRTY-THREE

The following day, I felt faint and wondered if the baby was coming. Just the day before, I wondered how many weeks until the baby's arrival. Now, I wondered how many days, how many hours. I rested a hand on a crate and breathed deeply. Marisol rose from her bed and looked at me. She limped toward me and moved me back to bed. Then she took on the role of cave mother for the day. When I tried to help, she said, "Nuh-uh-uh," and ordered me back to bed. I sank in and out of sleep throughout the day. Milo periodically checked on me.

It must've been late afternoon. I was muddled with grogginess. I leaned to my side. Marisol was by the common fire with Milo and Ginny. Milo wouldn't stop talking. He had laid out all his sticks and rocks and told Marisol each one's name and rightful place in the world. "And this one flies. See? Brrmm!" Marisol didn't know I was watching quietly from the dark corner. She focused on Ginny. "Can you say Mama? Just like Milo does." Ginny grunted and reached for one of Milo's rocks. A sad sigh resonated from Marisol's breath. She rested her face in her palms, asking Ginny over and over again to say Mama or anything, but she never did. When Marisol saw that I was awake, she came to me. She moved wet threads of hair off my temples. I was sweating and breathing long, tempered breaths.

"Do you think it's time?"

"I'm not sure," I said. "I'm feeling calm at the moment."

She felt my forehead. "Are you sick?"

"No. I'm enjoying watching you play with the kids."

"Well, I'll keep going then. Rest."

At night, Milo had trouble falling asleep. He kept flying his arms in the air and plopping them down carelessly.

"Come on," I said. "Lay your head here and let me tell you a story."

"About a doggie?"

"Sure, why not."

"Okay."

We lay side by side, wrapped in layers. For a long time, my monotone voice reverberated inside the cave as I told him a story about a doggie. In my story, the doggie visited a deliciously warm beach with white sand and a soft ocean breeze. Milo stared at me.

"Close your eyes. You have to imagine it in your mind."

"Okay. What's that mean?"

"It means you see pictures even though your eyes are closed."

"Okay."

I spoke slow and soothing. "And the doggie swam in the warm ocean water. And he was so happy and peaceful. He decided to take a nap on the creamy, soft sand. Oh, it was so warm and nice."

"Mama?"

"Yes, baby."

"I wish I was there now."

"Me too."

When Milo was asleep, I visited the fire. After a day of resting, my energy levels returned. Marisol was sitting, working on a basket.

"I liked your story," she said, smiling coyly.

"Oh, you heard that. God."

"You're a good mother."

"Puh," I groaned. "I don't know. I'm just trying to make it another day."

"I know." She paused. "Me too."

When I tilted my neck to look at her, I noticed her hands were still bothering her. She took breaks to rub her fingers. I took her hands into mine and kneaded her rough fingers and calloused knuckles. Her fingers were small in my hands. It was delightful to hold the hands of another. I imagined Felipe's hand, overbearing and hairy. And Milo's hands – smooth and tiny, never staying in my grip for long. Marisol's fingers were delicate. I didn't want to squeeze them too hard; they seemed to be whittled out of wood. She looked up at me with wishful eyes. I tried a couple of times to talk about something. But I never knew where to start. Soon, Marisol got on the subject of Ginny's speech. "She should be talking by now." She started rubbing at her elbows.

"Hurt there too?"

She nodded.

She continued talking about Ginny as I moved onto her elbows.

She twisted her neck side to side, savoring the massage. "I should be doing this for you," she said.

"It's okay. It's calming me. I haven't been this calm in a long time. It's good for me. And the baby."

"Okay."

"You shouldn't worry about Ginny. She's fine. She's perfect."

"I didn't speak until I was six," she said matter-of-factly. "I just...I don't want her to struggle like I did."

"She'll talk."

"If I just heard her say Mama, I'd feel better."

"She's still a baby."

"I know."

Marisol shifted around to massage me. "We're going to keep that baby inside you as long as we can," she said. "Okay?"

"And then what?"

"I don't know. I'm sorry."

"If Mosey gives us all she's got, I think she can get us to Sweet Gum. You and Ginny should come." I had talked to her often about Sweet Gum, but never so directly.

"We should wait for spring," she said quietly.

"You're suggesting I have the baby here?"

"Yes, Liv. I think that's the safest thing."

"What if it comes early? What would we do?"

"The same thing those NICU machines did for Milo. Give the baby food and keep it warm."

"And then you'll go with me to Sweet Gum?"

"Do you want me to?"

I moved her feathery hair over her ear. "Yes."

Marisol cleaned up the cave and did some last-minute chores before sleep. I made sure my gun was stored safely in fabric and kept high up on a platform on the wall. Marisol put our leftover fish and horse inside one of her baskets and tucked them securely into one of the crates. She wrapped a hand-woven fur scarf around my neck and rubbed my arms. It was time for sleep. And yet, we didn't want to be apart so soon. We stood outside the cave's opening with Mosey and looked out at the night.

"Are you okay?" she asked. I nodded mutely while stroking Mosey. My horse, who once had free will. Now, I tied her up. I loved her, but it was foolish to think she'd always be there for me. For us. I didn't like to think about her end. And this, I realized, as Marisol reached for my hand, was the problem with falling in love.

CHAPTER THIRTY-FOUR

In the night, there came a flash of light across my eyes. A long stream of fluorescent light snaked over me and Milo and then throughout the cave. I blinked, forcing myself awake, heavily disoriented. The light was followed by an intrusive orange flare, one after the other, lighting up the cave like a festival. I sat up and held on to Milo.

"*Marisol!*" I screamed. "Oh my god."

"What is it, Mama?"

"Stay down. Oh my god. Stay down."

We were being invaded. Patrollers moved into our cave, waving sizzling flares, hollering at each other to search the cave. How many? Two? Four? Five? Ginny began wailing with a searing ferocity. I grabbed Milo and got to my feet. My gun. It was still lodged in the tall rock wall. Why hadn't I slept with it? A man with frigid hands cuffed his fat fingers over my wrist, pressing into my skin.

"Get off me!" I shouted. "Marisol! Marisol! Men are here. Men are here."

"*Liv!*" she yelled from across the cave.

"Stop moving," the patroller said. "Come here."

The patroller's hand was firm on my wrist. I could not move to my gun. I held on to Milo with a tense grip. We were jerked violently out of the cave and stood shaking in the cold, dark night.

"Mama!" Milo cried. "Who are they? Mama!"

The patroller kept us close.

"Get your hands off me," I growled outside in the moonlight. "We aren't bothering anyone here."

The man was dressed in navy colors, his eyes shadowed by a helmet. "We're following orders. Everyone must report to the camp. For safety purposes, ma'am. We cannot have you out here in these conditions. Especially with minors."

"Horseshit," I said.

"I'm just following orders."

"Yeah, I got that."

"Load them up!" he yelled to the others.

There was barely headroom in the truck; they threw us into it like luggage. The windows were blacked out. Little light. No handles. No buttons. Marisol and Ginny were practically on top of me and Milo. Ginny's cries were ear piercing. I held Milo's hand and pulled his head into my chest. "We're gonna be okay. Mama is here. We're gonna be okay."

Soon Ginny stopped crying, but she hiccupped as she tried to catch her breath.

"Where are they taking us?" I whispered.

Marisol was breathing deeply. "The closest encampment."

"The one you escaped from?"

"Probably."

"Do you think there's someone we can talk to?"

"No."

"Are we going to stay together?"

"They'll assess us and see where we fit in. I don't know if we'll be in the same group."

"What about the kids?" I tried to hold Milo's ears shut.

"I'm not hopeful."

"Marisol, please."

"Liv, I'm out of answers."

"Do you have anything on you? Bring anything from the cave?"

"Nothing. You?"

"Nothing."

There were times in the cave that Marisol would talk about the women who lived in the cave before me. She spoke so highly of them; so much so that at times I was jealous. Then I realized how silly it was to be jealous of them. She spoke of their survival skills – fishing, hunting, weaving, foraging, first aid. Mostly she lauded their fire-starting skills. When she learned I had a fire-starter on me, her eyes grew big as walnuts. For our first couple of days together, it's all we used to cook our food and water. Then, a day came when she said she no longer wanted to use it.

"You want to go back to sticks and tinder?" I asked, cocking my head.

"Yes. I don't want to get used to instant fire. What would happen if we lost the fire-starter? Then I'd be out of practice building a fire by hand. You can lose an object. You can't lose a skill."

"Fair. Can you teach me?"

"Of course."

It took me two weeks to master the art of making a fire.

The truck hobbled down the mountainside. Our ears popped as we sat in silence, each of us imagining what lay ahead. I looked at my sweet, scared boy. Milo was sitting quietly, hip to hip with me, watching. He would not take his eyes off me. The white of his eyes flickered in the dim vehicle. Milo was trying to gauge my reaction. It was my job to remain calm. For him. For the baby inside me.

Soon the truck was driving onto a paved road. It felt strange to be moving so fast. I became queasy. Milo stared at me. His nails dug into my arm.

"You didn't ask me," he whispered.

"Ask you what?"

"If I brought something from the cave."

"Sorry. Did you?"

"Yes, Mama." He showed me his leather bag slung over his shoulder. It was the bag we'd taken from the dead men so long ago, the one that housed his growing collection of sticks and rocks. He had kept it right by our bed every night, always in the same place. He was more prepared than me – just like Felipe. He opened the flap, but I couldn't see what was in there. I put my hand in and jostled through the cluster of sticks and our compass.

"Good," I said.

"I have my magic acorn too," he said. "From Dada."

"Just what we need. Keep it safe."

Sometimes Marisol would talk about the encampment, but I always asked her to stop. Milo was always listening, always asking questions. But when she did get the chance to talk about it, her stories disturbed me so much I had to ask her to stop for my sake, too. She showed me her arm, the burns she received after defying orders. "If it weren't for Zed, we never would have made it out of there. As terrible as he was, he is the reason I'm alive."

"Do you think the other women escaped?" I asked her. I meant her friends, the ones who were re-captured. I wondered about them.

"No, Liv. They're probably not alive anymore."

"I'm sorry."

When the truck came to a complete stop, I wrapped both arms around Milo and said, "We're going to be okay. Everything is okay." A patroller opened the door, sending the light of dawn into our tired eyes. The patroller looked at us, but his eyes were vapid. Gone. He jerked us out of the truck. This was not a man. Not anymore.

CHAPTER THIRTY-FIVE

We moved into a stone-gray building, patrollers on either side of us. I held Milo on my hip to keep us walking quickly. There was a large steel door that opened into a sterile foyer. Inside, fluorescent lights were harsh on my eyes. There was steam pouring through vents and bloodstains on the floor. It was burning hot inside. It smelled like death. Hordes of people in gray jumpsuits walked through, led by patrollers in navy suits with guns. Everyone seemed to be coughing. Only the patrollers wore masks or helmets. We walked down a dark hall. There were screams coming from the other side of the building.

We rode an elevator that hissed softly and clunked to a stop. The patrollers moved us to a new level. Marisol held my hand. I moved Milo to my other hip and pushed his head onto my shoulder. I whispered to him periodically. *Shh. It's okay.* I looked all around, searching for the nearest exit. My eyes landed on a door that seemed to lead to a fire escape. On top of the door's exit sign, there was a bird's nest. I skirted my eyes toward the door, motioning to Marisol. She shook her head at me. I pleaded with my eyes and was about to run off without her, when a man began storming down the hall, naked and yelling. He was shot dead on sight. I pushed Milo's head into my shoulder and trembled. His body shook against mine.

We were led down a narrow, dismal hallway. We passed a series of doors, each one fitted with a murky windowpane. The rooms were labeled with faux gold plaques. Each label listed the name of a president: Van Buren, Adams, Monroe, Lincoln.

Lincoln.

I tried to peek into the room, but we were hurried along to the end of the hall where we were shoved into what seemed like a dim conference room. The walls were gray. The floor, gray. The room, sterile. No art. No windows. Nothing. We were told to sit in the cold chairs that were at a metal table. The door slammed shut swiftly; the patrollers left us in the room alone.

"Mama, where are we?" Milo asked, lifting his head up from my shoulder.

I ignored him and whispered to Marisol, "What's going to happen?"

"They'll assess our strengths through a checklist."

"What if we don't have strengths?"

"Then we're food."

"Mama, what's that mean?" Milo squeaked.

"What about the kids?"

"Labor."

"Impossible."

"Not impossible."

"Ginny's going to perform labor?" My voice was growing louder, more annoyed.

"They'll select caretakers to raise them until they're capable of labor. Individualism does not exist here. They see their work as steps for the greater good. For the future. We want to be strong, Liv. We want to be chosen for labor. Just do what they say. Show them our strengths."

"I'm fucking pregnant."

"Great. They'll see you're good for bearing children."

"How did you escape before?"

"Zed led us through a back door."

"Where is it?"

"I'm sure they've boarded it up by now. They learned their lesson from that escape."

"Where is it?" I asked.

Ginny cried.

A man with gray hair and emerald eyes came through the door. He was weathered but not old. He looked into our eyes as he walked toward the opposite side of the table. We weren't going to be there long. I was certain. I didn't care what Marisol said. No matter how much I loved her. The man looked emotionless, but not threatening. Not like the others.

"I need you to write your names here," the gray-haired man said. "And where you were from before the Shift, and where you've been since. And please fill out the questionnaire." He slid us paper and pens. It felt strange to hold a pen in my hand. It felt strange to have to answer questions while the world around us was sinking into the sea. Marisol tried to write her name, but her fingers cramped up and she dropped the pen. The echo of the pen felt louder than a firecracker in the bare room. The man paid attention to this and wrote something in his notepad.

Marisol tried again, fumbling. I wrote my name with ease.

New patrollers came in and dragged us to a room with showers. There were women, men, and children already in the shower room. It was crowded and steaming hot. We were ordered to strip and bathe. Our clothes were thrown into a pile. Marisol and I looked at each other, naked and cold. I still held on to Milo's leather bag. A patroller tried to pry it from me. The gray-haired man entered the room and intervened. I handed him my son's leather bag of sticks. "Please, don't throw this away. My son's sticks are very important to him. This is hard to explain, but they represent his father, who we lost. Please. I beg you." The man didn't say anything back, but he took the leather bag and wrapped it over his shoulder. Then he left.

Stripped down to nothing, we showered. We wiped away the earth from our skin. Dirt caked to our bodies was peeled away.

Afterwards, we were given gray clothing and black socks. No shoes. Milo's clothes barely fit him. He was swimming in them. And cold. We were forced into a cafeteria. This too was crowded. Marisol and I hooked elbows to stay together. There was coughing, sneezing, crying. We were given bowls of bread and a few cans of condensed milk. There was meat; it was square shaped. Nothing like I'd ever seen before. Or tasted. I looked at the boy. He looked drugged. He wasn't eating.

"Go ahead," I said. "Eat. Before it gets cold."

"What is it?"

"It's food."

"Fish?"

"No, I don't think this is fish. It's bread."

"Bread?"

"Yes, you used to love bread. Try it."

"What's this?"

"It's milk."

"Mama milk?"

"No, not mine."

"Whose?"

"I'm not sure. Maybe a cow."

"Cow?"

"Milo, just eat. Please."

"Why?"

"Because we need energy."

"Why?"

"Because we need to figure out how to get out of here."

Marisol looked at me. She put her hand on me. "Please, Liv. You saw that man shot down. That happens a lot. They like when people try to escape. I heard Lincoln say that during one of his reports. It makes it easy on them – they know who to send to the slaughterhouse first."

Milo sat, staring at his plate. Was he listening? I was about to speak when an announcement came over loudspeakers. The message was muddled, but it seemed clear as day to the patrollers. Milo screamed and cried.

"What is that?" he whimpered.

"An announcement. It's okay."

We were shuffled into a room with other women and children. No men. A patroller shoved plastic jugs of water through a small square opening in the door. People ran toward the water jugs. Later, I went to the door and tried to pry open the small square panel, but it was impossible. We stayed in the room for hours. Though we were clean and had been fed, this was hell. I longed to be back in the cave, back in the treehouse. Dirty and starving, but free. I held Milo in my lap. I kept my breathing tempered, trying not to let the stress get to me. *Keep the baby in, keep the baby in.* A patroller came while we were asleep.

"Marisol," the patroller grunted into the room.

"Yes?" She rose, groggy from sleep.

"Come on."

"Where am I going?"

"Fieldwork."

She leaned into me in the dark. She kissed me on the cheek. I pulled her back by the sleeve.

"No, Marisol. Don't."

"I have no choice."

I pulled her aggressively toward me and kissed her lips with all I had. She rose with Ginny toward the door.

"Leave the child," the patroller said.

"What? No. I can't."

The patroller called for backup. "Come on, miss." They pulled her out of the room, yanking Ginny from her arms like she was a challenging weed. Marisol screamed and then the door was shut. I went to Ginny and brought her back to the dark corner where Milo and I were camped out. In the corner of the room, I whisper-sang to Ginny and Milo, who both lay their heads on my lap. Ginny was shivering with fear, not even capable of crying. Milo ran his hand through her auburn hair. I stopped singing. Ginny fell asleep.

"Mama, where are we?"

"Prison."

"Why?"

"I don't know. We're not staying long."

CHAPTER THIRTY-SIX

We sat on the cold gray floor with a pool of urine around us, wearing the same gray clothes we were given upon arrival. Ginny and Milo had both wet themselves in the night. I wasn't sure how much time had passed since they took Marisol away. A patroller hooked up a small heater that puffed hot air into the room every forty-five minutes.

"Mama, when we eat?" Milo asked.

"I don't know. It's been a long time."

"Why?"

"Because this place is run by animals."

"Mosey?"

My eyes welled upon hearing her name.

"No, not Mosey."

Later when the children were asleep in the corner of the room, I felt a sharp pain in my ribs. There were some mattresses in the small room, and far too many bodies to occupy them. When my pain grew obvious, some women dragged a mattress from the back and laid it out for me. It was the first sign of empathy I'd seen since arriving. The women and children in the room barely spoke to each other; conversation led to intervention. Intervention led to separation. The unknown. The patrollers would call individuals by name. Whoever put up a fight was forced to comply. There were whispers about what happened on the other side. I tried not to listen to them.

I lay in the darkness, moaning, thinking about all the things left behind at the cave. I should have slept with the gun next to me. The patrollers would have been dead before they reached the fire. *Boom, boom.* Done. I leaned into the mattress and cried silently. A woman came over to me and noticed that I was in pain. "She's in labor!" She got up and pounded on the door. No one came. Then all the women, and any child who was left awake, pounded on anything with a surface. Finally, the man with gray hair came to the door. The woman pointed to me. The man with gray hair motioned me toward the door. "Will I be able to come back?" I asked. He nodded. I followed him, leaving Milo and Ginny on the mattress, hoping he was telling the truth.

The building looked like it had been abandoned years ago. Was it once a school? A prison? It was hard to tell. We passed a room that reeked of rotting flesh. Through the window, bodies were piled on top of one another. I turned my eyes away and could feel my body trembling as I walked. The man leading the way down a dark corridor put his hand behind my back with a strange hurriedness. He looked me up and down, eyeing my bump down to my swollen feet inside my unwashed socks. He scooted me inside a room. The *Lincoln* room. I took a seat on a wooden bench, holding my belly. There was a slender candle on the man's desk. The man took a cigarette from his pocket and lit it. He inhaled and then blew white smoke in the opposite direction of me.

"How much longer do you have?" the man asked, whispering.

"Any day I think."

"Shh, lower."

"Sorry. Is there a doctor here?"

"No, there's not. Not the type of doctor you need."

"Who should I see, then? Who can help me?"

"No one. What's your name again?"

"Liv."

"Liv, if you have that baby here, you'll never see that baby again."

I stared at him for a while. Why was he telling me this?

"I don't understand."

He took another puff. "There are islands appearing in the east." The man was speaking hurriedly now. His voice grew bolder and louder, until he seemed to realize it was much too loud. He paused. "The head patrollers – the government – whatever you want to call these sick bastards – they want children and babies on those islands. It's part of their re-population strategy."

My voice was stuck in my throat. "Well, what about their mothers? Won't they go too?" The idea of moving to a new island, a clean island with food, with Milo, was beginning to sound enticing.

"The mothers aren't invited. They have enough women already. What they don't have are enough children."

The man's voice was beginning to sound familiar, comforting. This was the man on the radio. The informant. *Lincoln.*

"So, what will become of the mothers?"

"They'll stay here. They'll work. They'll produce more children if need be. They'll make the food or become food themselves."

"What do I do?" My voice was quavering. My legs were shaking. I couldn't stop them.

"Tomorrow the doors will unlock at three p.m. The patrollers will be at a meeting. You will *run.* You will tell everyone to run. You will run away from this camp. You will not look back. You will have your baby in the wild. You will keep doing what you were doing before you were brought here. If you ever see a drone again, say EEMA Pass. It will bypass you. It's a code."

"What does EEMA mean?"

"Emergency Evacuation and Mass Asylum."

I couldn't form the right words. I stuttered, trying to find what to say. "What if we're caught?"

"No one will be around to catch you. Like I said, the patrollers will be in a meeting. I'm the one who arranged the meeting. I should know."

"Won't they see you unlock the doors at three p.m.?"

"No, all the doors in this building will unlock automatically. It'll look like a glitch in the system."

"Why are you helping us? Why are you different? Is this a trick?"

"It's not a trick, Liv. Not all of us have fallen for the propaganda. Some of us create our own way. Have our own thoughts."

There was a long silence. The man offered me the end of his

cigarette. I refused.

"I'm going to douse this place in gasoline during the meeting," he finally said. "I know how to do it strategically so that the others won't know or smell it."

"Will you be in the meeting?"

"No," he said, sounding a little frustrated. "I have others on my side. That's not important. Listen carefully. This is what you need to know. The left of the building will be lined in gas just before three. The right will not. This will give you time to escape. Run right. Right. Do you hear me? The room they keep the children in, the ones they tear from their mothers, is on the right side of the building, just down the hall from your room. The patrollers reside in the left. I will ensure that when you escape at three, there will be no patrollers guarding your door. Before they even realize anything, I'll light their side of this building on fire. But you must ensure you get everyone out quickly because the fire will travel quickly. There is no doubt."

I didn't know what to say.

"Do you understand? I will burn this place down after you've escaped. These people have no right to play God."

I searched his eyes. He was serious. And I trusted him. But I couldn't do this without Marisol. "Yes, I understand," I said. "But do you know what happened to my friend Marisol? The one who came with me?"

The man hung his head. He didn't speak. My chest tightened. Pain returned. I couldn't breathe.

"I'll take you back to the room. Are you okay for the night?"

I swallowed. Nodded. I was shaking, everywhere. I tried to calm myself, to go numb. I could not let stress get to me. Not yet. I needed the baby out first. I pretended what he said meant nothing. Nothing at all. Marisol was just out fishing. She would be home soon.

"Liv, before you go. I want to give you something."

I looked at him as he pulled Milo's leather bag of sticks from a drawer and returned it to me.

On the way back to the room, we passed the exit that once had the bird's nest atop the exit sign. Now, the bird's nest was on the floor. The sorry thing. For some reason, I scooped the nest into the leather bag.

"Mama?" Milo whispered as I nestled back onto the mattress.

"Shh, we have to sleep now."

"Where did you go?"

"I had to go pee."

"I have to go pee-pee too."

"Go in the corner. It's okay."

During the night, Milo and Ginny inched closer to me. Ginny was tucked at my legs. Milo held on to my belly. I found myself reaching into Milo's bag of sticks, holding on to every one. Our only possessions. These belonged to us. We'd found them. These had meaning to us. They were important. Special. I understood how Milo felt now. Large, small, thin, fat, long, prickly, delicate sticks. All kinds. I came across an acorn in the bunch. Milo's magic acorn. The one from Dada. I squeezed it and waited for sleep to come.

CHAPTER THIRTY-SEVEN

In the morning I was awoken by a stream of white puke sopping down the crook of my neck. Ginny leaned over me. We'd been graced with a couple cans of condensed milk, and it didn't seem to be doing well in her digestive tract. I got up and went to the lone sink, which was at the back of the room. There was a line. The smell of milky vomit was growing stronger. It nauseated me; I threw up on the spot. Those in line for the sink turned to me with disgust. I went back to the mattress, unclean. Milo had woken.

We were not provided breakfast. At some point, we were moved like a herd of deprived goats to the cafeteria room. No one spoke. A woman in line, who had been feverishly mumbling in the night, dropped dead while walking. No one turned to look at her. When we were seated at a table, I kept Milo and Ginny close. I didn't want anyone looking at them, memorizing their faces, their hair, their tone of voice. I kept my head down too. A bowl of gray porridge was placed in front of us. No spoons. We took turns sipping from the bowl. I wondered if Milo knew how much more he deserved. Ginny too. As I sat there feeding the children, I recalled a dream I had in the night. Marisol was in it. She was by the frozen lake, slipping further away from me. I tried to warn her. Of what? I wasn't sure. Even now some part of me wished I'd never stumbled upon her. Some part of me wished the same of Felipe. Then, I reminded myself that would mean no Milo. No Ginny either. There would be nothing. Just myself. Just my animal heart and animal body, surviving. Like the lone mountain cat searching for a meal, belonging to only herself.

On the way back to our room, I held both children on either hip. I ignored the pain. I ignored my breathlessness. When Milo tried to speak, I shushed him. He put his head into my milk-soiled neck and sobbed. When patrollers eyed him crying, I squeezed his leg, begging him to shut up. We passed a room filled with children. Through the frosty glass windowpane, I saw poorly clothed children playing with trash on the floor. There were no adults in the room. I felt faint. Were those the chosen children set aside for the islands? Momentarily, I imagined giving Milo and Ginny up. Perhaps the new island would be full of wonderful opportunities for them. Food, shelter, toys. Milo had been able to move on without Felipe. He could move on without me too. Milo simmered down and softly grazed his fingernails against the back of my neck.

I spent the early afternoon trying to explain Lincoln's plan to the women. I was careful not to speak loudly or seem obvious in any way. Using my fingers, I signaled three o'clock. Milo followed me around the room as I visited each nook, each woman. No one wanted to listen to me. They sorted through their socks and bags of milk. The insane notion of creating order, making meaning in this place. The day was moving quickly. There was one clock in the room. I visited the door often, feeling the handle out of impatience, waiting for it to unlock. There was a camera above us, watching every move. Milo asked me about it.

"It's a camera."

"That's weird, Mama."

"Yes."

It was so peculiar, so strange to go from a densely dark cave to a fluorescent world with a security camera. *We should still be at the cave,* I told myself. *No, we should still be in Sea Isle,* I had to remind myself. It was getting closer to three. There came a girl – a teenager perhaps – who had caught on earlier to my warning about the doors unlocking at three.

From what I could tell, the girl was by herself. We spoke quietly to one another.

"The door should open soon," I promised her.

"And then what?" the girl said.

"Run right."

"And then where?"

"Anywhere but here."

"Can I come with you?"

I looked over her scrawny figure and noticed she had slender fingers that would be good for weaving. Surely, I could teach her everything I learned from Marisol. Oh, Marisol. How silly to think she was gone. She's just waiting at the cave. *Soon, spring will arrive, and we'll kiss once more.* I wondered how long I would need to play this game with myself.

"Do you like children?" I asked.

The girl shrugged. "I used to have brothers and sisters."

"Okay."

"Do you think it's true? Do you think the doors will open at three?"

"I'm hopeful, yes. Shh. We need to warn the others."

"I can help."

I was beginning to think it was nice to have someone listen to me. She would do well in the wild. A mother for Ginny, perhaps? *No, no. Silly Liv. Marisol is her mother.*

"Do you know the way out once we leave?" I asked the girl.

"No."

"In case we're separated, you make a right out of this room. You run straight until you reach a dead end, then veer left. Then run straight on to the exit."

"Do you need help with the kids when we run? Should I take the red-haired girl?"

I turned to her with a smile of relief. "Yes."

"Okay, I'll tell the others. I'll be discreet. Don't worry."

"Thank you."

The girl smiled and went to warn the others.

I looked out the pane of the door. There wouldn't be much time for her to warn anyone. A fleet of patrollers was marching down the hall right toward us. They weren't supposed to be here. They were supposed to be at a meeting. Lincoln's plan was not unfolding as intended. Something was wrong.

CHAPTER THIRTY-EIGHT

The patrollers stormed the long gray room and initiated a wordless battle. They concealed their faces with masks and decked their hips in weapons. Why were they here and not in Lincoln's meeting? My heart raced as more patrollers entered the room. They began ripping babies and children from the arms of mothers like weeds. They moved the children to the hall, where more patrollers were waiting to keep the children in line. Crying and shouting consumed the room. Terror. The fleet of guards pillaged the room, like they were ransacking a village. I ran back to my mattress where Milo and Ginny sat and pushed it toward the wall. I foolishly thought I could keep them hidden from this darkness. The women who put up a fight were shoved to the ground and smacked at any sign of noncompliance. Ginny began crying, and for some reason I looked to Milo for help. He put his small hand over her mouth.

"Listen to me. I'm going to talk very fast to you."

"Why fast?"

"Those men are going to take you and Ginny."

"And you too?"

"No, not me. Not grown-ups."

"But I don't want to go." He started to cry.

"You know how Mama always tells you it's okay to cry?"

Milo nodded.

"You cannot cry here. You must be good. Be invisible. Help Ginny."

"Mama, please. I don't like this."

"You take care of Ginny, okay?"

"Mama."

"You're smart, Milo. You're going to be okay."

"No."

"Milo, please, baby. It'll just be a short while."

"Promise?"

"Yes."

The boy wiped at his eyes and looked over my shoulder. He looked like his father.

"Mama?"

"Yes."

"I love you."

"I love you too."

"I go with the trollers, and then I come back to you?"

"Yes."

"And…and then we go to BeezBo's house?"

"Yes."

"And then we see pictures of Dada there?"

"Yes, exactly."

"And Dada be there too."

"No."

The patrollers came to our corner of the room. Two of them looked at me sternly, eyeing my pregnant body, and then they overtook me. I was thrown to the ground. The patrollers hoisted Milo and Ginny into the air, and each was tossed over a shoulder like a sack of horse feed. Ginny wailed mercilessly into the patroller's ear. *Good*, I thought. *Scream until blood sprays from his head.* Milo, on the other hand, remained quiet. He lifted his head and stared at me solemnly until he disappeared into the hall.

There was no way I could let this happen. I wiped away blood from my head and stood wobbling. The baby in my belly moved in a circle. It pushed into my ribs. It was pleading to jump out of my skin. I fought the urge to lie down and let the baby push its way through. I tripped over my feet. Dizzy and delusional, I leaned against the wall, surveying the room. I felt ready to collapse. The room was stripped of its children. Crying was in every corner of the room. There now only remained a few patrollers. Then came the young girl.

"It's almost three o'clock," the girl said, shaking my arms.

I looked at her, but I was too exhausted to speak.

"Hey, are you listening? It's almost time to run."

"No," I said breathlessly. "This wasn't part of the plan. Patrollers weren't supposed to come. They were supposed to be in a meeting. Something isn't right."

The girl shook her head. She was determined to get out of here. "I'll go after the children first," she said. "You follow."

"We have to think about this carefully. We can't just run cold."

"I can't stay here. I've been here since the start of the Shift. I'm done being a lab rat."

My head was spinning, wondering what happened. Lincoln said the patrollers would all be away, not ransacking our room and taking our children. What had happened to his plan? "No, I think we need to—"

"You said a right. A left at the dead end. Straight on to the exit. Right?"

"No, something's wrong."

"I'm going."

There was no getting through to her. When all but one of the patrollers had left the room, the scrawny girl ran toward the door, managing to skirt out before it locked shut behind her. I hobbled toward the door to watch what I could see through the pane. She didn't get halfway down the hall before she was shot down. She lay on the gray-tiled floor, pooling blood. I slunk down, breathing heavily. The baby was coming. It was too soon. Much too soon. I cursed through the coursing pain. Why couldn't I do what I needed to do? Keep the baby contained. I played out the scenario in my mind – the baby would come early. It would be small. It would be of no use to the patrollers, to this place. To the islands. Nor would I.

I slowed my breathing and got to my feet.

CHAPTER THIRTY-NINE

I thought about the pilot as I stood at the door. I wished I had asked him his name. It would be easier to curse him out once the baby came. Alas, he was also the reason Milo and I escaped the floods. Curses and praises, at once.

I thought of the night we evaded the floods in his helicopter. Felipe had to just about drag me off the bed. The drink the pilot had given me before our act untethered me from reality more than I would have liked. The drink was violently strong. It crept in like a thief. I'd only had half a cup or so, but it was enough to affect my judgment. Sitting like some used rag on the pilot's bed, Felipe stared at me with anxious eyes.

"Are we ready?" he asked. "The waterline is almost at our floor."

The pilot nodded. "Yes, we'll take the stairs up to the roof."

"Are you ready, Liv?"

I was trying to stop the room from spinning. "Yes."

"Where's my turtle?" Milo whined.

Milo's stuffed turtle. He called her Mama Turtle.

I looked over my shoulder, as though Mama Turtle could be lying on the pilot's bed. "I don't know. Felipe?"

"Fuck Mama Turtle. Let's go."

"Dada, why you say that?" Milo began crying.

Felipe breathed deeply. "Sorry, I shouldn't have said that."

The pilot zipped up his jacket and eyed us with annoyance.

I always knew where Mama Turtle was. At the time of my sex appointment, however, I wasn't exactly thinking of Mama Turtle's whereabouts or bringing her to his hotel room.

I held on to the flimsy comforter to keep from falling over. "Did you leave Mama Turtle in the room?"

"Even if I did, I wouldn't go back for it," Felipe said. "It's underwater now."

"We should go," the pilot said curtly.

"No!" Milo cried. "*Mama Turtle!*"

I stood and almost collapsed. The pilot helped me. Felipe eyed us both with unease. I held Milo in my vision. His sad face wrinkled with disappointment.

"I think we dropped him in the stairwell," Felipe said.

Milo wiped his eyes. "Get him."

"It's really time," the pilot said. "I won't wait."

Felipe looked out the window at the rising water. "I'll be right back," he said.

I surveyed the room of scared women. No one wanted to be in the room, no one wanted to leave, either. I lifted my head and looked at one of the mothers on the ground, crying. Doing nothing. Just crying. Some of the other weeping mothers looked to me. God knows I was creeping up to them earlier telling them about Lincoln's plan. Their eyes drilled into me saying, *Where is this master plan of yours?* I shuddered, feeling my abdomen send a message of pain up to my brain. An old woman who was childless came up to me and rested a hand on my shoulder. She watched me carefully. I tried to center my vision on her wrinkled face.

"Everyone's been talking about what you said. About the doors unlocking at three."

"I didn't think anyone was listening."

"Everyone was listening. We were all too afraid to respond."

"There's no use now. There was a fault in the plan. The patrollers weren't supposed to come here. Something went wrong. I don't know what, but I don't trust to leave this room with the patrollers still out there." I flinched and lowered my eyes to my belly. "My baby is coming."

"You don't look ready yet. You're too small."

"I don't make the rules."

"What happened to the plan?"

"I said I don't know. I don't make the rules with my body or this place. I don't make the rules anywhere."

I breathed in and out slowly, trying to calm down.

"Are you okay? Should I get someone?"

"I'll be okay. I'll let you know. I'm okay for now."

"Okay. I'm sorry," she said. "We were all just so hopeful for a short time. I guess we go back to being hopeless."

She walked away with sunken shoulders. Her back was soiled with sweat. I was reminded of Felipe. His back was always sweaty. Always working, toiling, fixing, preparing. I slunk down against the wall, ready to lie on my back and let the baby emerge. Surrender. I lay on the cold floor and looked up at the ceiling. Another nest was tucked into a ceiling board. No bird. There came a loud sudden shot from outside the door.

I didn't want to trust the pilot with my life. But I had no other choice. The wind was forceful when we stood on the roof waiting to enter the helicopter. If a journalist had come up to me and asked me what I was doing, I might've said I'm not sure. All I knew was that I could smell the water. And Milo's hair was keeping my cheeks warm. I could've been on top of a mountain waiting for a ski lift. Or standing in line at the convenience store. The pilot's drink was deceptively strong. He guided me by the elbow, closer to the craft. Felipe came from behind me, stuffing Mama Turtle between Milo's face and my chest. Milo squeezed his precious stuffed turtle.

I opened my eyes and stared at the bird's nest, thinking about Mama Turtle. Her fuzzy green shell and black plastic eyes. Milo loved her. Felipe knew that and went back for her even though the flood waters were rising. I caught my breath and raised myself off the floor. The pain exited momentarily. A break. I hobbled to the door. The handle was locked. But I managed to pull my face to the pane. I looked out. The scrawny girl was still on the ground, dead. But there lay a new body next to her. Lincoln's. Shot. His memorable gray hair filled with blood. I gasped, feeling my heart quicken. Hope fizzling. My body shook with stinging fear. Yet, this was good too. I knew that I was no longer waiting for him. It was time to resurrect my own plan. I thought of Felipe running back to rescue Mama Turtle in the stairwell. If Felipe could run through flood waters to save a stuffed turtle, I could figure out a new plan to save us all. I staggered toward the old woman and grabbed her by the shoulder.

"There's a new plan now," I said. "There is still hope. Maybe I do make the rules after all."

"I had a feeling."

"How did you know?"

"I could see it in your eyes. Mother's eyes."

The old woman smiled. I looked up to the bird's nest and then sniffed the air.

"Do you smell that?" I asked.

"Smells like gasoline."

"It does, doesn't it?"

CHAPTER FORTY

Crossing the room to the mattress, I felt weak. I wondered if the scent of gasoline was getting to my head. The old woman was watching me. She flared her nostrils. The scent was getting to her too. Or, at the very least, we had both awakened to it. Lincoln had completed *part* of his plan. The gasoline. And then he was shot. Did they discover what he was planning to do? The old woman and I were both suddenly distracted by the shouting of patrollers in the hall. What was *their* plan? What would they do with our children? I turned to the room and took in the sad scene of huddled, crying mothers. I walked on toward the mattress. Tucked under a urine-soaked sheet was Milo's leather bag of sticks. I centered my breathing and searched the bag. I pulled out the bird's nest that I'd recovered from the hall and set it down for the time being. Then I dug around for two sticks. The first stick: sturdy and slender with a pointed tip. The second: wide and husky with a boat-like center. I took the slender stick and began rubbing it into the wider stick, back and forth, faster and faster.

The stick broke. I dug inside Milo's bag for another. And another. I raised my head and met the gaze of the old woman. She looked at me as though I were deranged. I got to work again. My arms moved furiously as I rubbed my new stick into the groove of the other stick. I closed my eyes and thought of Marisol. How she cheered me on during my first fire. I felt as though my arms were going to break at the seams. "That's when you know you're close," she'd insisted. In the cave, when I had finally created smoke, I felt like I had just created life. Marisol smiled proudly. She knew that I had.

When I glanced up again the old woman was kneeling on my mattress. She appeared deeply agitated.

"What the hell are you doing?" she whispered.

"I'm getting us out of here."

"By killing us all?"

"No. By freeing us all. No one is coming to save us. We have no guns. No weapons. We have nothing. But we have fire. Or we will."

"You're going to kill us with that."

My arms were weak, and the old woman was making the mattress wobble. I thought of shoving her off. But then, I'd be no better than the patrollers.

"The doors will open at three. We'll bust out once it unlocks. I'm told one side of the building is lined in gasoline. I'll throw fire to the gas line, and then we'll run to the children's room or run out of here. The patrollers will be too distracted by the fire to come after us. There's no other way."

"What if it kills us first?"

"What if the patrollers kill us?"

"You're crazy. This is crazy." She paused. "But – I've seen too many people disappear already. Who knows who's next? I'll hide you from the camera. Don't stop."

I kept rubbing. For a long time. I thought of the Pennsylvania hotel. There was this woman who was so weak, so sickly, she had no way to call for help from her room. But she did have a lighter. She lit her bed on fire. The smoke caught the attention of someone in the hall who kicked her door down. Sometimes, the only way to save yourself is by taking control of the fabric of life itself. Sometimes you must use the weapons of God.

"There," I said. "Smoke. Pass me that bird's nest."

"My god. Okay."

The woman passed me the bundle of twigs, hay, and grass. She held it close as I tended to a growing ember.

"I need to transfer this to the nest," I said.

"I don't know how to help you, dear. I was a schoolteacher. Not a survivalist."

"Good. We're going to need schoolteachers once life gets back to normal. Keep the nest steady."

"Okay."

"Come on," I said to the embers. "Come on."

When I went to transfer the ember to the nest, the lady dropped it and the spark of fire diminished.

"I'm so sorry! Old hands."

I stared at her without words, and then I looked toward the camera above. I didn't have much time. I didn't know who was watching or paying attention, but I didn't care.

"That's okay. Let's try again."

I looked at the clock. Fifteen minutes until three. I got to work on the fire once more. The slenderest stick had become dull at the tip. I pulled out a sharp rock from Milo's bag and began whittling the tip of the stick to make it sharper. The woman stayed by my side, and she massaged my shoulders. From above, it might have appeared she was merely consoling a sobbing mother. I scraped the stick into its base repeatedly. Too much time had already passed.

I tried it a couple more times. A final push into the base created a mist of smoke. I raked the stick into the core until sparks formed and the old woman helped me transfer the coal into the tinder nest. We both held the nest and watched it bloom into flames with a delicate whoosh. I reached forward as she tilted her hands, and I blew on the flames to make them larger. We didn't have much time until the nest would burn out.

"Come on," I said. "Let's go."

"What are we going to do now?"

"We're moving it to the door. We'll wait until the door opens. Be careful as we walk."

"What if it doesn't unlock?"

"Then we figure something else out."

"What if it reaches the children?" she asked.

"I trust Lincoln was strategic with the gas placement. I've listened to him for months. He's good. *Was* good. The children will be safe if we can get to them in time."

"Who the hell is Lincoln?"

"Don't worry."

"You're crazy."

"I know."

Two minutes until three. The fire was starting to weaken. I blew on it lightly. We shuffled closer toward the door. The other women joined us, forming a circle of shared purpose.

"Now we just wait," I said once we arrived at the door. The hall just outside our room appeared empty, but we heard shouting in the distance, fighting. I remembered Lincoln's words. *Not all of us have fallen for the propaganda. Some of us create our own way.* I wondered if there was a revolt. Perhaps those who knew of Lincoln's plan were keeping guards away from our room. We all watched the clock. "I know this could backfire," I whispered toward the old woman. "If you don't want to help me anymore, you don't have to."

"I just helped you light a bird's nest on fire. There's no turning back."

"Okay. This is how we live. This is the way out. We can do this."

"We can do this," she echoed.

The other women in the room whispered it as well. *We can do this.*

The room felt like it held its breath, every woman's gaze fixed on me, their hopes and fears resting on my shoulders. Wedged in the corner of the room, feeling my labor pains come back to me, I waited for a sign that everyone was prepared. Silence draped over us. The clock's second hand seemed to echo like distant thunder. As the hour hand struck three, I reached for the handle, heart pounding. Nothing. A collective sigh. Flames crackled, dying. A minute passed. Then another. Just as I was about to quell the flames entirely, the door handle still in my hand loosened with a satisfying click.

CHAPTER FORTY-ONE

In the time between lighting the nest on fire and waiting for the door to unlock, Felipe's face came to me. He had been in my thoughts a lot lately. He was always furious in my visions. Always trying to fix something. Get something done. I was never quick enough or prepared enough in his eyes. Not even in my own imagination. In the end I hoped to remember him smiling. It was his smile that first caught my eye. I met him before he became an electrician, before his obsessive need to prepare took over. Back then, he was just my mechanic. The boy in the filthy green suit who alternated my tires, changed my battery, and who always updated my car's chip. There were times I visited his shop, complaining about a phantom squeak, feigning ignorance. He smiled back then, especially the day I came in for a flat. When he realized I actually knew how to change a tire myself, he crossed his arms and stared at me, eyes twinkling. My ruse vanished right before him.

In the room, the old woman looked at me with wide eyes, waiting for my command. My anxious chest had replaced the pain of my contracting uterus. I blew on the nest to enlarge the flame.

"Run," I whispered to the room. I leaned on the door handle and moved into the hall. Patrollers were at the far end. Once they saw us, they immediately began charging, pushing away other guards who seemed to be mutineers.

"*Go!*" I shouted. The women spilled out of the hall as I ran toward the patrollers with my flame. The man in front lifted his gun to fire right as I tossed the nest on the floor where I saw the shine of gas. The fire followed a gas trail that spread from one end to the other, engulfing the oncoming patrollers. I ran back to the old woman who had stayed. Smoke instantly filled the hall.

"The fire is going to take over the whole building. We need to go, *now!*" the old woman pleaded.

I pulled my eyes away from the burning bodies, thinking of Felipe, and I followed her and the others who had managed to escape the room. We moved like gazelle toward our children. The fire was traveling quick.

The mothers and I made it to the room where the children were kept. They were abandoned by whoever oversaw them. The room was safe from the flames but starting to fill with smoke. Milo ran to me crying, holding on to Ginny. We were together again. I could've wept. I held his face and said, "See, I promised I'd come back." Then I picked him and Ginny up and followed the mothers and children out of the room and back into the hall. A group of mothers hurried the children from the smoky room toward the exit and disappeared down a fire escape. I followed, but the door had already locked shut. Holding the children, I looked around, searching for another way out. At one end, the growing fire paid no mind to the sprinklers above. On the other end, patrollers worked to tame the fire while shooting down escapees from other rooms. Lincoln's open room came into view. With the children, I burst through a cloud of smoke and tumbled into Lincoln's room and shut the door quickly behind me. It was safe for the time being. There was a patroller kneeling in the shadows of the room. I gasped.

The man watched me but did nothing about my entering. "Lock it," he said.

"Okay."

"The fire will come to this room eventually," he said.

"I know. Why aren't you trying to escape? What are you doing in here?"

"Surrendering. I knew it was coming. Lincoln warned me. I've been waiting."

The flames crackled behind the door. More screams. The door rattled as patrollers tried to get in. The man looked up from the dark ground, his cheeks streaming with tears. After a while he said, "I've seen the worst of this life. I cannot see anymore. I'm ready to go. This is the greatest blessing I could have received."

Milo and Ginny began to weep out of fear.

"I'm sorry," the man said.

"I never said you were wrong."

He looked up but said nothing.

"Can you help us?"

"What for?" the man asked. "What does it matter?"

"Perhaps you'd like to leave this world with something good to claim. To erase all the bad."

"I'm going to die. It doesn't matter."

"Help us, goddamn it!"

The man looked away. I set the children down and began frantically searching the room for something; I don't know what. I wasn't thinking clearly. I looked out the window wondering if it was possible to jump. We might make it, but the baby inside me wouldn't. Then I went to the man and grabbed the collar of his shirt.

"Can't you do something? Anything! Help us!"

The man gagged. "There's a key on the desk."

I moved to Lincoln's desk.

"Yes, I see it. What's it for?"

"There's a truck right outside. Look out the window. Runs on electric. Should be fully charged. It's yours."

I rushed to the window again. Smoke was seeping into the room now. The children coughed. A black truck emblazoned with the word EEMA waited in a barren field outside the building. Two stories down. I turned in a circle, looking for something that could help us get down safely.

"Jesus, are you pregnant?" The man had finally noticed.

The man got up. Milo and Ginny ran to my legs.

"Check the closet. There might be a rope ladder in there. Ever since the floods came, rope ladders have been in demand. Every encampment has them. We've saved so many people from the floods with those ladders, only to treat them like dogshit once they get here. Pathetic. We were once the good guys, you know."

I ran to the closet. It was packed with junk. More smoke was leaking into the room now. Milo and Ginny started to wheeze. Finally, I found the ladder in the corner of the closet. I launched it out the window and hooked the top beneath the sill. I didn't know how I could carry both children down. The man watched me as I frantically tried to pick both children up. More smoke crept into the room. The man was just standing there, watching us, tears forming. He began to cough. Then, he rushed to us, taking Ginny from me as I secured Milo on my body. Milo wrapped his arms and legs around me.

"I'm coming too," the man said, still holding Ginny.

"No, give her to me."

"You'll fall holding both kids. I have her. I'll bring her down safely."

"How can I trust you?"

"I might not care about my life, but I can't be the cause of one more death."

Ginny began crying. I eyed the man intensely. There was no other choice.

"Follow right after us," I said. "Don't let go of her."

The man fumbled to secure Ginny and get himself over the edge. "I promise."

I moved down the ladder with Milo.

"Mama, what are you doing!" Milo yelled.

"Shh."

"Mama, I don't like this!" Milo cried.

Ginny cried louder.

"Hold on to me. *Do not let go.*"

The man and Ginny were right on top of us as we inched down the ladder. I begged Milo not to let go of me. I looked up, relieved the man was holding on to Ginny and that we were all almost on the ground. The fire was now billowing through the window we just escaped from. When we were nearly at the bottom, the fire claimed the rope ladder and we plopped like logs onto the snow-covered ground. I looked up, searching for my breath. The children rolled into the snow as they tried to regain their footing. Fire consumed the building. I looked at the man, who got to his feet.

"Thank you," I said.

"No, thank you for giving me an ounce of redemption. The truck is still yours."

"What are you going to do?"

He didn't say a word. He turned around, walking toward the fiery building.

"Where's he going!" Milo cried.

"Don't look."

I got to my feet and picked up Milo and Ginny, who were still crying, traumatized. I held both children by their arms and dragged them across the snow. The children coughed and cried the entirety of my dash to the truck. "Almost there," I said. "Quiet."

The truck opened with the key. I sat breathing in the driver's seat. I put the children on the floor of the truck, scared they would be seen by some roving patroller. I started the truck, surprised by its machine noise. It had been so very long since I'd driven anything except a horse. I pulled away from the flaming building, toward a back road that looked unassuming and barren. The road descended into blackness. There was a marsh that was hard to see. One more inch, and we would have ended up in the swampy waters. Swiveling away from the dark pool of muck, I pulled us onto another road and drove until my breathing regulated and the children quieted.

CHAPTER FORTY-TWO

Ginny fell asleep as I drove. Milo crawled into the passenger's seat and kneeled to face the endless road ahead of us. The dawn ascended as the sun rose in the east. The amber sunrise was comforting on my eyes. It marked our direction and cemented that we were headed south. The mountain ridge came into view. I would follow it until I felt safe stopping.

"Mama," Milo whispered. "There's a car up there."

"I see it."

"Who is it?"

"I don't know."

"Mama, no one is in that car."

"I see that."

"Where'd they go?"

"I don't know."

We crossed several more abandoned cars. I created stories in my mind about what happened to the cars haphazardly positioned in the road. Poor souls stopped, forced into compliance, taken to the EEMA encampment. Or other encampments. How many more existed? There was no way for me to know. The truck's radio brought forth only static. I knew nothing. I longed for Lincoln's voice. Marisol. Felipe. Mosey. I took hold of the boy's hand.

"Whose truck is this?" Milo asked.

"Ours."

I drove on, waiting for the baby to kick. Nothing moved. I moved my hand around my belly. Milo copied me.

"Your belly is cold."

"I am cold."

"Me too."

I played around with buttons, blasting heat. Milo climbed closer to me and surveyed the mountainous view through our glass window. He looked down at Ginny every now and then, as did I. We drove onward, as I had no plans of stopping. I tried to look for signposts, but they were few and far between. They'd either been burned in fires or removed entirely. I knew I was headed south.

The road was covered in slush. Melted snow. I looked through the rearview mirror and eyed the backseat. Along the black leather seat sat duffel bags, suitcases, a rifle. I'd not seen these items in the darkness.

"Mama, where are we going?"

"Bisavó's house."

"Where is it?"

"At the end of the mountain range."

His eyes went to the passenger seat window and he pressed his nose into the glass. I spoke about Bisavó's house to keep Milo calm, to set his hopes on something. "She has a beautiful house with chickens and goats. She has the best view of mountains and the freshest air you will ever breathe. You were there when you were a baby. Once we took you down to a stream and gave you a bath and a little frog jumped onto your leg. Everyone laughed."

"Who laughed?"

"Me and Dada."

He liked hearing about that.

I drove until Ginny woke up wailing. I pulled the truck off to the side of the road. I ensured the truck was locked and then put the safety blinkers on out of habit, not that anybody was around. "What's that?" Milo asked, enraptured by them. I turned them off to save energy. After a moment, I reached for Ginny. I held her against my chest and rocked her until her eyes settled on a flying hawk who landed on a snow-covered pine. If Ginny could speak, she might tell me off. She might realize her terrible fate and how I played a part. I wished I could convey to her that I missed her mother too.

"Can we eat something, Mama?" Milo asked.

Ginny whimpered and sniffled. I climbed into the back to see what the man had left us with.

The man's duffel bag was filled with clothes, bars of soap, toothpaste, crackers, peanut butter, and canned food. Inside his suitcase there were forms of EEMA ID, cologne, shaving cream, money, credit cards, a wedding ring. We ate crackers with peanut butter. I stared into the void out the window, dissociating from our reality. Milo held up the man's money and asked if it was a toy. I laughed and told him it was. What did money matter when people were food and children were captured in front of your eyes? What role did credit play when cities were burned and flooded? When people were pulled out of their cars and put into camps. As the children explored the truck, I checked the rifle. Loaded. I pawed through more of the man's belongings and found clothing for me. Men's clothing. Perfect for my big belly. I found wool sweaters meant for children. I scavenged the man's wallet, finding photographs of children. His children? Oh, what became of them? I reluctantly dressed Milo and Ginny in warm wooly sweaters, fully aware of the bleakness of putting these recycled clothes to use in this way. After our snacks were finished, I drove on.

Long before night, pain came like an explosive. I had to pull over and lie on my side, ordering the children into the backseat. For some reason, I opened the man's glove box and started looking for something, I don't know what. I found a map booklet. Water spilled between my legs as I flipped through the booklet, trying to keep my mind engaged and away from the pain. Milo and Ginny peered over the seat. How far along was I? Seven months? Eight? I had no idea. It was tortuous to think about. I only knew it was not nearly nine months. How would I keep myself and this baby alive?

"Mama, you sick?"

I huffed. "The baby is coming out."

Milo jumped up and down on his knees. "Baby is coming! Baby is coming!"

I sat up groggily, looking through the rearview mirror. Ginny paid no attention to Milo. She looked out the window, surely wondering when her mama was coming to pick her up. I cried. For Ginny. For many things. I imagined leaving the two of them in the truck. Milo was so mature for his age. He'd help her. They'd help each other. A drone would come.

CHAPTER FORTY-THREE

In the late afternoon it began to snow. The pain had subsided. I needed to find a place to prepare for the baby's arrival. I needed fire. A fire would be stronger than any heat the truck could provide. I couldn't make it to Tennessee with the baby still inside me. I needed to get it out, fast. I drove slowly down a pulpy road. We listened to the comforting drip of static on the radio. I shifted my hips to keep the baby in a comfortable place. Ginny was falling asleep in the backseat. Milo stared forward as though something inside him had broken. He was a mix of emotions – sporadic excitement that dissolved into long eerie stares.

I pulled off into an exit and came upon an abandoned town as the snow transformed into rain. The stores along the main street were spread apart and skeletal – they'd been looted and burned long ago. We passed an archaic shop that was boarded up with planks and half burned. The store appeared bare through its large window, but it was the most stable out of all the buildings in the town. I craned my head to get a better view, noticing empty boxes and cans scattered haphazardly on shelves, as if a pack of wolverines had ransacked the place. I paused outside the store, thinking. Milo reached his hand over my cheek, spooking me. "Look," he said. Ahead, a human body lay sprawled on the street. Half a human body. I shrieked and put my foot to the pedal. I swerved away from the body, and then I hit the brake quickly. The body was a shell of a human, mauled long ago. Whoever burned this town came and went some time ago. I reversed the car.

"Mama, who is that?"

"No one. Don't worry about it, sweetie."

"What is that?"

"It's a store."

"What's a store?"

"A place where you buy things."

"What's buy?"

"I'll explain later. Baby is coming."

"Mama?"

"Yes."

"Ginny is wet."

"Jesus."

"She went pee-pee."

"Okay, I'll clean her up soon."

"I help."

"No, it's okay." I breathed in and out harshly.

"Why you breathe like that?"

"Because I'm in pain."

"Because of the baby?"

"Yes."

"Oh."

I parked in the back of the store's lot, in a field of mud and snow. The smell of earth and cold wet snow hit my nose as I hobbled out of the truck. Darkness was descending. Ginny was still sleeping. I pulled Milo out of the truck and locked Ginny in with a beep. We followed a cement path to the side of the store where a broken window allowed us entry into the small store. Dressed in prison rags, holding my son, in labor, I yelled into the void of barren shelves and random ransacked objects like empty boxes and money registers. "Hello, is anyone in here?" I held the man's rifle at my side. *My* rifle. We stood. Milo clung to me. He looked at me curiously. He didn't speak. There was a noise from across the store. I placed Milo down and shot the rifle at the sound. A raccoon skittered across the floor, his nails scraping over cheap navy carpet and through random piles of brown grubby paper – receipts, computer paper, notepad paper. It hightailed through a broken window in the front of the shop. Milo ran to my leg as I settled the rifle back to a locked position. I told Milo to find paper and pile it together. But he wouldn't let go of my leg. I laid the rifle on the ground and started to collect paper for a fire until Milo followed. This was once a quaint store. It had a gritty old-fashioned fireplace at the back of the room and a broken rocking chair. A novelty shop for mountain tourists, I assumed. Perhaps hikers came here to sip hot tea and hot chocolate after a formidable hike. Perhaps they bought maps and handmade souvenirs here.

After we collected a good bit of paper to act as tinder, we went back to the truck. I waited for a long time outside, observing our surroundings. Nothing. It was very cold. It was dark, and I didn't know how much longer I had. I sought to make the fire, nonetheless. I struggled on for some hours, hunting for sticks outside, and then led both children inside the shop where I got to work making a fire. The shelving units in the shop provided for a good game of hide and seek between the two.

The pains came and went. Huddled by the fireplace, I rubbed sticks in between contractions. The children sat, watching me. When I writhed, they were quiet. Milo stared.

"Are you gonne die, Mama?" he said. "Or are you pretending?"

So he knew what dying meant? What did it mean to him? I wasn't sure.

"Baby is just coming."

"Mama, I scared."

Ginny started to cry.

"I know. It's okay. Soon, it'll be okay. I promise."

The fire finally came. The darkness vanished with the fire's orange glow. When the pain subsided, I hobbled to the truck and brought in all our resources. I made bed piles out of the man's clothing and heavy coats. The duffel bag would be a place for the baby. The fire was so warm. But I was so tired. The children were tired too. The racoon returned, sending the children shrieking. I shooed it until it fled out a back window. The children sat close to me, my angels. The children began to sink to the floor. As they began to fall asleep, I told them that Mama would be busy getting the baby out while they slept. In the morning, a baby would be born. They didn't care. They fell into dreams, and I positioned them close to one another for warmth. I was granted hours of peace. It surprised me. In the deep penumbra of the shop, I thought back on my old life. I remembered waking up to cold gray light in the morning, tickled by Felipe's hair, and my quiet walk down the stairs where I'd get our coffee ready for the day.

Two days. I labored for two days. Maybe three. I hardly slept. The racking pain woke me every time. I rasped for air.

"I'm so sorry," I said into the grim darkness.

"It's okay, Mama," Milo answered.

In the afternoon, Milo and I collected more branches for our fire. The boy whispered as Ginny slept behind the cashier's booth. Just behind the rows of shelving where candy may have once been laid out for impulse buys or a child's swift hand. "Did the baby go back to sleep?" Milo asked.

"It may have," I answered. Two days, three days. The baby wasn't coming. I was dying. This was not labor. This was death. I dropped to my knees upon my realization. "Mama, you bleeding," Milo said. I touched my pants and pulled blood away. I kneeled, looking out the window as the sun shone through backward letters and discount deals. A ray of light peered through a percent symbol, making me squint. I slid my pants off and rested a hand on the candy counter. I wanted to tell my son I loved him more than anything in the world, and that I was so sorry for everything that had happened. But I couldn't speak. I reached my hand between my legs. Something felt off. I dragged a finger across my groin and felt the softness of a baby's head.

CHAPTER FORTY-FOUR

Standing in a lagoon of my own discharge, I pushed. It was too much for my feet. I squatted into a frog position, holding on to a rim of plastic that once held chocolate bars and breath mints. With my other hand I cupped the soft, emerging head. My encampment pants were tossed to the floor. Milo grabbed them and dragged them around the store. Ginny followed, giggling. The children were strangely uninterested in what was going on with my body and moved on to running about the dusty shop collecting pieces of plastic and other odds and ends. I yelled for them to stay away from the fire. The baby began to move sluggishly through my body. Like bowels removing some great and poisonous beast, my body spasmed beyond control. I feared for the other children. Too many dangers. The fire. The rifle. I waddled horribly toward the fire to guard it. I kept the rifle near me. Crouching, I put a hand on it, keeping it from the children. The fire warmed my backside. As the baby tore through the cavity, a grizzled man with a revolver suddenly appeared at the shop's broken window. The opening to our newfound home. He obliviously tried to inch his way into the store. When he noticed me by the fire, his face lost color. He did not expect to see a pregnant woman giving birth by a fire in an abandoned store with two children milling about. I had parked the truck far away earlier. I did not want to draw attention. The man raised his revolver with shaky hands. Before he could blink, I shot him in the stomach and fell back on my free hand, moaning, screaming, until the baby moved through the final groove and parachuted into my waiting, open palm.

Ginny was crying. Always crying. Milo ran to me as I panted feverishly.

"Mama, why you shoot him! Mama, what is it?" he said, hoarsely. "That's the baby?"

I struggled to breathe. "Yes."

"But…but…where did it come from?"

"Shh. My god, my god. Jesus. Oh my god. Oh my god. She's a girl. She's alive."

The baby hiccupped and let out a raspy cry.

"Give me that sweater. Hurry!"

Milo ran to our pile of clothes. "This, Mama?"

"Yes. And that shirt. Those pants too. Bring it all."

He fumbled with the clothing.

I wheezed for air. "Hurry, Milo."

Milo dropped the garments at my shaking legs. I began to layer the baby, holding her close to my chest. I cried as I crouched there on the floor holding the baby. A sinking, deep cry that sometimes came without sound. Milo placed a hand on my shoulder. Ginny quieted and drew near, eying the new alien creature in my hands. Uninterested, she moved toward the dead man at the broken window.

"Ginny, stay with me. Milo, you too. Please, I need you both. Don't look at that man." I tried to stop crying, but it was difficult. "We're a family now. The four of us." I spoke feverishly through choppy breaths.

When the baby was still, I eyed every part of her. Tiny. Not smaller than Milo when he was born, though. She was bigger than him. I was farther along. I was well past thirty-two weeks. Could I have been thirty-five? Thirty-six? No clue. I just knew she made it, and so did I. I could see her ribs, throbbing through her skin. I wiped the pulp from her body and covered her head with cloth and a chunk of a wool sweater. As for myself, I was filthy – discharge, blood, excrement. I looked toward Milo and his tired, long face. Some new gap had appeared between us. It was palpable.

I moaned horribly.

"Mama, what?"

"The placenta is coming."

"What's that mean?"

"Shh. More rags, Milo!"

The dead man lay on the glass shard the rest of the day until I mustered the energy to drag him far beyond the souvenir shop to leave him in a ditch.

In the early dawn, the newborn slept by the fire, bundled in more layers than prehistoric limestone. I had no experience cutting umbilical cords, but I had heard of lotus births – leaving the cord intact with the placenta until it falls off naturally. I wrapped the placenta in cloth and laid it beside the baby. Milo and Ginny slept too.

As the morning stretched on, the children began to stir as the sun poured through the broken glass. The baby cried. She was distressed. Everything blurred. Visions of death swirled in my mind. Minutes passed like hours as I settled the baby in my arms. She could not be placed down. It hurt her to be without human touch. My chest. My warmth. I wanted to give her to Milo and ask him to take care of it.

"Come here," I whispered to her. I cradled her small body, swaddled in materials of all kinds. "Time to eat."

I attempted to give her milk from my breast. Her wailing mouth would not click into position. I had been without milk since the woods. Now my body was springing forth milk, filling my chest with fierce intoxicating tingles.

"What you doing, Mama?"

"I'm trying to feed her."

"But that's *my* milky."

"It's her milky too."

Milo began to weep. "But I want it to be mine."

"But you can eat food now. She can only have milk."

He looked up at me with red eyes. He was tired.

"Come," I said. "You can have some next. Maybe you can teach her."

"Okay." Milo looked at me. "Mama, who is she?"

"She is your sister."

"What about Ginny?"

"You have two sisters now."

In the following days, we foraged wood just outside the shop and we picked through food left behind by the man from the encampment. And once the umbilical cord detached from the baby, we ate the placenta too. We sat by the fire and licked our fingers after dinner. I opened a new jar of peanut butter for dessert and passed it between the children. The boy held an empty can of tuna and drank boiled snow water from it and then passed some to Ginny. Ginny left us and went to the window where the dead man had once lain.

"Ginny, come back!" Milo yelled.

"It's okay."

"Why?"

I watched her look out the window. She struggled to form a word. Her voice was stuck in her mind.

"She misses her mama."

Milo looked at me and then toward Ginny. "Her mama is gone?"

"Yes."

"Like Dada?"

I looked down. "Yes."

My silent tear fell to the baby's cheek. She was sleeping. Her lips were quivering, sucking. I used the opportunity to place my nipple into her mouth. She accepted and nursed in her sleep. I looked up, brimming with a smile. Milo looked as though he wanted to throw her in the fire.

"Come here."

I brought him into my lap and kissed his forehead.

"What's her name?"

"I don't know. What do you think?"

"Um. Ginny."

"But that's Ginny's name."

"Ginny two."

"Ginny number two?"

Milo laughed. "Yes." Ginny came over to us.

"Ginny, what do you think the baby's name should be?"

She opened her mouth. Nothing came out.

"What she say?"

"She didn't say anything."

"Why she don't talk, Mama?"

"Because she doesn't want to."

"Yes, she does."

"Okay, well maybe you could ask her."

"Ginny," Milo spoke softly. "What's the baby's name?"

Ginny opened her mouth. She struggled to make sound. Then, a sweet noise came through. "Muh-Muh."

Milo looked to me, shocked. "She said Mama!"

"She did. My goodness."

Ginny came to me, smiling with a newfound pride. "Muh-Muh."

Surrounded by three pure souls, the fire snapped behind me. We soon lay down in a cluster of warmth. Rain fell softly on pine leaves outside. I watched it through a sliver of glass. Somewhere in the middle of sleep, Milo raised his head in the twilight and said: "Mama, can we call the baby Pee-Pee?"

"No," I whispered.

"Okay."

"But what about Pine?"

"Um. Okay."

He put his head on my shoulder and went back to sleep.

Pine.

In the night I settled Pine in the duffel of soft clothing, close by the fire, smiling to myself. Milo was the spark, the harbinger of Ginny's speech. Or maybe Ginny was beginning to realize she had to speak. She must. Perhaps she thought it was the only way to bring forth her mother. I looked toward the dark rain and thought of Marisol.

CHAPTER FORTY-FIVE

It was late into the night when the fire died. I lumbered through the shop with Pine clung to my chest as I collected wood. Milo came to me in the dark.

"Mama, I went pee-pee," he cried.

I whispered toward the small shadowy figure at my knees, "Okay, I'll be right there, sweetie."

"*Mama, I went pee-pee.*"

Pine wriggled against my chest and moaned. Ginny stirred. This was a dilapidated room full of crying children. I set to putting logs in the fireplace even though the crying was relentless. Utter numbness consumed me.

"I know. I know. I'll be right there. Please. Shh."

Logs clunked into place.

"*Mama!!*"

I turned like a hissing snake, with gritted teeth. "*Shut* up, *Milo.*"

The room quieted.

The next day Milo hid from me and spent most of the morning burying himself beneath clothes and rags where I could not see him. I cursed myself out as a terrible mother. My own son afraid of me. This wretched soul. I held Pine. My back was to the children, my chest toward the fire. I wept into her soft head.

We were sheltered from the wind and rain, far away from the camps, no floods, no drones – and yet, I was incredibly afraid. More fearful than I had been in months. I was afraid of myself. I couldn't sleep. Sometimes, I imagined a hunched figure lingering at the window's opening. I boarded up the entrance as best I could, but the idea of someone coming through again rattled me to my brittle bones. Other times, I heard whispering in the shop. But it was just coming from my own mind. My thoughts looped too. When I muttered a phrase in my mind, the sentence recycled itself over and over again, like a spinning clock. If I said to Pine, "Oh my sweet girl," the phrase would go on and on in my mind. *Oh my sweet girl, oh my sweet girl, oh my sweet girl, oh my sweet girl.* Endlessly. I had to yell at myself out loud to make it stop. My voice. Or a shell of it, rather, was my own monster. Other times, I imagined myself accidentally dropping Pine into the blazing fire. When I held her and walked near the fire, I told myself over and over: *Hold her tight. Hold her tight.* I was afraid of my guns too. Afraid I might do something with them that I would come to regret.

In the late afternoon, the sun shone with a heavy thickness through the glass. I placed Pine in the duffel bag and positioned her in the sun. I went to Milo to ask his forgiveness. He showed me a box of crayons discovered beneath the carpet. "Look, Mama!" We colored on the walls until I noticed the sleepiness on his face. We pulled our rags over to Pine and the three of us napped with her in the warm sunlight.

Days passed. The snow had long melted into the earth. Our only water supply came from the rain. It rained often, thankfully. The day's thread of light was growing longer. We needed to leave. We had been at the shop too long. Marauders would come eventually. When it was light enough to see the small blue veins peeking through Pine's skin, I rested easy, knowing she was growing plump as babies do. Every night I feared her death though. The dent in her head from where she moved through my birth canal was still faintly visible. Her eyes were open and hunting for milk. There was much to consider with leaving. The truck's energy source was low. I did not know how much life it would give us. I feared driving on main roads. I was certain the truck's heat would not provide the same sense of intimate warmth as a fire. The children had a home here. A shelter.

But Milo was scaring me. He woke every night with a new terror to speak of.

"Mama, I scared."

"Close your eyes and think of nice things. What nice things can you think of?"

"Nothing. Nothing nice."

"Clouds are nice."

"Don't like clouds."

"Hide and seek is nice."

"Don't like hide and seek."

"Oh, but I think you do."

"No, Mama. I don't like anything."

Sometimes in the night, I wondered if Felipe was watching over us. There were some nights that went perfectly smooth. The children slept. I slept. Those were the nights Felipe was with us. Some nights, the looping thoughts let me rest.

Sometimes in the morning, I caught the sunrise. One morning I went out in front of the shop. A nearby poplar appeared ready for spring's return. I picked up a blade of grass and brought it to my line of sight. I wanted to see something colorful.

194 • ELIZABETH ANNE MARTINS

CHAPTER FORTY-SIX

Some days I was filled with abundant energy. Where did it come from? A mystery. Perhaps some evolutionary hormones rising in me? Sometimes, I stared at the baby like she was made of gold and spoke so sweetly to her as though the world were pure and perfect. When I spoke in my sing-song baby voice to her, the children liked to watch me as though I were a circus entertainer.

"What should we do today, Baby Pine? Drink some milky? Shadow puppets? How about we look for some caterpillars? Oh, my little Piney-Whiney."

Milo turned toward Ginny, who was occupied by a green crayon. "Mama is silly," he informed her.

I bounced Pine, wondering who she resembled. I couldn't see the pilot's face in my mind anymore. My voice was practically filled with helium now. "Aren't you the cutest baby in the world? Oh yes, you are. Yes, you are."

"Mama, why you talk like that?"

I tickled Pine's nose. "Boop. Boop."

"Why you talk like that!"

"Because Pine likes it."

"You sound weird."

"That's okay. Who do you think Pine looks like, Milo?"

"Like me."

"Yes, of course. Just like you."

I left Pine in the duffel bag while she slept and went on to create order in the shop. I organized the children's playthings, folded our clothes. By now, I'd fully investigated every crevice of the small shop – the back office, pantry, every cabinet and drawer, the grimy basement. The basement only had room for one person – plus a couple of vacuums. It was once the raccoon's den. The raccoon no longer came, but she left behind some canned food she must've pilfered from who knows where. The cans were dented with marks from the raccoon's attempts. It wasn't much food. But enough to get us through a couple weeks. The basement smelled like rodent dung and mold. I never went down there. Only to remove the raccoon's storage and bring it to the main room and onto a shelving unit. Now, I circled the various shelves we used for storage. I crouched down and inspected our food supply.

Milo appeared, looking hungry.

I sighed. "We don't have any food left."

"Maybe peanut butter?"

"None left."

"Crackers?"

"No."

Pine whimpered in her sleep. I went to her. On my way, I saw a herd of deer walk past the shop. The warmer weather was bringing them out of the shadows and into this nowhere town. I would need to hunt. But how? Hunting and fishing with Marisol was one thing. Hunting with two toddlers and an infant was another. Milo got to Pine first.

"Can I hold her?"

"Really? You want to hold her?"

Milo nodded enthusiastically. His half-sister. As I settled Pine in Milo's lap, I thought about what would've happened if I never met the pilot. Would help have come to the Pennsylvania hotel? A less horny pilot perhaps? Someone who didn't require an act of lust before saving us. It was hard to believe there would have been another way.

"Shh. She's still sleepy."

"Why?"

"Baby's really like to sleep. Here, put your arm under her head."

"Like this?"

"Yes. Use your whisper voice."

"Okay."

Milo fell asleep holding Pine. I placed Pine in the duffel bag, and then I walked back to the shelves to survey my supplies. I stood on the perimeter of the shop when Ginny appeared and buried her face into my legs. I quickly bent down to see what was wrong. "What is it?" I asked her. She looked up at me with a pout. "Are you okay?" I asked. Ginny turned her head left to right. She tried to make noise. "It's okay," I assured her. Soon, she said *Muh-Muh* in a gravelly voice. I picked her up and held her close. "Oh, I know. I'm sorry," I whispered. "I'm so sorry."

We crossed the shop. Ginny's face melted into my neck. Her tiny cheeks were clammy against my skin, and I felt tears soak into me. She cried quietly. Normally, if Ginny wanted to cry, she would cry. She would open her jaw and let the recesses of pain and sorrow fly past her teeth like some desperate hawk shooting into the sky. She tried a couple more times to bring forth sound, but only the sad faint whisper of *Muh-Muh* came through. I patted her back. She wiped at her eyes. We walked over to the fireplace and listened to the sparks crunch and sizzle before us. A log fell into the pit with a low whoosh. I sat down on the cracked rocker and put Ginny's head on my chest.

"Shh. Shh. Sleep now."

Her head was stiff. She would not let her neck fall loose.

"Do you want me to sing you a song?"

Ginny rose and looked at me. A somber look. It did not feel as though a toddler was looking at me. A soul was staring at me. Searching. Wondering. Who was I to her? A mother? Or the woman who made her mommy go away?

She stared at me for a long while. I let her. I didn't look away. If she needed to get better accustomed to my face, I would keep my head high all afternoon for her.

"I'm Liv," I whispered. "I told your mommy I would take very good care of you. I told her I would love you like you were my own little girl. And I will. I will not let anything bad happen to you. You're safe with me."

Ginny raised a hand to my lip and felt around my face. I smiled. She did too.

She fell asleep in my arms by the roasting fire. I eyed my pistols on top of the mantel. My mind twisted in knots, thinking how I was going to get out of this place. How was I going to find food for us all? I pried Ginny off me and placed her by the other children. I wiped away dirt and dust from her grubby skin as I left her. I mostly looked at the boy as I stood above them all. There were times that they all slept so well together. Would it be possible for me to hunt our dinner during naptime? I went back to the shelf that kept our food. Nothing. Some peanuts. I moseyed to the mantel of guns. I had no other choice.

CHAPTER FORTY-SEVEN

There were times I vowed never to speak to Felipe again. Never to kiss him or touch him or see him. Our relationship was like water. Hard to hold in place for a time and always changing form. He had his temper. I had my apathy. I measured us against other couples far too much. Probably my greatest fault. He didn't know what I wanted. And I didn't know what he wanted either.

I paced the shop, thinking about his face. The dark contours. Pepper-like stubble on his chin.

I ruminated on our darkest times.

And our greatest intimate moments too.

Memories rattled inside my head. I went through the files on my parents too. A drunk father. A critical mother. Not good enough for either of them. Only when I played sports did I manage to catch my father's eyes. Only when I prayed did I catch my mother's. Conditional, conditional love. Baseball and God.

I was quite young when my parents said goodbye to me. I thought I was pregnant. Some stupid guy, I told them. It was bad enough to be pregnant in those days. It was sudden death to be *young* and pregnant. I was told to leave home, to be with the *stupid guy*. The baby did not manifest, but my parents' true colors did. I began seeing Felipe shortly after. Alone, friendless, without a baby. Years later, before Milo, I told him about my pregnancy scare.

Felipe said, "If I was the father of that baby, I would have demanded respect from your parents."

"Yes. Well, good thing you weren't."

"Why? I'm father material, you know."

I didn't answer. I wasn't sure I wanted to think about babies ever again.

"I'd love to be a father someday." He looked at me, holding my gaze.

I looked away. "No one is having babies on purpose anymore."

He picked my chin up and held on to my hand. "I don't care about everyone else. I care about us."

"Why? What's the point?"

"Love. Family. You and me."

"I don't know, Felipe."

"Do you love me?"

"Yes, of course I do."

"Why?"

I started to cry. I didn't want to cry. I hated crying. "Because… you always save me."

"You always save me too."

Once the seed of a baby was planted, I couldn't stop thinking about it. Yes, maybe there was a way. Maybe it would be good. I became obsessed with the idea in fact, with the idea of loving someone so wildly and so unconditionally…the way I wished to be loved.

When I learned I was pregnant, I thought I'd be ecstatic. But reality hit. I grew motionless and gray. A baby. No money. A world in crisis. I didn't know the Shift was coming, but it's as though my subconscious did. Some fiber inside me knew to expect chaos very soon, to preserve my energy for days to come. When Felipe was around, I tried to hide my growing ennui. His energy for our new baby left no room for my nihilism.

"Can we name him Vincent? After my grandfather."

"Sounds very formal," I said.

"Well, maybe he's destined to be formal."

"I don't think so. Not if he's coming from us."

"I've come up with everything so far. What have you got?"

"Something easy. I like easy. How about Milo?"

"Milo? Yes, of course. Milo."

Felipe worked without pause my entire pregnancy. There'd be days I didn't see him at all. He wanted to ensure our baby would be born into a net of safety. His burning appetite for security turned into an obsessive-compulsive need to stockpile, hoard, and protect. He became his true self. As did I. His switch went on while mine turned off.

The more the children slept, the better I felt. I could see my plan. My thoughts were clear. I knew what had to be done. My checklist: a good meal, something to last a while, and a heated truck. The truck I had. The meal, I did not.

"Mama?"

"Jesus, you scared me, Milo."

"Sorry. Mama, I thirsty."

"You already drank this morning."

"I thirsty again."

"Okay, shh." I creaked across the terry cloth carpet to our water section on the shelves. There was a quarter cup left of rainwater filling a mason jar that looked like it was once used for peach preserves. The boy reached his hands up.

"This is the last water until it rains."

"Can I have it?"

"Yes, just remember that it's the last one. After this, we won't have any more until it rains or until Mama goes hunting."

"And we need water."

"Yes. To live."

"To be together."

"Yes."

"More water coming?"

"That's the plan."

Milo looked at the cup and walked away. He went back to the nest of clothes and rags and lay down next to Ginny. In a couple days, if I did not find food and water, we would all be dead. I visited the mantel and checked on my pistols. Now, I just needed the targets. Things had been quiet lately. Even birds no longer came. Had the wind swept the deer off this land? No raccoons in sight either. No sign of life except three children and a desperate mother. I walked around the shop. This was my birthing home and nothing more.

"We are only home near food and water," I said out loud. "We have to leave this place." Milo eyed me strangely from across the room.

The children all slept very long. Even Milo went back to sleep. Death was too close for comfort. Their bodies were in preservation mode. Our bodies always know. Milo woke up when the moon appeared. Shifting in the den of fabric, awakening from some uncertain dream, he looked at Ginny and Pine first, and then toward me. He leaned over the girls and said nothing. Pine's lips quivered, searching for a drink. I gave her my breast. Moonlight hung in the glass window, turning our faces blue. *I will hunt in the morning, I will hunt in the morning*, I told myself over and over, like a mantra, so that I would not forget. Breast milk was the only thing on the menu for now.

"That's Pine's milky now?"

"It's everyone's milky. You come drink too."

"But Pine is—"

"I have two boobs, Milo."

"What about Ginny?"

"When she wakes up, she will drink too."

"You have three boobs?"

"No, Milo. Just come drink. It makes the milky strong when everybody drinks. Come."

"Okay, I save some for Ginny."

All the children awoke in the night having slept into the late afternoon and early evening. Night had turned into a clouded nightmare. Everyone was starving and Ginny and Milo were rightly acting up over it. It had not rained recently, and the earth was hard as limewood. At some point in the night, out of desperation, I dug my hand into a mound of dirt outside the shop and procured some bugs. The children thought I was

202 • ELIZABETH ANNE MARTINS

insane to offer it to them. When they refused, I stuck the bugs inside a mason jar. The children drank from my breasts every three hours well into the dawn until sleep finally came for them. I swallowed the bugs whole and held Pine by the fire until late morning.

CHAPTER FORTY-EIGHT

We sat in the heated truck for a long while doing nothing but waiting for an animal to cross our path. There was a gravel street that curved toward a back road. In the daylight, I moved slowly down the rubble road that was surrounded by blackwater trees. Pine was sleeping, strapped to my chest by a makeshift flannel sling. In the backseat, Ginny played with paper dolls, which I had cut into shapes earlier. Milo sat next to me, pulling at my sleeve.

"Where's the deer?"

"I don't know. We have to wait for them."

"Where are they?"

"Hiding."

"Mama! Look!"

"What is it?"

"Doggie!"

"Oh, that's not good."

"Why?"

"Dogs mean people are nearby."

"We don't want that."

"Right."

I drove us to a new road, far away from the stray dog. We came upon a highway surrounded by open woods. I thought of driving onto the smooth road and speeding in the direction of Sweet Gum; but I was too deliriously hungry for a journey into the unknown. Plus, the fear of encountering patrollers or marauders pulsed in the background. I knew I didn't have the strength to defend against anyone. Not yet. I kept my eyes trained on the woods, waiting for movement.

"I'm useless in the truck. I need to get out there."

"Why you need to get out there?"

"To see better. Maybe there are some groundhogs or birds I'm missing."

"What's a groundhog?"

"Milo, shh. I don't want to wake Pine."

"Because then she be too noisy."

"Yes."

"Okay. Mama?"

"Yes?"

"What's a groundhog?"

Milo moved to the backseat. I drove onto the overgrown grass on the side of the highway. I brought us closer toward the dense woods and parked in a bed of wild weeds. Pine stirred at my chest. I gave her my breast to quiet her moans. Pine suckled as I squinted one eye through the rifle's aiming hole. Nothing. When Pine fell asleep, I moved her carefully to the floor and covered her ears with cloth. The heat blasted on my body from the vents. I feared I was using too much of the truck's energy. The electric vehicle would need to be charged at some point, and there was no way for me to do that. The truck was warm enough for the time being. I turned it off for absolute silence. I lowered the window and raised the barrel of the rifle over the glass. The long brown snout pierced the crisp air.

In the distance there was a rabbit standing in tall grass, its ears folded softly behind its head. The rabbit crossed to a new patch of grass, lifting its head every so often. I followed it with my gun. Milo and Ginny were playing quietly in the back. One loud noise and the rabbit would be gone. The boy realized what I was doing and looked over my shoulder. He was going to ruin this moment. I had no choice but to try my shot. Right before I could feel Milo's hot breath on my ear, I pulled the trigger and shot the rabbit in the chest. I looked down at Pine, who awoke with a cry. I looked at Milo.

"Got him," I said.

"What?"

"A rabbit. Do you want to go get it with me?"

Milo began to cry.

"What is it?"

"I don't like shooting. Too loud."

"I don't like it either."

"I don't want to eat rabbit."

"You think I do?"

"Yes." He wiped his nose.

Pine's crying grew louder.

"Well. I don't."

Ginny looked over. She was the only one not in tears.

"We have no choice right now. I'm sorry. Wait here."

I scooped up Pine and left the truck. I moved with haste to the dead hare. I picked it up by the ears and walked back to my truck in the tall grass. For a moment, I was alone with my thoughts in the vast openness. I caught the scent of seawater momentarily. I sniffed again, and the scent was gone. My mind was playing tricks on me. The sight of the highway must've triggered the memory when we were stranded on the roadside, right before we were brought to the Pennsylvania hotel. I searched for the smell again. I couldn't be sure what was real or not. I needed to eat. We all did. The hare rode passenger side as we drove back to the abandoned novelty shop in silence.

CHAPTER FORTY-NINE

I carried armloads of dead rabbits, muskrats, and a goose from one side of the shop to the other. I worried the scent would attract larger animals. Men, even. I needed to cook it all and then save the rest.

Sweet Gum remained my goal, but I needed to ensure my body had fully recovered from pregnancy, that my mental state was stable, and that I was physically strong enough for the inevitable breakdown of the car. Until then, I decided to stay put. Days, maybe weeks, had slipped by. Time was a blurry concept.

The truck was on its final legs. But the truck was the only way I could hunt with three children in tow. I used it sparingly, only hunting when I absolutely needed to. Yet, I feared how typical it was becoming for the children to see me hunt and skin animals. They tired of me explaining how bodies work – the need for protein and such. I made sure they heard me say 'thank you' for the sacrifice of each animal, a ritual I had only recently begun. It was a practice I hadn't considered before, but with a watchful audience, it felt imperative.

The children liked goose the best.

I lit the fire and smoke curled over the stretched body of a scrawny muskrat. I fanned the blaze with a dated political magazine to keep the smoke toward the flue. The flames crackled in the dark fireplace. I admired their beauty. I was in a serene trance. I ignored the hunger wails coming from Pine. Milo came beside me looking like some docile troll in the night. His hair had grown out of control. He seemed mesmerized by the heat. Ginny tugged at my back, pulling me toward Pine. I went to the crying baby. I picked her up and breastfed by the hearth with the children. "Dinner will be ready soon," I whispered. "Very soon." We sat in silence, watching the muskrat bake over flames.

While the muskrat charred, I took Milo toward the window to capture some hints of evening light. The sun was making a delayed exit lately. Spring was here. I lowered Milo to the ground and fanned out his long hair. I took a shard of glass and began slicing at his browning locks and knelt over him until I procured a successful bundle of hair to show him. Then he looked up at me and informed me that was all that was to be done for the day. His hair was a mix of lengths. He would not let me chop it all in one sitting. A few more days and I would have the whole head. He turned toward the window and pressed his nose to the glass. Then he turned back toward me. "I saw people," he said. The second he said this, I fumbled toward the hearth and threw dirt over the flames. I didn't even need to confirm his statement. I trusted Milo, trusted what he saw. He knew our fear of people. Warmth was pulling people out from hiding, out of the cold. Perhaps the encampments were loosening their grip. We were lucky not to receive any unwelcome guests so far.

Not long before, we saw marauders near the woods where we usually went to hunt. They ducked from us – most likely fearful of the EEMA symbol on my truck. I feared they would make their way to the town eventually. If they knew a novelty shop with a fireplace existed and that a woman and three children were the only people occupying it, our journey would be over. Their presence meant we needed to be going, even though the truck wouldn't last the entire journey. At least, we had meat.

"We have to leave in the morning," I said.

"Why?" Milo asked.

"I'll explain later. Let's eat."

We ate the muskrat slowly, tearing meat off bones, savoring the satisfying dissipation of hunger. The dull cloud lifting from the gut, lighting the head and heart. There was a faux stone podium we used as our dining table. I sat in the rocker with Pine on my lap. The children knelt around the table, slurping meat off the bone. The warming shop groaned in the wind, like a scared animal warning us

of some impending threat. Milo smiled behind his muskrat toward
Ginny. Ginny tore flesh off the bone and smiled in return. The
children had come to form a bond that inspired me on my worst
days. I chewed silently, enjoying their volley of coos and noises.
It was starting to rain. The wind blew outside. The front window
rattled in the wind, shaking the frames of the shop. The fire was
gone. The sounds of the creaking shop always seemed more dramatic
when the fire rested. I rose to check on the glass window in the
front of the shop, tussling Milo's filthy hair as I lifted myself from
the rocker. I prayed silently that marauders would quickly come to
see this town offered nothing and be on their way. At the window, I
witnessed a man on horseback in the great distance jump off his steed
to inspect a far-off dumpster. He would find nothing in there. Just
some old empty boxes.

I wasted no time. I ran back to the children. I needed to hide them.
I needed to kill that man before he came for us.

"I want you both in the basement."

Milo spit out his muskrat to talk. "No! *Don't like* it down there!"

"There's a bully, Milo."

"No."

"Come on."

I opened the basement door and pointed strictly. Ginny walked
over dutifully. Milo looked on, enraged.

"Milo, if we hide, the bullies might think no one is here and leave."

"Why?"

"Why? Well, because there will be nothing here for them to take?"

"What do they want?"

"I don't know. Food, clothes, us?"

"Mama, you scary."

"Please, Milo. You have to listen to me."

"I eating."

"Let's play hide-and-seek. You hide down there and see how long
it takes me to find you after I count to twenty."

"Okay, Mama."

I guided them both into the basement and then moved slyly to the glass window. The man and horse were gone. He would surely make his way down the road until he came for us. After a bit, I moved the truck out front of the shop. If anyone stopped here, I wanted them to see the EEMA truck. *Nothing here except trouble. Be on your way. You come for us, you die.* This thought looped and looped until the wind and rain forced me back inside. I ushered the children upstairs.

"You're bad at hide-and-seek, Mama," Milo uttered.

While the children slept, I packed our belongings. I bundled our dried meat in fabric, and I collected wood and sticks that would be used for fire on our journey south. At some point in the night, the front window shattered, causing Ginny to scream. Milo and Pine slept soundly. My mind rattled as I tried to make sense of what happened. It was bound to break. Nothing I could've done. After putting Ginny back to bed, I moved to the broken window and looked out. An assemblage of marauders on horseback suddenly appeared. They clopped down the road, barely visible through the dark night and thick coating of rain and wind. By the grace of God, no one turned their head my way. I crouched motionless until the band of marauders left. Exposed, I fumbled back to check on the children behind the cashier booth. They slept on without a care in the world. I moved back to the open window with my rifle. I kept one eye through the rifle's iron sight until dawn. Then I took a break to set cans outside to catch rain. I went back inside and fell asleep beside a pile of broken window glass. In the morning, the rain stopped.

CHAPTER FIFTY

I rummaged around the shop for anything that could be of use on our journey. There was an old cigar box that might prove useful for storing berries or minnows. A stapler with a few staples left – good for mending clothes. An ancient Rolodex of names and numbers – a toy to occupy the kids. I was like a country craftswoman, coming up with ways to recycle junk. Junk that previous marauders tossed aside as useless. My plan was clear in my mind: I would drive as far as the truck would take us, and then I'd look for the closest water source. And then, we'd walk.

I packed the duffel bag with every item of clothing from the man at the encampment and all our food. As the children waited in the shop, I stuffed the truck like a festive turkey. I emptied the cans of rainwater into a small trash container and secured the top with shirt fabric and wrapped it tightly with an elastic band pulled from the man's underwear. I only sacrificed this one pair. The others were used as diapers for Pine and Ginny. I came back inside once everything was packed.

"It's time to go. Say goodbye to this place."

"But I don't want to leave." Milo clung to the brick hearth.

"Me neither. But it's too dangerous here."

"Not out there?"

"Come on, Milo."

"Is Dada coming here?"

"No. We're headed to Sweet Gum to see *pictures* of Dada. Remember?"

"Yes. Dada."

We ate goose meat in the truck. "I smell something," Milo commented, right before I rolled the windows up. It was ocean scent. So, I wasn't imagining it earlier. How strange to smell the ocean in the dry lands. Strange was the norm since the Shift. I had no promise the tides weren't coming for this land too. No promise marauders wouldn't take us apart, flesh and bone, once we were on the open road. No promise of anything. There was an unusual beam of hope in this. All things must end. The best one can do is prolong the inevitable. One's only job.

As I turned the truck on and skated onto the barren road, I thought of who I once was before Milo. At night when I couldn't sleep, I'd slip into the basement where an old digital piano sat in layers of dust. An old friend. I'd sit there and play songs I managed to remember from my lessons as a girl. I'd be − for the moment − at peace. Silly thing to think one once had hobbies or things that brought small moments of joy. And yet, driving down the road, free from some arbitrary point in time or place, I felt that long-gone archaic form of peace return.

We came upon a grocery store at the end of town. I had never driven past it before. I had only driven sparingly between the novelty shop and the woods where I hunted. I wish I had known about this store earlier. My fear of the unknown had obscured a treasure right down the road. The boy pressed his nose to the glass, staring at the faded yellow logotype letters. Some missing. Surely, nothing would be left inside the market. But what if there was *something*?

"We're making a very quick stop. Very quick. Come on."

I stood with the children in the market's front parking lot for about half a second, before a ten-man gang of marauders on horseback appeared from the back of the market. A trap. *Stupid Liv. Stupid Liv.* The horses surrounded us. Several men jumped off their horses and put my hands behind my back. Milo and Ginny attempted to stay close, hiding behind my legs. I tried to scream but was gagged with a rope. Pine was secure on my chest. These marauders were business minded. Cut-to-the-chase types. Not interested in conversation or concealing what they were going to do.

A man masked in black leather held my hands in a gloved grip. "We want the keys to that truck." He made orders to one of his partners. "Take her gun too."

His partner ripped the rifle off my arm. It felt like I was losing part of my body.

His other partner, dressed in red suede, answered, "She's got kids for Christ's sake."

"If you care, stay here and be their daddy."

My eyes bulged.

"Ma'am, we're not looking for trouble. Where are the keys?"

I tried to wrestle my way out. The men on horseback raised guns to me and the children.

I nodded toward my left pocket.

The masked man instructed one of his mates, "Hold her hands a second." He went into my pants pocket and procured the keys.

The man let out a deviant laugh as he waggled the key in front of his kin. "Load the gear in the truck. I'll drive this black beauty."

"At least give her your horse, you asshole. Did you think through what you'd do with it?" the man in red suede spoke assertively.

"I'm not losing my horse."

The man in red spat on the leader's shoe. "Asshole."

The masked man brought his spit-covered shoe into the red man's groin. "Hey," he called to one of his mounted horsemen. "Give her the deaf one."

The man in red held the space between his legs and spoke through his pain. "That's not fair. Why give her the deaf one? Give her mine, at least."

I mumbled behind the rope, trying to speak. I was continuously trying to get their attention.

"Let her talk, will you!" the man, still holding his groin, begged.

The rope was pulled out of my mouth. I struggled to breathe. At the raspy sound of my voice, Milo tried to talk to me too, to beg for understanding on what was happening.

"Well, what do you want?" the man in the black leather mask asked.

I struggled to breathe. "I want the deaf one."

"What? Really?" the man in red said.

"Yes."

"Great. We've wasted enough time here," the masked man said, turning toward the truck. "Let's get the fuck out of here. I'm sick of this nothing town."

The man in red brought forth the horse.

Tears consumed me. "Mosey. My girl."

But how?

"Do you know this horse or something?" the man asked.

"Yes, she was once mine."

"Oh, well she was wandering the highway, lost. She joined our pack quite easily."

"She does that."

"Stop talking to her! Come on!"

The man in red looked at me pitifully, as he transferred the reins of the horse to me in a slow exchange. He took my rifle off his partner and nonchalantly gave it back to me.

There was a brief second when I thought he might stay.

But he didn't.

When the gang of marauders vanished with their horses and our truck, I fell into Mosey's creamy neck and nuzzled my face into her soft skin. I wrapped my arms around her and cried despairingly. She pulled her head away and blew air. Oh, she was much thinner. Her ribs were like blades beneath pale skin. I imagined her journey. Had patrollers come back for her? Or did the marauders find her at the cave? I wish I could have asked her.

By the time I had enough breath to stand straight, Pine was ready for her next feeding. Ginny and Milo were turning blue with cold. I walked our growing family into the supermarket for warmth. But when I turned to Milo, the boy was crying.

"What is it?" I asked.

"Nothing."

"Tell Mama."

"No."

In the dark market, I managed to find some cans of potatoes and peaches. Mosey clopped around the abandoned shop looking for something, I don't know what. There were some dust-covered cans of soda that looked long forgotten. I found some tools in the back room. An old sheet, some plastic bags, a memory-foam bathmat, a bag of sugar. I hunted for a sturdy bag until I found something made of canvas that held receipts. I took pleasure in the echoes of hooves. Then, slow dread rolled in. The fuming hiss of despair. How could I do this? Fewer resources than ever. And more mouths to feed. Shuffling past the children like a train, I knew there was little time. As soon as the marauders realized how little energy the truck had left in her, they'd come back for Mosey. They'd come back for revenge. I had to get us into the belly of the woods once more.

CHAPTER FIFTY-ONE

Milo found a shopping cart. He tipped it over and spun the wheels, faster and faster. It was a larger-than-life toy to him. He burst into laughter over the squeaks the rubber wheels made. He caught the attention of Ginny, who was keeping tabs on Mosey. It had been a while since she last saw a horse. I went to the boy and lifted the shopping cart back up. "Get in," I told the kids. Milo got into the back and Ginny sat up front as I set off down a barren aisle. The children squealed as I strolled through the store – a slow amble with elbows resting on the handlebar. I imagined the shelves filled with food. Options upon options. I pretended there were people in the store. The boy stood up and asked me to go faster. "Do you want to keep this shopping cart?" I asked him. Of course, he said yes.

We ate some stray food I found in the market before going back outside. We stood in the market's parking lot as I knotted rope around the shopping cart and then onto Mosey's saddle. My plan was for Mosey to pull the shopping cart as though it were a wagon. I hoped my idea would work. The boy sat looking at me a long time. There was broken glass in the parking lot, and so I told the children to sit on the pale-yellow lines and not move. I knew I had little time before my rules became a faint memory in their minds. Mosey was an angel while I packed the cart with a few items pilfered from the market. Why was she so good to me? To everyone? I placed Milo and Ginny in the packed cart and mounted Mosey. We moved slowly onto the road; the cart rolled smoothly behind Mosey's clopping hooves. I smiled at my invention.

I knew I was placing hope in an impossible situation. But hope had got us this far. I could have quit. I could have done a million things differently. But why think about any alternative path? This was our path now, and it was clear and open for the time being. The mirages of my dead loved ones appeared to me, spoke to me. *Go on.* The forceful ache of momentum propelled me.

"Mama! Go faster! Faster!"

"I don't think we can go much faster."

"This is so fun!"

"I'm glad you think so."

"Where are we going, Mama!'

"Sweet Gum, Tennessee."

"Ginny, we're going to my BeezBo's house!"

Milo jumped up in the cart, making Mosey walk with a strange gait.

"Milo, honey, you have to sit in the cart."

Milo quieted and I eavesdropped on him talking to Ginny.

"You can come to BeezBo's house too. But...your mama not gonna be there. And Dada too. They gone. I don't know why."

Ginny started to cry. "Muh-Muh," she groaned.

"It's okay," Milo answered. "My mama helps you. I help you."

I shifted slightly, craning my chin over my shoulder. Milo was rubbing Ginny's back.

I looked ahead. The blue sky was fused with pink.

"We have to be quiet, kids," I said.

"Why?"

"Because I don't know what's out here."

"Are there bullies?"

"Maybe."

"Why?"

"I don't know why. Shh."

"Why is Mosey here?"

"She left the cave, like us. Do you remember the cave?"

"Yes. And then, bullies found her?"

"Yes."

"And...they took care of her?"

I paused. "Yes."

"And…they didn't hurt her?"

"No, I don't think so."

"But…you hurt animals, Mama?"

"Sometimes. Only to survive."

"Survive means we be together."

"Yes."

"Sometimes bullies are nice?"

"I guess so."

"And…sometimes Mama is a bully?"

I laughed. "Let's be quiet and figure out a good place to rest for tonight. Okay?"

"Okay."

The sky had three shades – navy, tangerine, and pink. On the road with a horse, a cart, a rifle, and a warm baby on my chest, I felt as though we might be the only ones on the planet. I kept my eyes trained on the ridgeline, looking for Heaven's Dome, the observatory tower that marked the way to Sweet Gum. Nothing. We still had quite a way to go. The children had been quiet for at least twenty minutes. I dismounted from Mosey to check on the children. They were falling asleep. I laid their bodies down on the memory-foam bathmat and used supermarket plastic bags as pillows beneath their heads.

By the time complete darkness came, the children were fully asleep in the cart. I nursed Pine in the middle of the stark highway and then placed her back inside the wrap. I mounted Mosey and we walked on. With the children asleep and the road set out before us, I decided to push Mosey onward through the night. I was adrenalized with the idea of being away from the desolate town, out of the novelty shop, away from the encampment. I felt my body had healed as best it could after Pine's birth. I was stronger. More aware. My mind was not completely restored from its looping thoughts, but there was improvement. I could forge ahead now as originally planned. We walked in lockstep with the mountain ridge that would take us to Sweet Gum. At some point, we would need to get back to our mountain trail, back to the coverings of trees and sources of water. The open road was too dangerous. I prayed we'd stay safe through the night. As we walked on, the scent of the sea followed us. I could taste salt in the air. My hair was dry – the way it gets when wind snaps through it on evenings by the shore. The sea was coming. The great beast of wet darkness following us. I could practically hear the lulling sound of waves washing over the dead town we just came from, over every sacred piece of earth. Or perhaps it was all in my mind. Hunger and little sleep clouded reality. The indifferent moon glowed regardless, and so I looked toward her and modeled her attitude.

CHAPTER FIFTY-TWO

In the night, the wind sounded like a crying woman. Who was crying? Marisol? My mother? I was hearing things out of extreme exhaustion. Suddenly, I felt phantom hands pawing at my feet. Nothing was there though. Then, a wisp of a figure appeared at the end of the road, its form almost translucent in the moonlight. The night was full of terror, and I was hallucinating. Oh, I needed sleep. But how could I? What if marauders came for us? Or pumas, bears, or a sudden heart attack? My thoughts began to loop again. *The night is terrifying. The night is terrifying. Death is everywhere. Death is everywhere.*

Mosey walked on without complaint. Every now and then she tested the road with her hooves, making sure she wasn't about to fall off some grand cliff. I turned toward the clinking shopping cart obsessively. The children slept. To ensure I didn't spill into complete madness, I envisioned Sweet Gum. Pleasant thoughts. I envisioned a soft pink bed with fresh linens. I imagined plentiful food, water from a spigot, a good book. I imagined Ana, Felipe's grandmother, taking me in her arms, telling me how brave I had been. I imagined her scooping up Milo, crying with joy as she studied his face. We'd both agree he took after Felipe. She would tell me her glass studio was still in operation. We'd marvel at her latest artwork. And she would feed us until we burst.

When the dawn came, I found myself nodding off. I picked my head up as Pine whined and arched her mouth for milk. Slow going. I was exhausted. I offered Pine my breast and slumped forward. I turned my head to inspect the cart. Milo was sitting upright, staring at me. He offered me a smile. It was like a shot of heroin. If I could somehow manage to find security for Milo and not completely ruin him, I would consider my time on Earth a success. Milo looked out at the ridgeline. There was a hawk swooping over the ravine as the grapefruit-colored sky boasted peaceful tones. "Good morning, baby," I groaned, barely audible.

"Where are we now?"

"I'm not sure. It doesn't really matter. We're not where we want to be yet."

"Why not?"

"Things take time."

The truth was road signs were all but gone. But I had seen one in the dark night that led me to believe we were on the right track.

Ginny woke up in shock, bobbing up and down in a fearful fit. Mosey walked on, unaware of the chaos she pulled behind her. I yielded her to a halt and tied her to a rusty guard rail on the side of the highway. I walked to the cart to calm Ginny.

"It's okay. We're safe. We're safe," I said. I massaged Ginny's back as she stared up at me from the cart like some deranged animal.

"She scared," Milo said.

"Let's get out and watch the sun rise for a bit."

"Okay."

We sat, each of us wrapped in our own pale blue apron. I had taken them from the market. We looked like wage workers on a much-needed break. We sat for a long time watching the sky. I looked for the words to explain our state. But none came. After a while Milo started playing with blades of grass.

"Maybe...maybe...Ginny misses her mama."

"I think you're right."

"Like I miss Dada."

"Yes. I think you're right."

We walked on when the sun was nearly overhead. I had food and water on my mind. There were no cars, no souls, to be seen on our journey along the road. I was certain the sea had come for everyone but us. But I knew it was only a matter of time. I spoke of nothing except pleasant things to Milo and Ginny though. A sudden burst of energy came upon me as the sun hung overhead, white and warm.

"Do you want to play a game?"

"Yeah!"

"Okay. Let's play a game called I Spy. I say, *I spy something*. And then you both figure out what I'm talking about. Got it?"

"Um. I don't know."

"Okay, let's just start. I spy something black."

"Um. The road!"

"Yes, now you got it."

"My turn?"

"Yes."

"I spy something brown."

"Hmm. That hawk?"

"No."

"I don't know."

"Ginny's poop!"

"Oh boy."

We played I Spy until my stomach groaned so forcefully, I was sure Mosey could feel it. I steered Mosey to the edge of the highway, where we were able to survey the mountain to our right, unrivaled in beauty. I held my rifle at my hip waiting for the hawk to fly right up to me and request to be shot and eaten. I pulled Mosey into the tall grass off the side of the road. There was a steep hill that would take us into a brush of woods. The mountain trail lay just on the other side. The shopping cart provided wonderful transportation for the children thus far, but there was nothing on the road for us to eat. And the cart wouldn't drive well over the hill. I needed to get the children onto the horse with me. I didn't know how it was going to work. I didn't know how I'd be able to carry three children and myself atop our gracious Mosey. I wondered how ancient mothers before me survived and traveled with little ones in tow. But knowing they did was all I needed.

CHAPTER FIFTY-THREE

I remembered waking once in a blue tent to the sound of sizzling pancakes on a skillet. I was on a camping trip with Felipe. We camped often, finding ourselves rekindling our romance whenever we were under the open sky. It was always our great reset. Later, we cuddled in sleeping bags in the open air, inching closer to one another beneath endless stars. Endless kisses too. Somewhere beyond our campsite, the lapping of river water kept rhythm like a metronome. Felipe pulled me to the shore that night, and we stood barefoot in the rugged sand and admired the moon's light waggle over the water. When we went back to the tent, I nuzzled my cheek into Felipe's stubbly chin, and I wondered how anything in life could ever be better than this. I'd later learn, nothing could. As much as Felipe and I had our problems, we always had our nights beneath the stars too.

When I was finally able to juggle the strange act of securing two toddlers and myself on a horse, both children were scared and crying. I needed to turn it into a game for it to work. *Who can sit tallest like a cowboy and cowgirl! Oh, Milo can! Now who wants to hear Mama sing a funny song about horses!* Tireless and strange work, but we were atop the horse, nonetheless. We came upon a great opening in the woods, where I began a fire. We laid our aprons on soft grass and watched the flames. Soon, slumber took us all.

In the morning we moved on until we approached a waterway with a strong flow. The rush of water reminded me of the Sea Isle Bay back home. A beach town now at the bottom of the sea. I looked toward the river. The water moved random pieces of litter in her stream now

and again. Driftwood and plastic bottles were among the most popular
objects to get stuck in the river's teeth. An ancient plastic milk jug lolled
down the river and landed at our feet.

"What's that?" Milo asked.

"An empty milk jug."

"For your milk?"

"No, milk from a cow. From a store."

Milo picked it up. "Drink here? Where's the milk?"

"Well, normally you'd pour the milk into a cup first."

"Oh."

"But I think we can use it to catch some fish. Remember
catching fishies?"

"Fishies!"

We stood on the rocky shoreline and looked out at the murky water.
The wind bouncing off the water smelled of sulfur. On the rocks there
were remnants of dried blood. We crossed to the other end of the shore.
Mosey lapped at the water. We passed over a bundled strand of fishing
wire, left chaotically in a ditch of sand. The fishing line was soaked in
blood. Something terrible happened here, but hard to say how long ago.
As the children collected rocks, I crouched by the water, cleaning the
line and untangling it. Pine slept on my chest inside a makeshift shirt
sling. When the fishing wire was unmatted I tied it to the handle of the
milk jug. I searched nearby mud for bait until I procured a fat moist
worm and stuffed it inside the plastic jug. I eased it into the water.

"Mama, what you doing?"

"Fishing."

"Can I try?"

I handed the fishing string to Milo, and we watched the malleable
container bobble in the slight waves. Milo dropped the string and
screamed. Ginny picked it back up for him and the two squabbled
over who was to hold the string. I said nothing as they debated.

"Ginny, share," Milo said.

"Muh-Muh!"

"My turn!"

"*Muh-Muh!*"

"Fine. Maybe…we both hold."

"Muh."

"You hold here. I hold here."

"Muh."

We kept to our little beach, each taking turns with the string, until we produced a fish. The children cheered as we pulled it in. It was tiny, but it would be suitable for the two of them. I killed it and then we set the jug back into the water for more. In the rippled water, more junk manifested, washing onto shore, or blundering senselessly in the billows. Every item, every factory-molded commodity – a rubber tire, an orange crate, a plastic bag – were now buoys in the inky water, awaiting new life.

CHAPTER FIFTY-FOUR

We moved back onto the mountain trail, the trail that would lead to Tennessee, and to Sweet Gum. We could only walk a short distance before the children had to reshuffle. It was an awkward and clunky mess. Naps, underwear changes, squabbles, time for comfort. In between toddler issues, I tended to Pine. Her eyes were opening more, absorbing light, the sweet and gentle sun. Her lips searched for the breast constantly. We stopped at every stream to fish and eat. Meanwhile, I lost my voice. My sense of self. I could only perform action. A machine. Voices moved in and out of my mind. Voices of Felipe. Marisol. My parents. Madness. *Do this, do that.* I turned my head, thinking someone was calling me. No one.

"Mama, why don't you talk anymore?" Milo asked me one morning.

"I'm sorry," I whispered.

"You sad?"

"No. I don't think I'm sad."

"What happened?"

"Sorry."

"Mama." He touched my hair.

"I think I'm just broken or something."

"Like a stick?"

I grabbed on to his hand. "Yes, Mama broke like a stick."

"I fix you."

Milo folded my hands into my lap. He brushed the lengths of my arms. He bent and kissed my knee. It was bleeding through my pants from an earlier fall. He looked down at my pants. More blood was pouring through. My period had returned. There was nothing I could do for it though. I let it soak me.

"Mama, you broke there too?"

"Yes. I think so."

"You need a bath."

I laughed. And for some reason, this gave me the energy I needed to stand up. "Yes, I think you're right, Milo. I do need a bath."

One day we found a large lake and my bath finally came. We had also found an empty nest with undeveloped eggs that we drank from. When Pine was asleep in the bag, zipped up to her neck for warmth, I moved my body into the lake. I was sore; it hurt to move. Treading water, I waved to the children, who hunted for worms in the shore grass. I slipped my hair under the clear water, gasping with cold. Pulling myself out, I looked up toward the spring sun. I was practically glittering in its glow, naked. Milo was right. A bath. I needed a bath in precious, restorative water. I slunk back into my clothes, feeling a modicum of revitalization.

Later, rain came. No shelter. Mosey carried us onward in the wetness.

When the rain ceased, we came upon a restroom building adjacent to the mountain trail. It was a small structure with a men's room on one side and a women's section on the other. Both doors were locked, but a glass window was half-shattered already. I gave the remaining fractals of glass a heave with my rifle's end and was able to climb through to unlock the door. Inside, I tried the faucets, but nothing came of course. I was shivering uncontrollably from the rain. At the very least we could dry ourselves at this remote station in the woods. I welcomed the children inside, and they pushed through like desperate geese in search of a warm nest. Milo asked if it was our new home. I told him no. Just a resting place for the night.

There was a stench of urine in the restroom. A sour smell of rot. Damp and soggy. The children didn't care. They played hide-and-seek between the stalls. Milo climbed the dull green sinks. When he found the mirrors, it was ecstasy. This was nothing more than a funhouse for him. As such, it was a funhouse for Ginny too.

I made a fire outside while the children played in the restroom. I tied Mosey extra tight to a tree limb and then cooked leftover trout. I would never lose her again. I was done gambling with her presence. I needed her more than anything. She was my partner. She stood in a lush patch of grass and grazed happily. I stripped naked and dried my period-stained clothes over the fire. I dried the children's clothes too. Once we were all re-dressed, we settled down for sleep in the restroom. By then, the scent was gone. I was accustomed to it. Nothing mattered anymore except hearing each one of their exhausted, tired breaths.

When day came, I waited until the children were ready for a mid-morning nap before moving on. I found a loose, ceramic tile from the bathroom wall that would be good for carving fish or meat and kept it as my own. Then, I adjusted my wrap to carry Pine like a backpack. This provided room for Milo and Ginny to lean against my chest. Ginny against Milo, Milo against me. They fell sleep as Mosey carried us further down the trail. Exhausted, they slept for a long time, giving us incredible distance. Mosey whinnied. Her hooves began to drag, and I knew she would need to rest soon too. I pet her silky hide often. There were times I wondered if she were full of magic, of goddess strength. And other times I became conscious of her frailty. Her boniness. I was about to nod off into Milo's sweep of hair when I noticed a signpost in the distance at a crossroads in the trail. I squinted to see its directional mark. *South. Tennessee.*

CHAPTER FIFTY-FIVE

Mosey carried us along the trail, only pausing for streamside drinks or to entertain a seductive patch of grass. I spoke often of my appreciation for her, hoping she'd feel the vibrations of good words in the air. Hoping Milo and Ginny would hear me, knowing good things don't come around like this often. "A miracle," I told them. One morning while Ginny and Pine were still asleep, Milo and I communed with Mosey, stroking her golden skin.

Walking on, I couldn't stop thinking about Felipe. His face whooshed into my mind constantly and stayed there like some hovering piece of driftwood. A weird gray look in his eye, wondering what was taking me so long to get to Sweet Gum. In the distance, the faint murmur of thunder rumbled, and I remembered one of our final conversations.

"Liv, if anything happens to me, do you know the way to Sweet Gum?"

I grabbed his sleeve. "I don't like when you talk like this."

"Just answer me. Do you know the way?"

"You follow the mountain trail. South."

"South, yes. Until you get to the observatory dome. And then you walk further south until you come upon the cliff with the waterfall. You take the narrow trail up the cliff. There's a rock formation by the entrance to the trail in the shape of an ear."

I blew air. "Yes, I remember the ear. What did your grandmother used to say?"

"That her mountain is always listening. Always waiting for tired travelers. She loved taking in lost hikers. We always thought of her as the family outcast – moving to a remote mountain – but looking back, she was just answering her calling."

"Hmm. You get it from her."

"Get what?"

"Your call of the wild."

"And Milo will too." Felipe glanced at me playfully. "And what is your calling?"

"I'm still waiting to figure that out."

In the late afternoon we walked along the trail for hours. The mountain ridge was to my right, a comforting friend. Below, a valley of trees offered peaceful views. I'd become better at getting the children seated on Mosey. I hoisted them over her saddle, belly first. They hung over her back like two fox skins, ready to be lugged home. Once they were both snaked over Mosey's body, I climbed into place with Pine on my chest. Then I shaped them into position and lurched over them like a wild mother hen keeping her chicks dry from the rain. By now, we had nothing on us except a rifle, a milk jug for fishing, one steel can for purifying water, and a compass. The duffel bag was gone, as I had left it in the truck that was taken from us. We had only the clothes we wore. Mine were still stained with blood, but I came to realize it was just a part of me. Nothing gross about it at all. Just me in another form. How special. I came to love my blood.

We went on. When starlight penetrated the black sky, I whispered to myself. Recalling memories, remembering old recipes, singing songs. I talked to the trees in the night. The wind had become an old friend. If a marauder happened upon our path, I'd greet him politely and then shoot him mercilessly. There wasn't much to it. Survival. It turns out I had found my calling after all. I spoke to Felipe, to the fervent air, telling him I'd found it. At long last, I'd found my calling. To live.

In the late morning, we came upon a deer on the trail whose legs were tangled in some sort of wire. The doe was on her side, unable to stand. The children woke from an awkward sleeping position on

Mosey. I hadn't slept in two days. How far had we come? We paused and watched the deer struggle. We dismounted the horse. Milo looked at me, wondering when I was going to shoot it. That morning, we had already enjoyed a hearty meal of fish. The thought of a deer felt excessive, especially when I spotted a weak, near-collapse family of wild turkeys close by. They seemed like an effortless option, and I wouldn't need the gun. Besides, I lacked the energy and tools to hunt and dress a deer at that moment.

"Mama, shoot," Milo said.

"No. Listen."

"I don't hear anything."

"Over there?"

"What is it?"

"She has a baby."

A baby deer rustled in the nearby brush, waiting for its mother. Holding Mosey's rope, I edged closer to the stuck deer. I untangled the wire from her legs until she was able to stand and limp toward her baby. Milo's smile was sunny as he watched the mother and child reunite and move down the valley toward the mountain. The deer could have provided a good meal, but I thought it was more important that the children see an act of goodness from their mother. At least one. We rested awhile until I squinted in the direction where the deer moved. "My god," I whispered to myself. "That's it." Heaven's Dome. The observatory tower in the valley of dense forest, just before the mountain ridge. The one that marked the path to Sweet Gum. It looked like a torch of light among the trees.

CHAPTER FIFTY-SIX

After eating turkey, we moved on, finding a steep hill that would provide a shortcut to Heaven's Dome – or so I hoped. It was a deviation from Felipe's trail, but it appeared as though it would cut our time in half. I paused momentarily to survey the route. I estimated it to be about one more day of walking. It seemed so close but still felt so far away. I could hear Felipe telling me to stay on the trail, but I ignored his voice. Our ears popped as we moved down the grassy embankment, off the trail. Misty clouds seemed to hover in the air. Mosey paused frequently, catching her breath. The boy was curious about the dome in the distance.

"That's BeezBo's house?"

"Just beyond it. It means we're on the right track."

"Why are there clouds?"

"It's fog."

We moved on but Mosey struggled. She was rightfully tired. She had done her duty a million times over. The hill we moved down became incredibly steep and I worried if it was unwise to be on top of an exhausted horse with three children. A dark horse came charging at us suddenly. Mosey lifted her head to him as he rushed by us. The stallion moved onto his haunches, much too close. Was this defense or a mating move? Mosey's feet began to slip. She neighed with annoyance. I tried to hold on to the children. But everything happened too fast. We fell off, as Mosey reacted to this foreign horse. I was much too busy ensuring that the children were okay to notice Mosey and the stallion scuffling. What did this horse want? Where did he come from? I hated him and how he bothered her. I fumbled for my rifle to scare him off. Mosey would be left alone and we'd get dinner. Mosey lost her footing and toppled down the hill, sliding against dirt and roots and rocks. My heart sunk. The stallion moved after her, trying to continue whatever he set out to do. I grabbed my rifle and fired at him, missing. The stallion ran off in fear.

As the stallion ran away, I tried to pull myself to my feet, only to realize my ankle wouldn't let me. I had landed on it awkwardly. The pain was too immense, I couldn't even process it. Shock. I arched my chin to get a look at Mosey, who had slid down the hill until landing in a rocky ravine below. She wasn't moving. I was desperately tired. I cared more about Mosey's well-being than my own ankle. I tried to get back on my feet, but the pain was strong. I succumbed to the pain and sat down. Pine began to cry, and I folded my body over hers. When she quieted, I listened for Mosey. Eventually, I heard the far-off rustling of her grunts. She was alive. I let out a sigh of relief.

Moments later, Mosey bellowed out with a fierce neigh. She was not one to make such noise. Milo was beginning to move down the hill. Ginny was following him, toddling awkwardly. I tried to scream toward them, but my voice was hoarse. I had no power left. "Milo! Ginny! Come back!"

They didn't listen.

"*Milo!*"

I worried they'd fall down the hill just as Mosey had. The hill was covered with hidden jagged rocks beneath wild grass. Why did I think a dangerous shortcut would be best when we'd already walked so far?

"*Milo!*"

I tried to stand. The pain hit me like a bullet. My ankle was severely hurt. I could barely move it inside my boot, but each twist sent a horrific jolt of pain through my body. I couldn't let it stop me. I needed my children. I stood up. Milo and Ginny were inching their way down the hill. Ginny paused to pluck at grass. She stuck some leaves inside her mouth. Milo had his eyes trained on Mosey. He was going much too fast down the steep hill. If he slipped, he would bust his head on a jagged rock. One slip is all it would take. I started to slide

down the hill, with Pine clung to my chest. I led with my good foot
and grabbed Milo by the collar just as he picked up speed.

"What the hell do you think you're doing?" I yelled.

The boy pulled away. He slid down the hill even more.

"Milo, stop." I held Pine tightly and continued sliding after
him, leaving poor Ginny in the mist. I would come back for her, I
told myself.

I grabbed on to his shoulder. "Why did you leave Mama? This is a
very scary hill to go down alone."

Milo shook his head ferociously. He wiped his nose. "I'm going to
BeezBo's house. BeezBo take care of me now. Not Mama."

"Why?"

"Because you're a bad mama."

I felt a hundred knives stab my heart at once. My ankle pain was
nothing compared to this. I didn't answer him. He was right.

Milo cried until snot spouted from his face. He sat in the grass
shaking. He cried and hyperventilated until he vomited. I wiped his
mouth with my hands. "I'm sorry this is hard, Milo," I said, crying
too. "Shh. Are you okay now?"

Milo held on to me, still shaking, and nodded. I put my hand
on his chest, feeling his rapid heart. When he was only a baby, his
heartbeat was irregular. Much too fast. A condition premature babies
sometimes get. I worried he wasn't going to calm down. His heart
clamored uncontrollably. Oh, what did I do? I couldn't live with
myself if something happened to him. The rifle in my hands suddenly
felt foreign and heavy. I dropped it to hold onto my son, hoping
the rhythm of my heart would calm him down. Yet, my own heart
thundered even faster than his.

CHAPTER FIFTY-SEVEN

We stayed at the bottom of the hill the rest of the day because neither Mosey nor I could stand. Mosey had not stood since her fall. I thought of leaving her there, but I wasn't sure how I'd walk the rest of the way with my ankle sprained. The children cried out for food. Pine cried out. I had no diapers for her; she barely went anyway. This was a problem. We slept to bypass the hunger. Pine nursed until there was nothing left. Milo's heart was still irregular. The next morning, I spread my hands over the boy's cheeks and smoothed down his matted hair. His cheeks were flushed, his eyes barely open. There was nothing I could do for him except hold him. I asked Ginny to sit down and hold Pine, giving me a free hand. But that was useless. She sat up wildly, dropping Pine to the grass. Milo ran to Pine and threw his body on top of her.

"I think she's okay," I said. "I'm worried about *you*."

"I fine."

I didn't believe him.

"Come here. I'll hold you both."

I took both children in my lap and leaned myself down into the grass. The children clung to me, motionless, and when the sun shone into my eyes there was a strange moment of bliss. I wondered if this were an afterlife of sorts. Lifting my head to see my bloodstained encampment clothes, I knew otherwise. There is no blood in the afterlife. Perhaps God was just taking away the pain moments before death.

Slumped in the moist grass, holding on to the children, listening to Ginny murmur in the distance, I fell asleep. I had no control. The warmth of the sun was so heavy on my eyes. I could not fight it. In my sleep, I imagined that this was our final day alive. A soft, soothing voice asked what I would like to do with my last remaining day on Earth. "This," I replied. "Hold my babies. That's all."

In my dream, Felipe visited me, shaking me violently. He screamed at me to get up, that I was failing Milo, failing *him*. I awoke to the sound of whipping air. Four helicopters flew overhead, sending my heart into a panic. EEMA helicopters. I froze. Milo ducked into my neck.

I lifted my head. "Ginny, where's Ginny?"

Ginny was crouched in tall grass, far off, crying. I held Pine in one arm, and I dragged Milo by the hand; I limped my way to Ginny. I grabbed on to her as the helicopters moved on, bypassing us, moving east. I held all three children in my arms until the whirr of helicopters subsided. I put my hand over Milo's heart. It was clamoring. Ticking. Ticking. I needed him to calm down.

My voice, barely there, asked Ginny what she was doing. "Eat," she said. I was too debilitated to comment on the fact that she had spoken a new word. I didn't even know what she was eating or if it was safe. I labored to swallow. I clenched my fists, wishing I could scream out in rage. We had made it all this way – all this way to lose to a hill.

Mosey puffed air. I turned my head to her as she nodded up and down – what horses do when in pain. I felt terrible ignoring her, knowing that Milo's heart was in distress. I kept my hand firmly pressed against Milo's chest. It was quickening. His heart, my heart. This was the end. Just like my dream. My final day on Earth. I was holding my babies; what I asked for. I looked up at the sky, hoping that the EEMA helicopters would return.

Another day passed. My foot was beginning to move better. I had taken off my boot and tied my supermarket apron around it tightly. We slept nuzzled up next to Mosey. When things were peaceful, I searched for food. I found nothing except bugs. At one point in the night, I realized that we would not survive another day without food. Mosey was dying.

And Milo had not moved all day. He had surrendered to long sleeps. In the night, I felt his heart slowing down. Evening out. My own heart seemed to slow down, suspended in blood. I fell asleep and dreamt of Marisol. Sweet Marisol. Her voice was like a quiet morning bird: "It would be a sacrifice of her love for you all," is all she said.

I awoke in sweat. My eyes flickered, adjusting to the light of dawn. I looked to Mosey. She nodded swiftly. She was in great pain. I rubbed her nose with my palm and inched close to her. I pushed my forehead into her nose and held her precious face. "I love you," I whispered. "I love you." I held on to her, soaking her face with my tears.

While the children slept, I picked myself up from the grass. I wiped my tears and labored to find sticks to make a fire in the distance. Once I was successful, I scooped each child up and moved them closer to the fire and away from the horse. The sun was all too bright. I felt exposed, like I was doing something dirty, something forbidden. I moved back to Mosey, clenching my rifle, crunching over leaves. I knelt to her and rubbed her ears. Her head was so soft and weary. She could not lift it. I moved behind her. Her poor ears.

"Thank you," I said, barely audible. Breathless. And then I fired.

CHAPTER FIFTY-EIGHT

Holding in tears, I ate. The children ate. Restoration came. It came to our stomachs, our nerves, our minds, our blood, our eyesight. I hated myself for what I'd done, but I thanked myself for it as well. It was a strange duality. It was also some kind of magic to see each child perk up. Each a flower raising its head after a cool drink. We left the hillside sometime in the afternoon. I hoped the day would be easier now that we had eaten. I hoped I could shake off the darkness that consumed me. As we walked, I replayed the shot in my head. Mosey seemed to cough as the bullet hit her. Her head fell forward with a clunk. She lay there like a woman in a grave, and I wept over her body with remorse. After taking what we needed from her, I covered her body in leaves and prayed near her head. I stroked her face, her ears, her nose. My dead loved ones came to me when I shut my eyes. I said goodbye to all of them. I petted Mosey for the final time.

When we got back to walking, I held Pine on my chest with a makeshift sling. Ginny and Milo wanted me to pick them both up, but my ankle still hurt. I held their hands instead and asked them to walk. I had my eyes trained on the observatory tower. I could hear it calling to me. I could smell Bisavó Ana's *balcalhau* and potatoes, her *porco preto*, her *pao de lo*. They were like phantom scents that beckoned me to keep walking. It was slow moving with each child stopping every now and then to inspect a rock, a root, a stick, a leaf, a bug. If I were alone, it might have taken me an afternoon to reach the dome. With three small children and an injured foot, it took an eternity.

In the night, we made it to Heaven's Dome. The observatory tower looked like a tall lighthouse, with an expansive opening at the top for viewing the beautiful mountainside. I touched the cold cement façade with a shaking hand. The observatory tower was locked. But even so, I wouldn't enter it anyway. I feared what resided up there. Marauders, animals, traps. I made a fire off the beaten path near a ravine. The children helped me gather wood. Ginny was asleep on a soft patch of grass before having the chance to eat a wounded hare I had found upon our path. I laid an apron over Ginny for extra warmth. The area felt barren, except for seagulls cawing nearby. I didn't trust the emptiness; I didn't want to take anything for granted. I had to assume trouble was everywhere, waiting. Marauders could be hiding. Bears could be lurking. Either way, it felt ominous to hear seagulls at sundown. In the night, Pine breastfed while Milo and I ate and talked.

"Mama, what's that noise?"

I paused to listen. The night air was filled with wind and bugsong. Somewhere, there was the faint echo of people. A far-off shout. A ripple of laughter. My intuition was correct.

"It sounds like people."

"What people?"

"I don't know. We should stay quiet."

"Why? I want to see people."

"No. No people. Never people."

It was dark, but I could feel Milo's eyes on me.

"Mama, you mean," he whispered.

In the morning, we walked on toward the great cliff that was the home to Sweet Gum. The cliff village resided just overhead. We just needed to find the narrow road to climb upward toward the town. Soon, we reached a thin waterfall and the rock pool. I had remembered this place. Flashbacks of Felipe came to me vividly. I imagined us swimming here. The wind coming off the water, flowing through our hair. A flash of Felipe's smile. He looked so dignified with his hair slicked back. His lips on my neck. On the rocks, there, the remnants of Felipe's happiness came to me. It came into my mind and swirled around like warm honey. I realized something standing there – there was goodness in our relationship. There was laughter. Respect. Love. I had thought so much of his evilness, my evilness. Underneath it all, there was pure and honest goodness between us. I crouched in the dry tufts of grass and watched the pool of water.

"Mama, what you doing?" Milo asked.

"Let's just watch for a while."

"But I'm cold."

"Okay, let's move away from the wind. Over here."

I grabbed his hand and Ginny's hand and we moved onto a big rock to sit. The supple grass around us thrashed softly. I stared at the waterfall and the pool of water it fell into. Endless energy.

"How long we gotta stay here?" Milo asked.

"Not too long. Just a little."

"Is this BeezBo's house?"

"We're very close. This is her special waterfall."

"Why it's her waterfall?"

"Because it is. Me and Dada used to swim here."

"In there?"

"Yes, in there."

"He was here?"

"He was."

Milo sat and watched the ripple of water.

"Are you still cold?"

"Yes."

"Do you want to leave now?"

"No."

We walked along the sweep of the cliff until we found the narrow path that would lead the way to Sweet Gum. There was a large rock formation in the shape of a jagged ear.

"The mountain is always listening," I told Milo. "What do you want to tell it?"

"Um. I gotta go pee-pee," he said.

"Okay, that's a good thing to say. Let's go."

We rested a great while before trekking up the mountainside path, our clothes flapping softly in the wind. Our dry eyes were caked with dirt along our lashes. Our bones were tired and longed for sleep. But this was the final stretch. The path was steep and narrow, lined with weeds and bones of birds like some gruesome warning of death. I cared not. This was our last moment to be strong. I pulled the children upward with everything I had. The muscles and bones holding up my foot begged for me to stop, but I didn't. I raged on like a bull, like a mother.

CHAPTER FIFTY-NINE

We arrived at the mountaintop village just as rain began to rattle on the tin roofs of houses within the community. There were seven or eight houses in view immediately as we rounded the cliff. Ana's home was deeper within. I was still gasping from our hike. I had to sit on the ground with the children for a moment. Pine needed to nurse. Milo was anxious. Ginny was starting to whine. The village was quiet. Far off, I heard the bleating of sheep and goats. I hadn't remembered there being so many houses before. I could remember three. Perhaps more were built since I had last visited. Or, perhaps, the memory is a funny thing. After Pine finished nursing, I held Ginny at my hip and clenched Milo's hand. Pine was on my chest. We followed a dirt trail through the village. A child herded goats into a pen in the rain as we passed. The child looked up, craning his neck to see us clearly through the gray weather. He ran inside his house.

Ana's house was cold and weathered in the distance. *Oh, I remember this place*, I thought. I remembered walking up the dirt path lined with gargantuan gray boulders, Felipe's hand clenching mine. I recalled the scent of smoke pouring from Ana's chimney. I remembered the stone wall that guarded her house, separating it in some fashion from the rest of the Sweet Gum community. Now, the stone wall was crumbling. The dirt path was filled with tall grass. There was no smoke coming from the chimney. We approached Ana's large wooden door. I knocked.

"Mama, is this BeezBo's house?" Milo asked.

"Yes."

"Where is she?"

"I don't know."

The rain was beginning to thicken. Ana was not coming to the door. I needed to get the children inside. Surely, Ana would not mind me barging in. I was family. I swiveled the handle with my calloused hand, but the door was locked. No marauders knew of Sweet Gum, I was certain, but perhaps that didn't stop Ana from being careful. I needed to find the spare key; could it be where she'd always kept it? Indeed, it was safely stowed in the chipped ceramic frog ornament nearby. I desperately wanted to get over with telling Ana that Felipe was dead. I opened the door and stepped inside with the children. I looked around. The quietness in the house was uncomfortable. The house smelled like woodchips, lemon, and faint smoke, as though someone had been cooking a scrumptious dinner hours earlier. I was starving.

Pine began to cry. She was tired. All the children were so tired. The house was freezing. I moved through the home, opening doors and plowing past a picture frame. I backtracked to see a family portrait of me, Felipe, and Milo. I had sent it to Ana for Christmas two years back.

"Who are you?" a voice said.

I turned around to see a woman with two children. The woman was holding a rifle and pointing it at us. I gasped, startling Pine.

I struggled to get my words out. The woman cocked her rifle.

"I came to see Ana."

The woman looked at me. She looked down at my bloodstained clothes. "You know Ana?" she whispered. "Ana Vela?" Then she looked at the picture frame hanging on the wall.

I moved Milo and Ginny swiftly behind me and ordered them to sit down. The woman's children stared at me. I wanted to scream for Ana. Did she know there were strangers in her home? I also wanted to ask the woman to say Vela again, Felipe's last name. My last name. It sounded so nice, even in the face of a rifle, to hear a piece of my name out loud. It was nice to be recognized in some way.

Milo touched my kneecap. "Mama, is she a bully?"

"Ana is my son's great-grandmother," I said, smoothing Milo's hair. "My husband's grandmother. My late husband."

The woman lowered her gun. "Felipe?"

"Yes."

"Oh, I'm so sorry."

"Yes, how do you..." My voice trailed off.

The woman lowered herself to a nearby couch and whispered to her children. "Go to the kitchen and prepare some bread and eggs." The children hurried off dutifully.

"Did you know Felipe?" I asked, my words somewhat bolder now.

"No. But Ana talked about him. She talked about you, too."

"Do you know where she is?"

I looked around. Ana's décor had not changed at all. The same bear-print curtains, and the same wooden furniture and flannel blankets draped carefully on the arm of the cottage-style sofa.

The woman looked at her folded hands. "Ana's not here."

"Where is she?"

"Would the children like a snack?"

"Can you please tell me where Ana is?"

The woman looked up solemnly. "I really think the children would like a snack. We just made warm bread."

I looked down at Milo, who was staring intently at the woman, holding on to every word she said. I grabbed his hand and massaged it.

"Okay, a snack sounds good."

"I always love warm bread on a rainy day," the woman said, standing up. She placed the rifle high up on a shelf and moved to the kitchen. I held Milo's hand and carried Ginny into the kitchen. The kitchen was lit warmly by candles on the table. The light bounced off the faces of the children. There was a large loaf of bread on the table. It looked like a Christmas ham.

"My name is Nova. The boy is Andre, and the girl is Daisy — named after the daisies that bloom here up on the mountain. He's six and she's four. Your little boy must be Milo."

I looked down at Milo, who appeared confused, uncertain if he should remain quiet or tell this woman everything he knew. He stared at her, grabbing on to the leg of a chair.

"Ana talked about Felipe a lot," Nova said. "Showed me pictures. Before everything went to hell in a handbasket, Ana invited me to visit Sea Isle with her. Said she missed her grandbaby and great-grandbaby. She even asked me if I'd assist her. You know, with her old age and all. It might've been hard to travel without a companion. I would have gone, but Daisy was just too little at the time. I wish I had just made the trip though. I feel like I missed my chance. I get lonely up here sometimes. And Ana missed Sea Isle. I feel like it was my fault. I'm sorry if I deprived you all of that. Now the world is swimming, huh? Well, that's what I hear."

For some reason, I laughed.

"Here, have some bread."

Ginny reached for bread. Milo stared at the little girl named Daisy. "Mama, I want bread," he whispered.

"Here you go, sweetheart," Nova said. "Take a seat." She pulled out two chairs and began to put Milo in one, then paused to ask if it was okay to pick Milo up under the arms. I nodded. I placed Ginny in an open seat. Both children tore into the bread.

The woman looked at me and handed me a soft piece of bread. "Look. I can't imagine what you've been through. And I don't know how to say this without making things harder."

I stared at her without expression. "Ana's gone. Is that right? Is that what you want to say?"

She kept her voice low. "Yes, I'm so sorry."

After the bread was nearly finished, Nova pulled out some potatoes from a drawer and began to cut them into chunks. I wanted to ask what happened to Ana and why she had a potato drawer in my grandmother-in-law's house. It didn't feel right to ask just yet. Not with the children around. Plus, I was exhausted. The house was cold. Everything felt off. I wanted the woman to give me a summary of what happened and then have her leave. I could scream. Part of me felt drained beyond comprehension and another part of me felt the need to hunt, to prepare. The least I could do was light a fire. I bit my nails, ready to claw at my skin. While Nova prepared something to eat, I asked if I could start a fire. Nova handed me a fire-starter from a drawer. *How easy*, I thought. I went to make a fire, wondering where we'd lay our heads for the night. I had planned on falling into Ana's arms, and then into her guest bed. I didn't expect to run into anyone else. But I guess that's what happens – people die and leave their homes behind. Treasures for the next in line. Nothing is permanent. And what right did I have to Ana's house without Ana around? It sounded as though Nova was close to Ana. Closer than me. Perhaps she was a good friend in Ana's final days. We'd have to look for somewhere new. I was so tired of moving. Milo came into the living room after exploring the cottage.

"Mama? Why are you here?"

"I just wanted to have a little quiet time with a fire."

"Can I have quiet time too?"

"Yes. Come up on the sofa. There's a blanket."

"Okay."

"Where is Ginny?"

"Eating something."

"Okay, good."

"Mama? Where is BeezBo?"

"Um. I don't know right now."

"Mama, can we go back to the treehouse?"

"The treehouse? From a long time ago?"

"Yes."

"No. I don't think we can."

"But I want to!"

I paused. "Sometimes, I think I do too."

CHAPTER SIXTY

In the murky evening, the rain stopped. The children fell asleep quickly in the spare bedroom. There was a small crib for Pine. Nova pulled it out from a closet. "It was Daisy's," she said. "Ana built it. She let us sleep here when we first arrived at Sweet Gum. She was very kind to us."

Nova and I moved outside by the chicken coop and sat side by side on a bench staring up at the night sky. I wanted to ask Nova about her life, how she ended up in Sweet Gum, and what life on a mountain was like. Every inch of me hurt with exhaustion. It was hard to form words. I hoped I didn't appear rude or ungrateful. Outside, the chicken coop rattled when a strong gust of wind suddenly beat against it. A howling coyote sounded from somewhere down below. Then there was silence. I held my face in my hands and wept. Nova ran a hand over my back. I never thought of myself as someone who would cry in front of a stranger. But I couldn't keep it in any longer. It hurt and it felt good at the same time. It was out of my control. I had dreamt of Sweet Gum for so long. Some nights, I pictured Ana's bed in my mind, imagining myself nestled among clean sheets with the children. In many ways, the imagining was what kept me going. I cried. I cried. Nova laughed, which surprised me. I picked my head up to see what was funny. I wiped my cheeks as I looked up and into the darkness.

"The chickens are quiet," she whispered lightly. "Usually, they make a fuss right after dusk, settling into their spots and all. But they're curious. See how they have their beaks through the grate?"

I stared ahead. In the faint moonlight, the chickens were indeed quiet and curious. They appeared determined to know what gossip was abounding. How nice to be in a place where distress is unusual, even to chickens.

I lifted my head to the moon. "I'm sorry. It's been—"

"Shh, shh. You don't have to explain. Don't have to explain a thing! I get it. I've been there."

I made a fire outside and we watched flames crackle in the air. Nova told me she was impressed with my fire-making skills. This made me smile in the dark. I pictured myself showing her more of my skills. Soon, the fire snapping put the chickens to bed. There was wind, but it was pleasant. There soon came a light rain, but it was agreeable and barely there. Nova told me of Ana's final days – how her chest twisted, and she wished for her glass sculptures to be preserved in some way. How Ana claimed her grandson would come someday. And when he did, the house would be his. I breathed out for the first time in a long while. Nova didn't have to tell me any of this.

The fire burned amid the rain and the smoke flourished in languid coils. Nova slipped out of her coat and laid it onto my shoulders. We watched the gray rain fall like gentle dust until the fire was snuffed out completely. As we walked back to the house, Nova told me her husband died in the floods. She had found Sweet Gum by accident. She intended on Heaven's Dome but found Ana instead. Nova had another home in the Sweet Gum community, but ever since Ana died, everyone in the community took turns caring for Ana's animals and homestead. This day happened to be Nova's turn. It was an honor and privilege to care for Ana's home, she told me. This was the agreed-upon opinion of the Sweet Gum community. Ana had been there for all of them, and they were pleased to be there for her.

When we got inside, Nova showed me to the bathroom, where well water came through a spigot into the tub. She left dry clothes on the sink for me. I bathed myself in cool water. I lathered soap in my hands, marveling at the suds. I plucked dirt from my fingernails and looked at my clean hands from multiple angles. When I was finished, I slipped into nightwear that was creamy on my skin. Nova met me in the hall to let me know I could sleep in Ana's bed. Andre and Daisy were on the floor, and she would sleep on the couch.

"Oh, thank you. That's kind. But I should stay with the children," I told her.

"You've had such a long trip. Are you sure? Won't it be nice to stretch out?"

I hesitated. Finally, I said, "The baby wakes up very early. It's best that I'm near her. The children know when I'm missing, too."

"You're a very good mother," she said. "But I'd think that even if you did take Ana's bed."

I paused in the dark hall and then grinned. I smiled because I believed her.

"Thank you," I whispered.

CHAPTER SIXTY-ONE

The days wore by, unaccounted for. Nova stayed with us, explaining the chickens, sheep, and goats. She extended her stay at Ana's house to assimilate us to this new world. Working with the animals kept my looping thoughts at bay; it took away the image of the burning helicopter still etched in my mind, and the looming thoughts of Marisol's last days. Of Milo's sickness in the woods. His desperation. Ginny's longing. Pine's birth. The animals were a lot of work anyway. I relied on Nova greatly. She invited us to visit the others in the community, but I wasn't ready. The exhaustion still lingered in my bones; the trauma forced my tongue to be silent. How could I talk to anyone? The time would come, but I would delay it as much as possible.

Along the mountaintop, animals emerged from hibernation. The cold was long gone, leaving a distant memory of hostility as new life germinated all around. There was a spring where the mountain began to slope that I found pleasure in visiting. The children and I went down the mountainside one day with our plastic milk jug to hunt for fish. Nova found it curious, explaining that there were plenty of eggs, sheep milk, and bread. "The children like fish," I told her. Treading on newly grown sprigs of grass, dipping toes into the fresh water as fish waggled through my toes, gave me a quiet repose.

The looping thoughts followed me everywhere. But there in the spring water, they seemed to disappear. There were some days in the mountaintop home, I hardly spoke at all. Whenever I heard Nova's voice, booming with jokes for the children, I wondered where she found the energy. I tried to leave my shell of silence and join this new family. The children seemed happy. It was perfect. And yet, I couldn't drag myself out of pity, out of some ragged, woeful mindset that had taken over every part of me.

One day, Nova and her children were gone, staying at their own cottage for the day. I awoke to glass shattering. Milo was in the living room, his hands covered in blood. "I wanted to hold Dada's picture. But it broke," he said. He had tried to bring down the picture from the wall. The one that I'd sent to Ana years back. I rushed Milo to the kitchen to wash his hands and bandage him with rags. I sat him on the kitchen counter. He was crying, reaching for the living room. He scooted himself off the counter and ran back to the pile of broken glass when I turned my back for a moment. I blinked away my own tears and ran after him. I tried to pull the photo from his hands to keep tiny shards of glass away from him, but in the act, the photo ripped. His cries grew louder and reminded me of our journey. The encampment. The fire. Everything came rushing back in that instant. My chest fluttered as I watched Milo sitting in a pile of glass, trying to fix the photograph of his father. Blood was scattered over the ripped picture, over Felipe's smiling face. Milo cried with a painful, scrunched face.

"My picture is broken!" he cried.

"I'll fix it," I said.

"You can't! Look!"

"I see. It's okay. I can clean the glass and find a new frame for the picture. Maybe we can make one somehow."

"*No!*" he shouted. "I want *this one.*"

Milo finally got up and came into my arms, unstable and crying.

"Okay. I understand."

After Milo calmed down, he took a nap. I stared at him. How could I fix his sadness? His hurt. How could I fill the hole his father had left? We had celebrated the framed photograph on the wall the first couple days after arriving at Ana's cottage. "See! I told you Dada's picture was here all along!" But it wasn't enough. I should have looked for more photos of him sooner, but I was distracted by my own depression. While Milo slept, I paced the home looking for more photographs of Felipe. *Felipe Vela.* My husband. My friend. My son's love. I could take my son across the land. I could save him from patrollers. I could keep him alive in deepest danger. But I could not bring his father back. After a thorough search, I realized there were no other photographs of Felipe, or anyone, in Ana's house.

Later that night when the children were asleep, I went outside to escape my own thoughts. I stared up at the moon and thought of her. Marisol. The woman from the cave; my savior no one would ever know about. I walked down a slope of grass as night wind played with my hair. I had a mug of hot mint tea in hand and sat down with a quilted blanket draped over my shoulders. I closed my eyes and imagined how she'd massaged my body. She had a hawk-like sense for when I needed her touch. I was gray and cold, sore, and bleak – and there she was. Some angel who smelled of pine needles and dirt, who caressed me, fed me, made heaven out of hell, brought me back to life, gave me the gift of fire. God, I missed her. She'd opened a foreign part of me, someone I hadn't known was there. I wished she were on the mountaintop with us. I wondered what she would do to help Milo, to pull his sadness out and bury it in a deep dark hole. *She would talk*, I thought to myself and laughed. Yes, talk. We needed to talk. I needed to; Milo needed to. Talk to others. Talk about Felipe, our journey, our fears, our wants, our silly thoughts. In the morning, we would venture into the community. Perhaps Nova might know where I could find a new photograph of my husband. Perhaps there would be others with souls like Marisol's.

CHAPTER SIXTY-TWO

The following day brought temperate winds that carried the scent of the sea. A misty salt air that came in waves and would seem exquisite if one didn't know where one was – that the smell of ocean should be foreign here. Looking out at the landscape, I wondered where the shoreline decided to stop. Would I ever visit it? Touch it? Swim in it? Would it stay tame, allowing the children to play in her waves someday? Or would it come for Sweet Gum, too? For us. For everything. I ignored it. There were no pressing decisions to make just then, so I dressed myself and the children in new clothes from Nova. We set down a dirt path toward the cottages of Sweet Gum. I was afforded a restful sleep the night before. Ginny was beginning to experiment more with her voice. Milo nudged her, telling her to quiet down – he was still upset over the broken photograph of Felipe. I worried about his recent emotions lately. The prolonged crying, followed by impenetrable silence. Pine was beginning to show off more of her character. She was a curious baby who seemed to marvel the most at leaves.

Smoke was pouring from Nova's chimney as we approached her house. "I'm always cooking something," she had told me. I knocked timidly on her door. She invited us in without hesitation. Walking through her home, I asked if she had known of any photographs at Ana's house. I told her I hadn't found any; I thought I had remembered photograph albums at Ana's cottage before. "Ah, I think I know," she said. "Ana brought them to my house one day to talk about her family. Come on, I'll take you outside to the yard to meet everyone and I'll look for them." She led us through her small, cozy cottage and toward a back door that opened into something of an outdoor courtyard. Wooden chairs, a dirt floor, a warm fire in the middle. There were mothers. Fathers. Children. Animals. Strangers. I felt blood rushing to my face. It felt like the encampment, like any moment we would be judged on our weaknesses and sent for slaughter. It was a small space with too many people. Nova made circular motions on my back. "*This* is Sweet Gum," she said with a cheerful laugh, motioning to the activity in the yard. She proceeded to announce names that instantly left my brain. I struggled with how my face should appear. Friendly, relieved, scared, appreciative, reserved? I wasn't sure. I wasn't used to putting on a face. Ginny began walking toward the fire, and I ran toward her.

"Welcome," someone said. I ignored the voice and went to Ginny. I sensed eyes on me.

At the fire, there appeared to be some sort of potato dish with greens. It looked delicious. Pine, who was in my arms, began to wail.

Ginny seemed in awe of the fire, reaching toward the hot wood. Milo sat in the dirt and began rubbing his palms into the ground. Pine's crying was terrible. I thought we must've looked like a circus act.

I was about to yank Ginny back when a mother got to her first. She pulled her by the hand, gently.

"Very hot!" the woman said. "I'm Beatrice. What's your name?"

Ginny looked at the woman. No answer.

"Would you like a toy?" The woman who went by Beatrice looked at me, as if to ask if it was okay. She was clearly the fun adult of the group. I nodded. Ginny nodded, too.

"What's your name, hon?" Beatrice asked again.

"Gin," Ginny said.

"Gin?" Beatrice clarified.

"It's Ginny," I said. Ginny said her name; or part of it. This was huge. "It's the first time she's said her own name." I swallowed a lump, holding back my pride.

"And it won't be the last," Beatrice said. "Come on, Ginny. The children are playing a fun game. We're building fairy homes out of sticks and rocks. Would your little boy like to play, too?"

I looked back at Milo. He stared up at me with anger. I thought he might still be mad about the photograph.

I turned to him. He had a fistful of dirt. He let it fall to the ground slowly. I could feel his sadness.

"Maybe soon," I said.

"Okay."

With Ginny occupied, I was able to calm Pine down. She needed to eat. I felt strange breastfeeding in front of these people. I could laugh. I could survive the floods and make it halfway across the land to Ana's house, but not breastfeed in front of a group of people.

"My baby is hungry," I called to Beatrice. "Will Ginny be okay with you if I go inside for a moment?"

Another woman came over to me holding a shawl. "Hi, I'm Mercy. Would you like a blanket for your baby? She's adorable. What's her name?"

"This is Pine."

"Lovely. Here you are, Pine." She handed me the blanket. Her soft, quiet voice was comforting. "We've all been there, Liv. Let us know if you want us to play with the little boy, too. He looks around my son's age."

"I'll ask him," I said. "Thank you." I walked toward Milo, who was still sitting in the dirt.

"Milo, I'm going to feed Pine inside Nova's house. Do you want to play with the kids outside? Or come with me?"

"Come with you," he whispered.

I looked up at Mercy. "He'll come with me. Thank you."

We walked inside and found a sofa to rest on. Pine nursed herself to sleep.

"Milo," I said, once Pine was asleep. "Are you okay?"

He paused, looking at the dirt under his fingernails. Soon, he spoke. "One day, you be dead?"

"Yes, one day, I will be."

"But will it be a mistake?"

"No, not a mistake."

"But I don't want you to go."

He began to cry. I wrapped my free arm around him and kissed his head. He wouldn't loosen his grip on a bundle of sticks that he had taken from outside. I whispered into his ear, "We are connected. We will always be together. Even if I am dead, you will always be able to hear me."

"How?"

"I will live in your heart."

He looked at his chest. I laughed.

Nova was coming down the hall. Milo dropped his sticks onto the floor and then scrambled to retrieve them all.

"I found the photo albums," Nova said.

Milo forgot about the sticks.

The next day, we visited Nova's house again. Milo brought his favorite photograph of Felipe with him. Ginny met with Beatrice and the children again. Pine was asleep in my arms. Mercy came late, cradling a chicken in her arms. The chicken was frail, barely alive. She sat down next to me, holding the poor chicken.

"My chicken won't last another day," Mercy said, tears welling. Those who were around the campfire – a group no more than five – consoled her. They understood the relationship this woman had with her chicken. Mercy looked to me. "We rely on the chickens for eggs. We don't normally eat them. Only when it's necessary. I don't know whether I should wait or not."

"She's suffering," I said, noticing the fowl's difficult breathing.

"I can't do it. I need someone else to."

I breathed in. "I can help you."

"Okay," Mercy said.

Milo, who was sitting on a log, playing with the dirt, looked up at me.

"Milo, can you play with Ginny and the children?"

"Okay," he said. He picked up his photograph of Felipe and marched toward the children, who were building fairy homes with rocks and sticks.

"Would you like to say goodbye to her?" I whispered to Mercy.

Mercy sniffed and stroked the chicken. She leaned over and whispered near the chicken's gold-orange head. I tried to look away to give them both space.

"I'll go around the house. And then I'll bring it to Nova."

"Okay," Mercy said.

She handed me the chicken.

We spent the afternoon eating. The sound of children playing was like medicine. Mercy perked up. I conversed with the other adults. I told them my story. I learned theirs. There was another woman, named Winona, who came from the Carolinas. A young woman called Theodora, who had grown up and lived in Sweet Gum her whole life – knew nothing else. Her partner had passed, leaving her with children. I met a young woman named Poe, who did glass sculptures with Ana. She had wonderful stories of Ana, she said. There was also a father called Cedric, who was utterly wonderful with all the children. There were five other children in the yard, all varying ages. This was a sampling of the community; there were more names and faces to learn. "You'll meet everyone soon enough," Nova said. "This is a small group here. The daytime group," she joked. "We're the ones with children. We sort of stick together." We took our time learning about each other, subconsciously knowing there'd be many more days to reveal these vulnerable parts of ourselves. There was time. Much more time, I hoped.

I sat with the adults by a warm fire on a hand-carved wooden chair well into the evening. The children played together, a game of chase and silliness. Milo played, too.

"Thank you for your help with the chicken," Mercy said. "I'm not very good at killing things."

"It's not my favorite thing to do," I said.

"Yes, but you did it so well."

I watched Milo play, running in circles, laughing as another little girl his age was coming after him. He wasn't holding on to anything. No sticks, no rocks, not even the photograph of Felipe. Free hands. I paused to stabilize my breath, hoping the sound of his laughter would stay in my mind the rest of my days, hoping my throat would relax enough for me to get my words out. "Do you see my son?" I asked her.

Mercy looked toward Milo.

"It takes a second to kill something," I said. "But it can take a lifetime to heal. Killing is easy. Healing is what's hard."

Mercy watched Milo, as did I.

CHAPTER SIXTY-THREE

Three months passed. The heat was palpable. The scent of sea came to me sometimes. Some folks in Sweet Gum talked about the scent of water, about the possibility of the floods reaching us someday. Others ignored the concept entirely. There were those who acknowledged the world had changed and others who went on living as though it were just another day. One morning, I stood on the slope of the mountainside with Milo when a band of EEMA helicopters soared past. The blue horizon was dotted with black metal buzzards. Milo crouched. I raised a hand over my eyes. Shortly after, a horde of geese flew by, headed in the same direction as the helicopters.

"Where do you think they're going?" Milo asked, his language much clearer now that he was four.

"Toward new land," I said.

There was constant chatter in the village about leaving Sweet Gum. The need to explore was strong. To find a power grid. To find communication. More civilization. Stability. For a short time, I was their only source of information. When I told them I had heard about islands rising in the east, it sparked a fire in some. Milo had caught wind of these conversations. I was silly to think he wasn't listening.

"Are *we* going to the new islands?" Milo asked.

"No."

The helicopters disappeared into clouds. The thunder of blades soon diminished. A new chapter was brewing. I could feel it. Things were beginning anew, just as they always do. This time, it felt like a positive shift. I had no way of guaranteeing it; it's just something I felt within.

My voice trembled, thinking I needed to do something, to act. I felt a change in the atmosphere as the copters flew past us. As much as I wanted to ignore it, I knew the time would come for us to leave Sweet Gum – for Milo, Ginny, and Pine to grow up and find their own ways, to face life below the mountain. I looked at Milo, who was fiddling with our fishing jug. "Do you want to leave this mountain someday?"

Milo's face hung. "Why?" he asked.

"Because that's what people do sometimes. They move on."

"Do we have to?" He started to breathe heavily.

"Oh, I didn't mean to upset you. I'm sorry, sweetie. No, we don't have to."

"Will Ginny leave too?"

"No, we stay together. Always."

"Why do you want to leave?"

"I'm sorry. I shouldn't have said anything."

I knelt and held him against my chest. I wiped hair away from his forehead and kissed him.

"I don't know why I say things sometimes."

He grabbed my hands. "It's okay."

"Milo, what do you want to do this afternoon?"

Milo thought for a moment while more geese flew by. "Can we play with the goats?"

"Yes." I kissed him again and then went back up the mountain. "Let's go see if Ginny and Pine are okay first. I don't want to trouble Beatrice and Mercy with them too long."

"Okay."

I kept watch of the mountainside for years. The movement of helicopters helped me understand what was going on in the world. It reminded me that there was still life out there; there were still survivors. I began to prep, slowly and without announcement. Candle wax was packed into containers, flour and potatoes and the season's harvest were put into crates; firewood was plentiful. I never put any of it to use, but it was there just in case.

We said goodbye to many in Sweet Gum who felt the need to explore, to return to civilization. And we welcomed newcomers just the same. One year turned to two, and then five years turned into twenty. Friendships formed, romances bloomed, conflicts were managed, ceremonies were performed, funerals conducted, babies born. When someone perished, we carried them to a peaceful grove in the mountainside where the ground was tender. Once, we even held a ceremony for Felipe. Marisol too. And Mosey. This turned into an annual ceremony. A celebration of sorts. There came a day when the children were grown that they started to tire of the ceremonies.

"We owe everything to a horse named Mosey," I told the children. I told them often.

"We know, Mom," Pine would say.

"Well, it's important."

The children of Sweet Gum grew up together. We taught them what we knew. They taught us more. As we soared through the years, the drive to leave Sweet Gum increased among friends, among the children. I had always known it was a matter of time. We were an army now. It was possible. We believed. The dry lands were stable. The water had stopped inching toward the dry lands, creating new coastlines along West Virginia, Kentucky, Tennessee, Alabama, and Georgia. Encampments vanished. The east was established. Patrollers went to the new islands or dispersed into rebels who helped survivors of the dry lands. Whenever a newcomer came to Sweet Gum, we learned more and more.

If it were up to me, I would have died there in the tender dirt in Ana's yard, surrounded by goat muck and chicken feed. It was a life I came to relish. But the children wanted more. Of course they did. As they should have. Maturity sneaks in like a thief. Upon realizing this, we made a plan. I put a hand on Milo's shoulder. "Do you think it's best for the baby?"

"Yes, Mom," he said. He carried a little boy in a sling.

"What does Ginny think about leaving?"

"She's ready. We're all ready. She thinks it'll be good for the baby, to have opportunities. We can always come back."

"I'm old now. Maybe I should stay here."

He looked at me curiously – as though I had just cursed at him. He searched his pocket and procured an acorn. "Here. Don't be silly."

We passed the ravine where I had last seen Mosey. I imagined her lying there – the children yards away, oblivious. Now, they walked ahead of me, looking back every now and then to make sure I was okay. Milo handed the baby to Ginny. Ginny paused, positioning the little boy to give him milk from her breast. Pine was impatient, claiming she could already see the new town and smell the shoreline. Others traveled with us, too. Mostly young folks. I let them walk on ahead of me. My knees were not as strong as they once were. We were in search of a town that welcomed survivors. If anything, we would say hello and return to the mountaintop. But the children – oh, I never stopped calling them children – I knew they wanted more than the mountain. We approached a hill, the one I remembered Mosey falling from. I watched Milo in the distance, examining the fields. I wondered if he remembered this place. He turned to me, noticing my delay. He whispered to Ginny and then he rushed to me. I didn't want to hold them up. Milo held an arm out for me. Together, we walked up the hill. We had only walked a bit, but I was already feeling exhausted. He peered down at me, his forehead crinkling like Felipe's. "You look tired. Should we rest?"

"No, go on without me."

"No, we stay together. Always."

"Okay, Milo."

So we rested, our backs against the grass, staring up at the vast and sunny sky. I closed my eyes for just a moment, peaceful, knowing he was there. They all were there.

ACKNOWLEDGMENTS

Thank you to the teachers and staff of Rosemont College who put the insane notion of writing a book into my head. I'd also like to thank the literary community of Philadelphia for being a constant source of inspiration, from your literary magazines to your bookshops – thank you for shaping me. My gratitude goes out to Vanessa McCutcheon for reading a first draft of this book. Your advice was the key I needed to press on. Thank you to Philip Turner and Ewan Turner for your first round of edits. I especially want to thank Ewan for the time and focus you put into each and every word. I am indebted to Don D'Auria for taking a chance on me and this book. I am so happy to have found a home with Flame Tree Press and to experience working with a kind and focused editor such as yourself. Thank you to Mike Valsted for further eyes on this book.

I would also like to thank my husband, Mike, for pulling me out of a deep dark pit anytime I wanted to quit publishing. Because of you, I found the will to believe in myself and keep pushing forward. Thank you also for answering random questions at unseemly times, mainly about fire and explosions. I love you. To my mother, Andrea, for being my ultimate cheerleader. I won the lottery with you, Mom! To my father, Michael, for always asking how my book is going even when it's not going. And to my sisters, nieces, and nephews, I thank you for a lifetime of inspiration and pure love. My deepest acknowledgment goes to my son, who was three during the time of this writing and will be six once these words become ink. If you ever come back and read this when you're grown, I want you to know that much like the mother in this book, I would also go to the ends of the earth for you. I'm not sure if I would force you to eat bugs, but who knows. I love you more than I can comprehend.

FLAME TREE PRESS
FICTION WITHOUT FRONTIERS
Award-Winning Authors & Original Voices

Flame Tree Press is the trade fiction imprint of Flame Tree Publishing, focusing on excellent writing in horror and the supernatural, crime and mystery, science fiction and fantasy. Our aim is to explore beyond the boundaries of the everyday, with tales from both award-winning authors and original voices.

•

You may also enjoy:
The Sentient by Nadia Afifi
The Emergent by Nadia Afifi
The Transcendent by Nadia Afifi
Junction by Daniel M. Bensen
Interchange by Daniel M. Bensen
Second Lives by P.D. Cacek
Second Chances by P.D. Cacek
In Darkness, Shadows Breathe by Catherine Cavendish
Dark Observation by Catherine Cavendish
The After-Death of Caroline Rand by Catherine Cavendish
Dead Ends by Marc E. Fitch
The Toy Thief by D.W. Gillespie
One By One by D.W. Gillespie
Black Wings by Megan Hart
Silent Key by Laurel Hightower
Hellweg's Keep by Justin Holley
Hearthstone Cottage by Frazer Lee
Those Who Came Before by J.H. Moncrieff
Stoker's Wilde by Steven Hopstaken & Melissa Prusi
Stoker's Wilde West by Steven Hopstaken & Melissa Prusi
Land of the Dead by Steven Hopstaken & Melissa Prusi
A Sword of Bronze and Ashes by Anna Smith Spark
Jubilee by Stephen K. Stanford
Screams from the Void by Anne Tibbets
The Roamers by Francesco Verso
Whisperwood by Alex Woodroe
Of Kings, Queens and Colonies by Johnny Worthen
Of Civilized, Saved and Savages by Johnny Worthen

•

Join our mailing list for free short stories, new release details, news about our authors and special promotions:

flametreepress.com